Other book ⸻ Wyler (fiction)

*Deadly Errors*
*Dead Head*
*Dead Ringer*
*Dead End Deal*
*Dead Wrong*
*Changes*
*Cutter's Trial*
*Deadly Odds*
*Deadly Odds 2.0*
*Deadly Odds 3.0*
*Deadly Odds 4.0*
*Deadly Odds 5.0*

Other books by Allen Wyler (nonfiction)

*The Surgical Management of Epilepsy*

Deadly Odds 6.0 ©2023 Allen Wyler, All Rights Reserved

Print ISBN 978-1-960405-07-4
ebook ISBN 978-1-960405-08-1

Visit Allen online at www.allenwyler.com

Cover design by Guy D. Corp
www.grafixCORP.com

# STAIRWAY⇊PRESS
## STAIRWAY PRESS—APACHE JUNCTION

**www.stairwaypress.com**
1000 West Apache Trail, Suite 126
Apache Junction, AZ 85120 USA

# Deadly Odds 6.0

## Allen Wyler

# CHAPTER 1—Seattle

"YOU KNOW, DON'T you, that Collier is planning to rob us."

Gloria Kim said this so innocuously that Itzhak Mizrahi almost shoveled her words straight into the *blah-blah-blah* bin— blah-blah-blah being the price he had to pay for an occasional morsel of intel; in particular, classified tidbits from the managing partners' closed-door meetings.

*Rob us?*

She had his full attention now. As a card-carrying member of Motor-Mouth International, her unrelenting prattling could lull an amped-up meth-head into a coma.

They were sardined into his cramped office, Kim in the single visitor's chair, leg over knee, flashing a swatch of what might've been an attention-snagging thigh if the rest of the package warranted it. It didn't.

Fingertips pressed to her lips, she murmured, "Oh dear, you didn't know, did you," as a statement.

*Was she joking?*

He sat up in his chair now, studying her closely.

*No, it didn't look like she was joking.*

"No, I didn't," he finally admitted. "What do you know about it?"

As soon as the words left his tongue, he realized what Collier intended.

"Not much, really. Just that he's made up his mind," she murmured in a conspiratorially hushed voice. "He's been—

excuse the cliché—like a dog with a bone. Positively obsessed about it since Bertolli began his goddamn tirade about that ABA cybersecurity resolution. Claims it's time for us to finally get on board." Pause. "True. His exact words. *Get on board.* Can you believe he'd actually say that?" She chortled. "Especially this office?"

*Yeah, probably.*

If Collier finally came down on an issue, he tended to obsess it to death, so if office security was now the issue *du jour*, well...Kim was scrutinizing him, weighing his reaction, probably to use as a spicy addition for the next set of eager ears. When not racking up billable hours, her *raison d'être* in the firm was to serve as the office repository for headline-worthy gossip, particularly if it included prurient nuances.

"Good to know, Gloria. Thanks."

*There. That should satisfy her. At least for now.*

She beamed.

"Any idea how he plans to do it?" he asked, offhandedly, in an attempt to smokescreen the importance of the information.

"No, sorry, I don't."

*Yeah, she probably was sorry, but not over any deep concern for the security of the firm. Rather, for not knowing the answer.*

He realized he was nervously massaging the back of his neck and stopped.

*Did she notice?*

"Physically or virtually?"

She frowned.

"What?"

He paused to reword his question to one she might actually grasp.

"You know if he plans to break into our offices physically or just hack our networks?"

With a disheartened expression she shook her head.

"No, I don't really."

"Huh," he muttered.

The thought of some group of assholes trying to hack their firewalls or enter physically—even with the Security Committee's blessing—scorched his stomach. During the past four years as Head of Security for Larkin Standish LLP, he'd relentlessly plugged the colander his incapable predecessor had considered a firewall.

Not only that, but he'd tirelessly and selflessly invested countless hours training every employee—secretaries, paralegals, on up to the partners themselves—on identifying and neutralizing a broad spectrum of security threats from basic spear-phishing attacks to complex in-person social-engineering scams. And then regularly refreshed and updated their skills at six-month intervals, in a Herculean effort to meticulously maintain an ultra-high anti-intrusion awareness.

There wasn't a better group of security-conscious employees than his. Well, perhaps NSA or one of the other three-letter intelligence agencies, but security was, after all, their entire reason to exist. In spite of his employees' superlative training, the human factor was, without doubt, *the* weakest link in any organization's security. Including the NSA. All it took was for one employee's inadvertent mouse-click to infect the law firm's computers with malware.

So yes, Mizrahi considered any attack in any form a personal affront. An intolerable affront.

"Oh wait!" she said, raising an index finger. "On second thought, I *do* remember a whisper that…" A coy smile snaked onto collagen-enhanced L'Oréal lips. "He dropped a name…"

She pushed up from the chair, smoothed her black knee-level skirt, and glanced at the open door. Teasing him now with the dangling intel.

He followed suit, head cocked questioningly, humoring her and her adolescent game, knowing the information would follow, that she would never pass up an opportunity to drop choice gossip.

Turning toward the door, she posed, accentuating her ass.

After a beat: "Don't you find it bizarre that Collier's already picked a team in spite of not even interviewing them yet?"

Ensconced in her cocoon of blissful ignorance, she was totally oblivious to how stupid she came across playing her trivial games. The passive-aggressive cunt.

*Play along? Give her the satisfaction of jerking his chain?*

As much as it galled him, he *did* need the information...

"You don't happen to know their name, do you?" he asked as neutrally as possible.

*Of course, she did. Why else dangle it out there like a ball of yarn in front of a kitten?*

She turned to face him again with a broadening smile.

"Gold and Associates."

"Who?" Mizrahi could feel his brows furrow.

"Gold and Associates," she repeated, obviously enjoying his reaction, of one-upping the head of security. "Honestly? You don't know them?"

Her tone skated on the periphery of accusation.

He knew about all the local pen-testers. Well, all the *major* players. Which was beside the point. Arms crossed, he leaned against the gray metal four-high file cabinet, weighing the satisfaction of a snarky retort against prying more intel from her. Not an easy call, not with her pissing him off like this. But he did want the intel...

He shook his head.

"No, I haven't. They must be new to the scene. Obviously." Or else he *would* know about them. "Know anything about them? Their size? Track record? Anything?"

Smile broadening, she shifted her weight to her other foot.

"Nothing other than Webster speaks very highly of them," meaning Webster Collier, the firm's managing partner.

Mizrahi understood her games well enough to realize that she was now out of fresh information. Meeting over, he decided, so made a big deal out of checking his watch and frowning: a busy man with pressing responsibilities, his go-to ploy for situations like this.

"Thanks for the heads-up, Gloria," he said, pushing off of the file cabinet. "Sorry to cut our intriguing conversation short, but I'm now officially late for another meeting, so if you'll excuse me..."

He beelined for the elevator alcove. The bitch knew her way back.

# CHAPTER 2—Seattle

TO THE LEFT of the door jamb, an engraved rectangular white on black plastic placard denoted: Supervisor, Building Security.

Mizrahi knuckled the opened door. "Got a minute?"

Lorna Glass glanced at him from dual monitors.

"For you, Itzhak, always."

She then swept an open palm toward two mismatched, paint-chipped metal chairs to the side of her equally beat up battleship-gray desk. The spartan cinderblock office was perhaps more spacious than a storage room with about as much character as a cell in San Quentin. Her prized picture of ex-President Trump remained on the wall to the right of her desk. A statement of sorts, Mizrahi assumed.

Though, what exactly that might be was a genuine head-scratcher.

After a quick glance down the hall, he closed the office door then tucked into the closest chair, sat back with arms and legs crossed but said nothing.

Glass squeaked back in her desk chair, eying him over half-height reading glasses, waiting; an unspoken *Well?* hovering heavily in the cramped stuffy air.

Ah, he'd achieved the desired dramatic effect and had her

full attention.

After clearing his throat dramatically, he said, "My sources tell me we have an attempted pen-test in the works."

Sources. Plural. As if this bombshell intel originated from a more significant route than a single gossipy partner.

She nodded soberly as if taking his warning seriously, then shrugged.

"When you link *we* and *pen-test* in the same sentence, what exactly are you talking about?"

*Huh? Had he not been unambiguously clear?*

"The firm, of course."

Tilting her head a tad to the right: "Of course. So?" in an annoyingly dismissive tone.

He swallowed an instant zinger, realizing it could possibly be misconstrued, but found it difficult to believe that she could be so stupid as to miss the implication.

*Did she really need him to spell it out for her?*

Leaning forward, elbows on knees, he lowered his voice to a surreptitious tone.

"You apparently don't appreciate how valuable this intel is. If some doofus somehow manages to penetrate our security—which, I admit, is unlikely—it will reflect as poorly on your group as it might on ours. You *do* see this, don't you?" Now trying for the team approach.

She slipped off her reading glasses, huffed both lenses, began to nonchalantly buff them with the ratty blue eye-cloth that seemed to permanently reside next to the black desk phone, held them up to the recessed lighting, inspected them a beat before nodding approval before slipping them back on.

He continued to wait.

Finally: "Just to refresh your memory, Itzhak, my team's responsibility is to the building. Your team's responsibility is to Larkin Standish. Or did I forget something?"

*Rhetorical, so why bother?*

After a silent moment, she raised her eyebrows.

"No smart comment?"

When he still didn't answer, she added: "I'm simply pointing out the reason why our crew is denied access to any of *your* six floors. Am I not?"

Apparently finished, she interlaced her fingers across her ample belly and leaned back in her squeaky desk chair.

He began to rub his hands together in a washing motion, struggling to rein in an overwhelming urge to lunge across the desk and bitch-slap that smug expression off her self-satisfied face. Inhaling through flared nostrils, he reined in his anger and cleared his throat.

"Yes, Glass. We divide security responsibilities, but—"

She snorted.

"Divide?"

A quick head shake, then he said, "The point is that if my crew were to apprehend intruders in the process of *illegally* attempting to gain entry into my offices, it'll reflect very poorly on your responsibilities."

A bemused smile.

"Really? How so?"

"Because it'd be an undesirable statement about how well or poorly you manage building security, *that's* why. Don't forget that getting into our offices requires entering and transiting the lobby and then access routes, all of which are your domain. Or do you deny this?"

"C'mon, Itzhak, get real. Your firm maintains one of the few non-secure floors in this building." She spread her arms expansively. "You seriously expect us to monitor every person who crosses the lobby to hop on an elevator?" She coughed another sarcastic snort.

"Get real?" He reared back. "Get real? Think about it, Glass, do you think a pen-test would take place during regular business hours? No. *That's* real. And say one did succeed—and I'm not saying it will—but if it *did*, it'd show management that your team willingly allowed unauthorized persons to access our floors. Don't you realize how badly that this would reflect on *your* performance?"

He poked a finger at her. Then he realized that perhaps he could've taken a somewhat different approach, perhaps a *we're-all-in-the-same-boat* line.

She maintained her bored expression and in fact was beginning to again take on that silly annoying grin of hers, the infuriating one.

Shaking his head sadly, he pushed out of the chair, pivoted toward the door.

"Don't say I didn't warn you, Glass," he said over his shoulder before storming out. He stomped down the hall far enough to stop and mentally regroup and take two deep breaths to dial back his annoyance. Some.

*What was that bitch's problem?*

She should be overjoyed, even grateful for the time-sensitive intel. Instead, she'd blown him off like a fucking...he shook his head, at a total loss for words.

Dan Calvo's office was three floors below Glass's on the ground level, the door open. Mizrahi straightened his posture, ran his palm over his closely cropped salt-and-pepper hair, squared his shoulders, then knocked on the door but didn't bother to step into the office. This discussion could be conducted from the doorway.

Calvo, the on-site property manager, glanced up from some paperwork.

"Hey, Itzhak, what can I do for you?"

Palms pressed against both sides of the door frame, Mizrahi cast a quick furtive glance down the hall, to emphasize the confidential nature of his message.

He leaned in and said, "Just want to give you a heads-up. My intelligence sources have been hearing chatter that there's a potential break-in attempt directed at our offices. I haven't been able to narrow down precisely when this is expected to take place, but my best estimate is within the very near future," ending the statement with a wink, as if letting Dan in on a juicy chunk of highly sensitive information.

Part of him wanted to leave it at this, but another part just couldn't resist, so, in a low voice, he said, "Just warned Glass, but she doesn't seem the least bit concerned, which I found, well, disconcerting if not distressing."

Dan flashed his reflexive full-on smarmy-salesman smile.

"That's her business, I guess. But I certainly appreciate the heads-up, Itzhak. I assume that, as usual, you're right on top of things, making sure they're under complete control."

Straightening, Mizrahi slapped the door frame.

"That I am, Dan. That I am. Have a good rest of your day."

He headed back to the elevators.

# HONOLULU

# CHAPTER 3

ARNOLD GOLD ABSENTMINDEDLY nudged a withered palm frond from the base of a coconut tree with the tip of his gray Adidas kicks, as Chance, his beloved fifty-pound tan and black Belgian Malinois, sniffed out the latest p-mail along nearby shrubs.

Arnold glanced at the brilliant, cloudless sapphire horizon kissing the deep-blue Pacific. Another glorious afternoon of refreshing trade winds, T-shirt and cargo shorts temperatures, and nothing on the docket for the remainder of the day. A stunning portrait of the lifestyle he'd forged since fleeing Seattle two plus years ago in a harrowing escape from terrorists hell-bent on killing him. Funny the accommodations we're forced to make in response to the cards we're dealt. Some good, some bad, and some just flat-out lucky.

*Him? He'd hit the freaking jackpot.*

His iPhone began blasting James Brown's "Three Hearts in a Tangle," his custom ringtone. Slipping it out of his pocket, he saw NOAH CAIN bannered across the screen. Several months ago the Seattle lawyer had hired him to investigate and remove ransomware that was paralyzing his boutique law firm. The added benefit from successfully freeing their computers was gaining an enthusiastic advocate and referral source within the Seattle legal community for his fledgling IT company, Gold and

11

Associates.

"Hi, Mr. Cain. What can I do for you?"

"I'm not catching you at an inopportune time, am I?"

"No sir, not at all. Chance and I are just out for a walk, is all," he said, lowering himself onto the weathered bench at a nearby picnic table.

He and Chance loved this particular park for numerous reasons, but mostly because routinely no one else was here, so Chance could be off leash to explore as much as he wanted at his leisure while never wandering out of sight.

"Good, glad to hear it." Pause. "I have, what I hope, will be some excellent news. Are you familiar with the law firm Larkin Standish?"

A faint flicker of recognition struck a vague chord deep in his memory bank. Or was this simply the power of suggestion?

*Well, regardless...*

"Not that I know of. Why?"

"Because Webster Collier, their managing partner, just called to ask a few probing questions about you and your associates. In particular, he wanted to know if I have first-hand knowledge about your new service, the...help me out, I'm blocking on the name."

Arnold's ears perked up.

"You mean pen-testing?"

"Yes, yes, *pen-testing*." Mr. Cain emphasized the word, as if embedding it in memory. "Apparently, his firm's never seen the need to critically evaluate their security, assuming, I suspect, that their present measures are adequate. However, in light of the recent disturbing uptick in cybercrime, the managing partners believe it's now time to conduct an objective evaluation. Apparently, Webster is aware that we've employed you in the past, and so was calling to check on your work. He specifically asked about our ransomware case. I, of course, gave you a glowing recommendation. I believe I duly impressed him because he requested your contact information, which I happily provided."

Last summer, while working up that case for Mr. Cain, Arnold hit a grand slam: not only solving the ransomware issue but also uncovering a junior partner embezzling from the firm. (said partner was now out on bond awaiting trial.)

Since then, Noah Cain had been a very effective advocate, generating the bulk of their Seattle-based business via simple word-of-mouth referrals.

"I can't thank you enough for all your support."

Especially this potential reference, should anything come of it. Frustrating Arnold was his total lack of progress in landing their first pen-test. For without having at least one under their belts, it would be almost impossible to establish a toehold in this highly competitive narrow market.

"I'm more than happy to do it for you, and hope my word has a positive influence."

"Regardless of the outcome, I really appreciate your effort. Thank you."

Arnold suspected that a more eloquent person could easily manufacture a more accurate expression of gratitude but...it was the best he could come up with. Polished social skills had never been his forte.

More than once, his girlfriend Rachael had hinted that he was a textbook example of being on "the spectrum." A mild case, for sure, but a case, nonetheless. Then again, who the hell was "normal," anyway? Even she had issues that pushed a few boundaries...but, hey, that was only his opinion.

"Oh, a couple more things you should know before I let you go," Mr. Cain added, making it sound as if Arnold was the one anxious to get back to work. "Collier is a person who is painfully slow to reach a decision on important matters, but once the decision is made, he is quite anxious to wrap things up as quickly and flawlessly as possible. Perhaps this is one of the many reasons he's been elected managing partner of that firm for the past five years."

"Okay…"

Arnold watched Chance trot to another of his routinely visited shrubs.

"The other point is that apparently, I'm not the only lawyer to be questioned about you. I know Webster has spoken to several other clients of yours for similar evaluations. This is important to keep in mind because your company's reputation is spreading, so landing this job puts you squarely under the microscope. From what I hear, several other high-profile attorneys are now keeping a close eye on who he selects for this. Put another way, if Webster Collier should contact you, it's in the best interests of Gold and Associates to impress him."

Not subtle. Not subtle at all. Fair warning. Arnold nodded acknowledgement in spite of Mr. Cain being unable to see him.

"Got it, Mr. Cain. Thanks a ton for the heads-up."

Call finished, he wandered from the bench a few feet to stand and stare at nothing in particular, rummaging through Cain's words.

Gold and Associates, his boutique IT company, specialized, through nothing more than happenstance, in providing IT support to law practices too small to support full-time technicians; a niche that was growing, albeit slowly.

During a recent gig he met and eventually brought aboard his first associate, Prisha Patel. Together, they made the decision to add penetration testing to their portfolio of *a la carte* services, but unfortunately, they had yet to land their first gig. He suspected that it had to do with his decision to make their services known only through word-of-mouth rather than other means of advertising.

*His reasoning?*

He believed this route enhanced Gold and Associates unique boutique cachét, which in turn increased their allure and desirability. All it would take to catapult their new service-line into the word-of-mouth pipeline was to land their first job and then kill it. But nailing down that first puppy was becoming, like, freaking mercurial.

He wandered back to the weathered, bird-shit-stained picnic table, plunked down on the equally ratty bench, and began to brainstorm possible ways to increase the odds of nailing the contract should this Collier dude actually call.

*Oh, man, their first pen-test.*

He could already taste it.

## HONOLULU

# CHAPTER 4

SEMI-RECLINED ON his favorite chaise, Arnold waited for their conference call to start—with a vintage white ceramic Starbucks mug of freshly brewed steaming Kona blend on the table to his right, a Surface Pro hot against his thighs and wearing a Logitech wireless headset muffling bird songs.

To his right Chance was snoozing on the deck. The small digital clock in the lower right corner of the screen showed four minutes until the scheduled start of the meeting.

*What the hell, might as well sign in early.*

He was shocked to find Prisha, Lopez, and Vihaan already online chitchatting. He rechecked the time.

*Yep, early.*

"Sorry if I kept you guys waiting. Thought I was early."

Prisha answered for the group.

"No biggie, boss, just shooting the shit's all,"

Prisha Patel was Arnold's second banana in the chain of command. Vihaan Patel (her husband) and Carlos Lopez had yet to gain associate status. But within the next few days Arnold intended to discuss with her bringing Brian Ito on as a full associate. They'd recently hired him to help cover their Honolulu work. Especially if they were able to nail down the Larkin Standish job. Assuming, of course, they even got a shot to compete for it.

Because Arnold owned homes in Honolulu and Seattle, Gold and Associates website boasted "offices" in both cities. In reality, though, his Honolulu office was exactly this: the founder and CEO comfortably parked on the back deck with his Surface wirelessly linked up to his uber-secure internet network. Likewise, his Seattle office was nothing more than a laptop on the kitchen table. Show-stoppers? Hardly. Highly functional? For sure. Plus, he would quickly argue, the arrangement eliminated overhead. And besides, the group knocked out ninety-five percent of their work remotely.

Workflow went as follows: when a team member received a work order via email, they logged onto a cloud-based Gold and Associates Dropbox containing, among other things, a spreadsheet of all current and pending IT projects (like installing updates and doing routine system maintenance) along with relevant details. This way, every member would see what everyone else was working on and could quickly lend a hand if needed. A gonzo advantage to the system was allowing them to work at their own pace whenever they chose. For Arnold, the biggest benefit was that it *almost* eliminated any need for meetings like this one. He hated meetings.

Prisha asked, "What up, boss?"

Arnold debated how to broach the subject without pumping up anyone's hopes. Especially his own.

"Let me start by saying that nothing's definite, but earlier today I was called by a reliable source who said a major-league law firm has been contacting a few of our clients to ask for references. Word is, they might, and I emphasize *might*, be interested in pinging us about a pen-test."

A penetration test is when ethical hackers try to hack a company's security (a firewall for a computer network, or the back door for, say, a Ferrari dealership) using the same methods and strategies as malicious hackers or burglars. Only in these cases, the goal is to expose potential weaknesses and vulnerabilities that if remedied, would harden security and in some situations, be used to measure adherence to regulations.

A few seconds of silence ticked past before Prisha asked, "Who we talking about?" with a definite ring of eagerness in her voice.

"Before we get too worked up about this let's not forget we never did get a shot at the last contract that was rumored about. But the group's Larkin Standish and they're, like, a high-profile firm."

He already had their website up on his screen, so shared it with them all.

"Hey, check this out," he said, scrolling down the page. "They've got six freaking floors, dudes." Then, scrolling further: "More than a thousand partners in over twenty-one cities from Taipei to DC. How impressive is that?

"From what little I've been able to dig up on them, most of the partners are in this office and the other firms form some sort of loose affiliation that cross-refer and assist each other from time to time as needed, but one source suggested they have a few of Larkin Standish partners in some other offices, but that's beside the point. Point is, if we can finagle this, it'd be *ginormous*."

"How'd they find out we're looking to do pen-tests?" Lopez asked.

Arnold hesitated.

"Well?" Vihaan asked.

Arnold suspected Prisha understood. In fact, he would bet she felt the same.

Shaking his head, he said, "Sorry guys, that's classified."

After an awkward silence, Lopez mumbled, "It's gotta be Cain."

"As cool as this sounds," Arnold said, ignoring Lopez's dead-on guess, "this puts us in a good-news bad-news jam on account of word's out that we're being looked at." Pause. "And looked at not just by *any* firm. We're being looked at by Larkin freaking Standish, dudes." Pause. "And this puts us center stage in the spotlight. Which means potential clients are watching their selection process like eagles to see how it plays out."

He gave them a couple seconds for that to sink in.

"Which means we're sort of screwed, right? They hire another group, everybody'll be wondering why we were passed over. On the other hand, they hire us, everyone'll be watching how we do. That's good, right? Maybe...maybe not. Because then, if we blow it, we'll look like a bunch of bush-league clowns. Do that and we might as well kiss any hope of landing another pen-test adios."

"Put another way, be careful what you wish for," Prisha added. Then, almost as an afterthought: "What if we simply take a pass if they ask for a proposal?"

"And eliminate the risk," Vihaan added enthusiastically. "Just wait for another, less high-profile, less-risky offer."

Arnold nodded at the suggestion, having actually considered this. Fleetingly.

"The problem with taking a pass is I doubt we'd ever get another offer," Arnold said.

"Why do you say that?" Vihaan challenged.

"Because everyone'll know we chickened out. Think that's good for business?" Given that the question was rhetorical, he didn't bother waiting for a response. "Didn't think so. Bottom line: fortunately or unfortunately, it's looking like our one shot. Win big or go home." Then added: "Assuming they even contact us."

No one said a word.

"*But*...there's a strong chance they will, so I figure, hey, why not do everything we can to make us shine if they do. And the best way to do that is to be super prepared for an interview. And that requires us to scrape up every bit of information we can about them. My source says their managing partner—the person sniffing around about us—is a dude name of Webster Collier and he's a type-A who wants results, like, super fast. So it makes sense that if we really want to blow their socks off, we need to be ready to execute, like, blitzkrieg fast."

More dead silence.

Lopez: "Seriously? Even though we have no idea *if* they'll ping us?" adding a noticeable edge of incredulity.

Arnold nodded.

"Uh-huh. Dead serious."

More silence.

Prisha said, "I gotta ask, what specifically does getting a head start"—she made finger quotes—"mean? After all, our routine work's presently pushing saturation."

Arnold inhaled a long deep breath. This was going to be a hard sell.

"We need to put the majority of our effort into prepping for this by learning as much as we can about them. So much so that if we do land a contract, we're already fully prepared instead of starting from scratch. Yeah, it *is* a huge gamble for sure, but the kind that if we win, it's a reputation-maker."

Prisha: "You're out of your fucking mind, dude!"

Her full-force reaction jolted him, giving him pause. Of all of the team, he'd assumed—for whatever reason—that she would be the one to "get it." Why? Great question. Then again, how *had* he assumed she would react? Shrieks of joy? Cartwheels? After all, their workload was, well, admittedly stacking up. A blessing, for sure, but...

"I know, I know," he answered as placatingly as possible. "But if we're serious about shouldering our way into this niche, it's our only shot. And, for better or worse, I'm dead serious about this being a high-profile situation. Win this contract and do well, we'll be like serious players, right?" he added almost apologetically.

Silence. They weren't buying.

Forcing him to add: "Hey, am I thrilled our potential client's so high-profile? No. But they are and word's out. Like it or not, we *are* under the microscope. Now. Meaning we have no other option. If we have any prayer of doing pen-testing in

Seattle, we either nail this opportunity or toss our hopes right out the window."

"*If* we get the chance to submit a proposal," Prisha parried. "Or am I missing something?"

Vihaan—who seldom spoke during business meetings—said, "I dunno know, bro…with all the work piling up, why risk falling behind by putting all our effort into a vapor job, and in the process, risk pissing off our bread-and-butter paying customers? I mean, there's no reason to suspect our regular work's going to suddenly vanish while we focus on this other shit. What're we going to do if we end up with an unmanageable backlog? Think about that."

Again, Arnold nodded acknowledgement. After all, the dude just made a valid point. On the other hand, Vihaan's knee-jerk approach to life in general was maddeningly timid and conservative.

"I totally get it, Vihaan, I do. But I'm convinced it's a gamble worth taking. Look, land this job, kill it, and we'll lock down seriously awesome street creds. See?"

"Of course, I *see*," Vihaan said with uncharacteristic conviction. "I'm just saying we need to think long and hard about what you're proposing. There's a hell of a lot of *ifs* involved: *if* we're asked to submit a proposal. *If* they choose to interview us. *If* we're awarded the contract. Then the massive one: *if* we perform well. To me, it's just too big of a gamble. And, for the sake of argument, say we mess up anywhere along the line. We could lose our one shot at the pen-test market as well as the bulk of our regular customers. I'm talking about the accounts we depend on trickling in every day that make up our steady bread and butter business. Lose them, then what?"

Arnold decided *ah fuck it*. Time for a vote.

"I don't know what to tell you, dude, other than my gut says it's worth the shot. And besides, my source is like rebar-and-concrete solid. He wouldn't give me a heads-up if he didn't think we had a chance at an interview," he lied. "So, moving right along, Carlos, what's your vote?"

Lopez glanced away from the webcam, fingered his jaw, then returned to stare intently into the lens.

"I got to go with Arnold, guys. It'd be ultra-chill to go for it. I mean, say we don't get it," throwing in a shrug. "Think of all we'd learn from the exercise. I mean, even if we fail, we win. That's the way I see it."

"But," Vihaan whined, unable to surrender his position, "what about the *risk*? Blow any part of this and our future in pen-testing is toast. At least for this city it is."

"For sure," Lopez said with a that's-obvious nod, "but there's no way to break into the game without taking a risk. We either win the contract, or we don't. But don't ignore the fact there could be a shitload of reasons for not getting it. Hell, lawyers, of all people, should realize there's only one winner in this kind of selection process. That doesn't mean every team as passed over is a loser. No, man, it can be any number reasons teams didn't get it. Could be cost. Could be a bad interview. A bad hair day. Hell, could be just about anything. That's my two cents."

"Know what?" Prisha interjected. "I gotta go with Arnold too. For sure it's worth a try."

No one spoke for several seconds until Arnold said, "Sounds like we're going for it, right? Anyway, that's what I just heard."

"At the cost of neglecting our present work backlog," Vihaan said with doggedly righteous indignation.

"I take that as a no vote, correct?" Arnold said.

"Absolutely. I think it's too much of a gamble and I want that on the record," he said, punctuating the statement with an emphatic nod.

"*What* record?" Arnold asked.

"I'm just saying…"

Dead silence.

"In that case, it looks like we have three to one in favor of digging up what we can on the law firm," Arnold said in as neutral a tone as possible. "But to Vihaan's point, we can't afford to let our routine work slide, so, for the next few days I'd like you, Vihaan, to devote your time to keeping us up on the routine work as best you can. I'll put Gene on it with you."

Gene Ito—a new team member who was unable to make the meeting—was being considered for the position of Honolulu Associate, which would make him the only other Honolulu based team member.

How Arnold ended up with a home in Seattle and Honolulu went like this: he was living at home with his parents when they were murdered during a robbery of their strip-mall jewelry store. As if that wasn't enough, two years later his best friend Howie was shot to death in the kitchen by terrorists as collateral damage in their pursuit of Arnold. Arnold fled Seattle precipitously under an assumed name, landed in Honolulu, and reinvented himself under a false identity. That was, until his defense attorney, Palmer Davidson, cannily tracked him down. At which point circumstances forced him to default to Arnold Gold again.

The story got even more complicated. During adolescence, Arnold became infatuated with Howie's kid sister, Rachael. But after fleeing Seattle, he'd lost hope of ever seeing her again. As fate would have it, after resurfacing under his legitimate name, Arnold engineered a reason to start seeing her and one thing led to another...after she graduated from nursing school, he convinced her to move to Honolulu so they could start seeing each other seriously. She did, but initially was living in her own apartment. Until he finally convinced her to move in with him. Which she did.

The downside to this seemingly cool dual-city lifestyle manifested itself in the immediate aftermath of the infamous Noah Cain ransomware job. Initially, Rachael had no issue with Arnold flying to Seattle for the gig. However, when he stayed over for several days after the case wrapped up, she'd become, well, testy. In spite of explaining that he'd needed the extra time to resolve a few loose ends, her annoyance continued to smolder until ultimately hitting the flash point: last November when he was back in Seattle working a stolen-identity gig, she moved back to her apartment without any warning or discussion, leaving him hurt and confused.

After all, it was during this trip that he'd finally hired his first associate, Prisha Patel. A decision driven by 1) a glaring need for assistance; and 2) a glaring need to address Rachael's bitter criticism that Gold and Associates was patently ridiculous name if there were no associates. To stoke the fire, Rachael's reaction to Prisha's hiring? Jealousy. Go figure!

All of which seemed to drop Arnold into a bubbling caldron of conflict: yes, he was gaining traction in forging Gold and Associates into the business he envisioned, but at what cost? Losing Rachael? What kind of shitty deal was that? He *thought* he wanted both. However, a faint nascent inkling kept intermittently tickling his consciousness, whispering that that was impossible—which flat-out depressed him.

"Okay, boss, whaddaya want the rest of us to do?" Prisha asked, now sounding super-hyped at the prospect of moving ahead with preliminary research.

During the past few hours, he'd been agonizing over how best to sell Gold and Associates if given an opportunity to speak with Mr. Collier. Especially considering that Larkin Standish would damn well know they had yet to score their first pen-test. He decided his only real selling point was their past record of managing complicated cases, but that this, in itself, wasn't enough to elevate them above the competition. He needed a hook.

*What?*

"Prisha, I want you to start sniffing out everything you can about their security. Not just for the building but also if Larkin Standish has their own. I'm thinking a firm that big's got to have some, right? And while you're at it, see if you can get a bead on whether they have dedicated IT techs or outsource it. I suspect they have at least a couple in-house techs for the random shit that pops up every day." In replaying his last words, he decided to clarify: "I'm operating under the assumption that a group that size has at least a full-time SysAdmin"—referring to the System Administrator, the grand poobah—for a network. "We good?"

"Roger that," she said flipping a casual salute.

"Oh, almost forgot," Arnold added, "try to see what you can find out about what type of comms building security's using. As many details as possible"—he gave a fling of his hand "you know... radios or push-to-talk phones, whatever. And if radios, what frequencies? Oh, and if they're encrypted. That kind of shit. Got it?"

"Roger that too."

"Since we're on the subject of comms, and since this'll be our first of many"—he wanted to put a positive spin on it, as if they'd already inked the contract—"we need to decide what type of gear we need moving forward. I'd like you to come up with a recommendation. You know, phones or radios? Since it's a major investment."

*Phones or radios?*

Good question, now that he'd thought of it.

"That's not budgeted," Vihaan noted correctly, totally in character. "And it could get expensive," said the fiscal conservative of the group. "Or, rather, it will get expensive."

"No doubt, but we need to deal with it, and we *can* cover it. And besides, this should be a onetime expense, right?" He wasn't ready to leave this issue hanging, so before Vihaan could protest any further, he asked Prisha, "Any off-the-cuff thoughts about it?"

Prisha hesitated a second. "Since I'm now taking point on this, I say go with radios."

"Why?" Vihaan asked.

"Couple reasons. As you said, hopefully, we'll need them for more than just this one job and I don't think we wanta leave a record of cell numbers for someone to discover. Also, I don't wanta risk our conversations getting snagged to by a Stingray or one of the newer systems."

Stingray devices—also known as "cell site simulators" or "IMSI catchers"—were cell phone surveillance tools employed by law enforcement (and anyone else who might have one) to listen in on cell phones. By mimicking a cell phone tower, they trick any nearby phone into disclosing their locations and identifying information.

"Yes, we can minimize that risk with burners," she continued, "but if we end up doing more than one job, that could get pricey if we dump them each time."

Her arguments made a world of sense.

Arnold said, "Totally agree."

Lopez: "Me too, but say we go with radios, do we want encryption?"

"No," Prisha said emphatically. "That can be a huge issue if one of us accidentally messes up the key. Do that, our entire comm system goes tits-up."

"Good point," Lopez said. "But how do we keep people from catching us with a scanner?"

"Easy enough: we use programable PL-tones." She cut off the obvious question by adding, "That's not encryption *per se*, but it's as effective. Works by adding a subaudible tone to the signal so only radios programmed to receive that tone can hear it. Bingo, scanners can't listen in. The obvious downside is the initial cost will be higher than a round or two of burners. The upside is, we can use those babies all we want."

No one seemed to take issue with her logic, so Arnold said, "I'm sold. Vihaan, Lopez?"

Both agreed.

"Good. Then that item's off the list. Okay, next: Carlos. I want you to do a deep dive into getting as much information on as many partners and top-level administrative employees as you can. Start with Webster Collier and work right down the food chain. You good with this?"

"Got it."

"And what'll you be doing, boss?" Prisha asked.

Arnold gave a sly grin.

"I plan to hack their network."

Prisha guffawed.

"Yeah? Before we're even contacted? That's not only like super ballsy aggressive, dude. That's skating a hair over the line."

"Naw, not really," he said, trying to sound dismissive, in spite of getting her drift loud and clear. "After all, that's what they're going to hire us to do, right?"

*If we're lucky.*

Prisha scoffed.

"Dude, let's hope that's how it plays."

Ignoring the implication, he asked the group, "Okay then, we good?"

Everyone nodded at their webcams.

"I know I don't need to say this, but I'll say it anyway. Not a word to *anyone* about this. Understood? There's way too much at stake to afford an unforced error."

# HONOLULU

## CHAPTER 5

MEETING OVER, ARNOLD powered down his tablet and headphones, swung his legs over the edge of the chaise, and eagerly took the hot Surface off the bare skin of his thighs. Although using the tablet computer out here was super convenient, it got way too freaking hot during Zoom calls.

After schlepping the equipment back onto the kitchen counter and plugging in their charge cords, he leaned against the counter to wrack his brain yet again on a convincing way to pitch the powers at Larkin Standish that Gold and Associates should conduct their pen-test.

Hopefully, an enthusiastic endorsement from Mr. Cain had fueled Mr. Collier's interest enough to at least listen to a pitch. But what he really needed was a hook. What?

*Stay positive, dude. It'll come.*

*Yeah, easy to say…at the moment, you need to focus on a way to hack their network.*

He grabbed a yellow legal pad and thick-lead mechanical pencil and stormed back out to the chaise to brainstorm. Okay, so the paper-and-pencil thing was, like, ridiculously old school, but for some reason he could brainstorm more productively when doodling out random thoughts where he could look at the words and think about them.

Settled in, he began by scribbling out the names of his

favorite scams. In particular, ones that would be applicable to a high-security, high-rise building like the one housing their offices.

Although he didn't have a detailed layout for their particular floors, a cursory internet search yielded a standard floor plan for the building in general. In it, it showed the location of major core support systems such as elevators shafts, stairwells, and lavatories. It would serve as a great starting point. As for the specifics of the firm's six floors, he suspected that, except for the greater square footage, it was probably similar to the other law firms he'd worked for. Just more offices and conference rooms.

One major distinction, he suspected, was that a firm this large would have their own IT staff instead of outsourcing it to Bangladesh or some such place. Which made it likely that one of their floors contained a dedicated room for their servers and on-site backup devices.

Three quarters of an hour later, still comfortably semi-reclined on the chaise, he was zeroing in on an attack strategy. Before another distraction could bump his ideas from memory, he dictated an outline into his iPhone, checked that it was indeed recorded, then wandered back into his office to type out the plan in greater detail and store it on SAM.

With his notes securely saved and backed up, he emailed Mr. Cain asking for a call when he had a free moment. With all immediate tasks off his plate, he kicked back in his plush, black leather gaming chair to focus on the next items of business: dinner, Rachael, and Chance.

He padded back out to the deck where Chance was still curled up snoozing, dropped onto the chaise, and called Rachael.

Truth be told, having to call to make a dinner date seriously sucked. He preferred the way things had been when she was living here with him; a time when decisions like this one could be hashed out during breakfast or blossomed organically throughout the day. But now, having to call to make an appointment? It seemed so, hmmm...weird, unnatural, so unnecessarily businesslike. He caught himself staring at the sniper spot again.

*Damn. Would he ever stop doing this?*

"Arnold?"

He snapped back.

"Hey, sweetie, you free for dinner tonight?"

"Sure. What're you thinking?"

Easy enough.

"I'm thinking of picking up a couple dishes at Gulick's to eat here?" Just like old times...Gulick's deli, a great little Japanese place for killer take-out.

"Sure, that works...ah, have you and Chance gone out for your afternoon walk yet?"

She knew that Chance, like most doggies, loved a routine, so if this improved his life, Arnold had no problem providing it. In the years prior to Chance, Arnold's life had definitely been way more free-range. Then again, maybe he was just becoming an old fart by sort of liking a more structured life...

"Not yet, I've been dealing with a few issues. Why?"

"Since they close at three thirty, why don't I come over in about twenty minutes and we can pick up something *en route* to the park. Sound good?"

That Rachael. Always organized and efficient. He loved this about her. Probably one of the traits that made her a good ICU nurse as well.

"Perfect. We'll be ready to go by the time you get here."

Butt propped against the counter again, drumming the iPhone on his palm, he replayed their conversation. She sounded so...what? Warm? Well, no, not warm exactly, but certainly...different, a change he couldn't quite tag in spite of sensing it. Leaving him with a vibe that stoked hope that she might be edging back toward the way things were before her abrupt return to her apartment.

But this last thought gave him serious pause.

How *would* he react if she did drop a hint about moving back in?

Great question. One he'd never even considered before. Well, not directly. Certainly not consciously. Although, he suddenly realized that the thought had been marinating just below the surface of consciousness. Did he *really* want her to live here again?

*Wow!*

The days immediately following her precipitous departure—those times when he was finally able to rise above the shock and hurt of rejection—he was able to start to perceive enough contrast to appreciate the emotional turmoil she'd been putting him through while she was living here with him. It was like the resounding quiet one hears after turning off a white-noise generator. As difficult as it was to admit this to himself, embryonic qualms had begun to break surface; questions like: Did she embody the person he truly wanted to hang with in life? Boy, coming up with an impartial answer to that one was challenging to admit, but at the same time, he knew the answer would come, and when it did...he shut his eyes and shook his head, trying to refocus on the more important issue: the gig.

Okay, say they landed the Larkin Standish contract. Or any other Seattle pen-test contract, for that matter. Except for the drone he'd purchased for the Ramesh Singh take-down a few months ago, his Green Lake place had no essential hacker staples in stock. And, by the way, he'd crashed that drone, so it didn't even count. Bottom line: if he really meant to get serious about preparing to rock and roll on this gig—or any other one for that matter—he should remedy that situation, like, pronto.

Back in his office, he nestled into his chair again and began writing out a list of essential stock for the Seattle house, using the potential pen-test as a frame of reference. And was shocked to realize how many supplies were needed. But in all fairness, so far, their Seattle work hadn't needed what would be required for something as serious as a pen-test.

He logged into his Amazon account and ordered a set of programable Wilshin RFE 125KHz RFID cards: standard programable key cards for opening doors or gates. The next item: a Flipper Zero, a handheld device to read and program the key cards just added to his shopping cart. He closed his eyes and wracked his mind.

*What else? Ah, yes.*

He added five Hak5 USB Rubber Duckys to the cart. Then, spent another moment reviewing the list and decided that, for now, he had everything he needed.

He purchased his order.

*Done.*

His iPhone started in. It was Noah Cain. The timing couldn't be more perfect.

Leaning back in the chair, he crossed his legs, and answered with: "Thanks for calling, Mr. Cain."

"What may I do for you, son? Any word from Webster Collier yet?"

Arnold's pulse accelerated. Hacking into the Larkin Standish network now hinged—at least in its present iteration—on Cain's response to what he was about to ask. Although he wouldn't let on what he needed the information for, exactly.

"Not yet, but that's what I want to speak to you about."

Arnold went on to pose his questions.

Call finished, Arnold logged onto the website for the King County District Court, located the probate section, and brought up the case he was searching for.

*Rats!*

Only authorized persons could download the record. He thought about that a moment, decided, fuck it, and began snapping off screenshots of the relevant pages. He logged off and phoned Lopez.

After explaining to Lopez the information he was searching for, he added, "Dig up every scrap of news, documents, or any other chunk of information you can about the McDonald case. In particular, I need the name of the defendant's lawyer. Start with the screenshots I just posted to our Dropbox for the relevant names and dates."

"How soon you want this?"

Arnold thought about their priorities.

"Tell you what, it's not urgent-urgent, but don't put it so far down in the queue that you end up ignoring it, okay? But if we land that contract, we'll need it for sure." A split second later, he amended the statement: "Forget what I just said. We need it now *in case* we get the contract."

"Gotcha."

# HONOLULU

## CHAPTER 6

ARNOLD STOOD BY the open door of his silver Mini surveying the park.

*Perfect: no one in sight.*

He opened the back door, letting Chance bolt from the backseat and streak straight for his favorite cluster of shrubs. Rachael was already out, standing next to the passenger door. With no one else around, Arnold simply kept Chance's black nylon leash in hand. Just in case. Among his many reasons for loving this particular site was how infrequently other dogs and people used it, making it super cool for Chance to have free rein to nurdle leisurely from shrub to shrub exploring the world as only doggies can. Besides, he never wandered too far away, certainly never out of direct sight.

"The usual table?" Rachael asked.

"You bet," Arnold answered, leaning into the car, grabbing the white paper sack with their bento boxes of fried rice, teriyaki chicken, and pickled veggies.

A second white paper bag held their bottles of mineral water. Shouldering the car door shut, he trailed Rachael to the shaded table of weathered wood splattered with gray and white bird droppings. He spread out a couple of paper towels as place mats, plunked their paper sacks on top, then settled in on the bench beside her, their backs up against the table edge to admire the stunningly expansive one-hundred-and-eighty-degree view, the gentle breeze pleasantly cool. Arnold could hear the distant rhythmic crash of surf against the jagged formations of black lava far below while inhaling the salty tang of marine water.

"Damn. Just about perfect," he said, putting both elbows on the table behind him, eyes tracking a heavily loaded container ship plodding relentlessly across the horizon.

"Yes, it is. Gorgeous."

They stayed like this, silent, gazing out at the vast cobalt blue, as Chance continued his systematic exploration of all the usual suspects.

Need to tell her, dude.

After all, as business manager, she should be made aware of potential new accounts.

How she ended up in that job was, well, convoluted. Months ago, for pragmatic and somewhat selfish motives, he'd cajoled her into accepting the role.

Why did he do that?

Well, because he was such a total slough doggie when it came to the business of staying on top of the business. He needed someone who could look after all those niggling little details. When he was just starting out, that part was a cinch. He *was* Gold and Associates. But as accounts grew and Prisha started work, he desperately needed to offload these responsibilities to a responsible detail-oriented adult. Detailed, current, task-oriented...all aptly described Rachael. With three twelve-hour shifts a week, she had the time to manage the business. So yeah, that was his selling point when offering her the job. But he'd also had an ulterior motive: he'd hoped that by involving her in the business, she wouldn't become so irritated over his business travel. It was that simple. Yet simple things tended to become complicated, didn't they.

*Yeah, you really do need to tell her, dude. Why wait?*

After a tranquil interlude and careful inspection of an itchy spot on his right wrist, Arnold offhandedly threw out: "I got wind today of a possible gig in Seattle." Then he quickly added, "or a pen-test," hoping that this might give the news a bit more luster.

Then he cringed in anticipation of blowback over yet another business trip. To his surprise, she didn't say a word. He nervously side-eyed her.

She gazed at the view for another thirty seconds or so, until speaking in an unexpectedly neutral tone with eyes never wavering from the stunning view.

"Who's the client?"

*Wow, so un-Rachael. Or...was the volcano still fomenting, building sufficient force to explode?*

"Larkin Standish."

*As if that meant something.*

Then, hoping to impress her with the eminence of the job, he added: "They're a major-league law firm," but even the instant replay sounded, well, anemic.

Cringing, he side-eyed her once more. Her face remained impassive; her stare fixed. Then it was eyes forward again, hearing only the rustle of palm fronds in the gentle salty breeze.

Finally: "Would you like me to set up an account for them?" she asked calmly.

*Too calmly.*

Not at all what he was expecting. He turned now to look directly at her. For sure something was developing in those placid brown eyes.

"Naw," he replied. "Not yet," returning his gaze to the ocean.

"Why not? You sound like it's a pretty sure thing. Easy enough to delete the account if things fall through."

"That makes sense but...it's just that I don't want to do anything to, like, possibly jinx our chances."

Now, it was her turn to look at him, eyebrows in questioning arcs, intense dark brown eyes boring into him. He met her gaze and raised his eyebrows too.

*Two can play this game.*

"What?" he asked.

"Are you serious? About the jinx business?"

"I'm just saying..." with a shrug, his face starting in on the space heater thing.

"You? Superstitious?" she scoffed before turning toward the view again. "I find that very difficult to buy. You, of all people."

She shook her head dismissively.

"Hey, what can I say? You know how much I want into this line of work. And this job's a reputation-maker. Land this one and Gold and Associates will be emblazoned in the legal community's collective brain."

She slowly shook her head.

"Here's the thing I totally don't *get* about this pen-test fixation of yours: what makes a person want to break into someone's personal space—computer or business or whatever—to steal information? It's too totally weird. It's sick." Before he could respond, she raised her hand. "I know what you're going to say. We've been down this path a bazillion times already. You do it to help people improve their security. Yada yada yada...but that's like saying you want to become a peeping Tom so women will learn to close their blinds."

"Ah c'mon, Rach, you know we see this thing way differently. Let's not ruin a beautiful afternoon by arguing about it."

He returned this gaze to the cargo ship but couldn't shake her question. Why *was* he so emotionally committed to getting into that space? Since she'd first questioned his motivation, he'd been asking himself the same thing, but doubted he could ever come up with an objective, complete answer. He suspected that whatever the reason, it was far more complex and nuanced than the purported straightforward business decision he claimed.

After all, the team wasn't hurting for work, as their backlog clearly proved. So why take on the thrash of the new service? He suspected it came from the indelible emotional impact that his parents' murder had on him. Since then, many of his choices in life portrayed a rich tableau of its emotional aftermath.

A prime example: his elaborate, unabashedly over-the-top security systems. In both places. His rationalization? To protect SAM, his most valued and valuable possession. And although he dearly loved Chance now, he'd originally purchased him to provide an additional layer of security that sophisticated AI enhanced electronics can't. But Rachael knew all this.

After another drawn-out pause, she said, "Let me ask you this: if you do establish a name for yourself in this thing, would it require more business travel?"

*Uh oh.*

He'd been wondering how long before this subject would rear up, particularly since business travel was *the* hot-button issue fueling their present, uhm, relationship disharmony? The disharmony, he believed, was keeping her from moving back in with him.

"Let's not get ahead of ourselves, Rach. We haven't even landed our first contract."

"I understand that Arnold, but that doesn't invalidate the question," she said harshly.

*Too harshly.*

"I'm sure that if, God forbid, you don't get *this* contract, you'll eventually land another one. It's inevitable. I've seen you when you get this focused on something. So please just answer the question. I want to know."

She was facing him now, dead-eye serious, arms folded defiantly across her chest.

Well, hell, he'd known damn well this question lay just over the horizon. Hadn't been able to predict when it would crest but knew it would. Eventually. And to be honest, he was more than a little amazed it'd taken this long. Running his tongue over his incisors, he carefully crafted a reply.

"*If* we're lucky enough to establish a presence in this area," he began, aiming for as much positive yet ambiguous spin as possible, "we'll only accept Seattle jobs. Well, a few Honolulu ones maybe, I guess...but we'll certainly emphasize Seattle, since that's where the bulk of the team lives." He raised a hand before she could protest. "Remember, business is generated by word-of-mouth, so it's extremely unlikely we'd ever be offered a job outside of Seattle."

She shot him a dose of doubtful eye before returning to the view, clearly not buying his shuck-and-jive.

*Well, what had he expected?*

With their empty bento boxes and chopsticks discarded on the table between the chaises, Chance—the consummate diplomate—curled up equidistant between them, snoozing, Arnold semi reclined on his chaise leisurely sipping his favorite BV Rutherford Cab.

So far, the evening had been (surprisingly) perfect: a full stomach, a gentle cabernet buzz, deliciously temperate weather. Rachael—with the back of her chaise angled to forty-five degrees too—was staring languidly across the ravine but toward the evening sky instead of the sniper spot.

*What's not to like? A perfect evening, perfect opportunity. Ask her? Why not? See how she reacts.*

"Rach?"

"Hmmm?"

"Ever consider moving back in?"

He turned just enough to catch her reaction from the corner of his eyes. She remained perfectly still, staring, mute as he listened to the distant growl of jet engines from the general direction of Daniel Inouye airport intermixed in the rustle of palm fronds.

*Tick-tick-tick. Okay...*

After three or so more seconds, she turned to face him straight-on: "No."

Simple. Straightforward. Emphatic. Catching him completely by surprise. Well, not really, now that he thought about it. It did help clarify a prowling suspicion.

She eyed him a moment longer, before adding: "Here's the thing: I'm simply not comfortable with that level of commitment."

Arnold glanced at his wine glass in hand, his mind flashing the brain equivalent of the Blue Screen of Death, his face a portrait of stinging embarrassment. Although he'd suspected her answer, hearing it was, well, sobering.

"The thing is, I love this feeling of total independence. I'm not ready to give that up."

*What could he say? Nada.*

Besides, he was still reeling emotionally from facing reality dead-on.

"I love the security of knowing," she continued, completely oblivious to the effect her emphatic declaration had on him, "that if problems develop between us, I still have my safe place."

WTF?

"Wait?" he said, with a wave of his free hand. "Did I actually hear you say, *safe* place? What? Like I threaten you?"

He was staring intently at the sniper spot now, unable to meet her eyes, anger gusting inside.

*What had he ever done to make her feel threatened? Ever?*

Okay, he got it that their relationship had drastically changed, but to feel threatened by him?

She sighed.

"No, not physically."

"Then what?" he asked, genuinely perplexed, face still burning.

"No, that's not at all what I mean, and you know it."

He turned to stare at her: "No, Rach, I don't know what you mean," allowing his burning anger to seep into his words.

She turned away, blowing through pursed lips, returned to

him, eyes still hard.

"Like I said, I'm just not ready for that level of commitment."

No, do not say it.

But couldn't resist throwing it out there just to hear her answer: "Okay, I get it, so here's my offer: move back in and keep the apartment as a safety net. I'll cover your rent. In perpetuity, if that's how long it takes, okay?"

He hated himself for suggesting it, given his growing questions about their relationship, but by now a point needed to be made. He seriously resented the safe place remark, so...

He picked up a subtle sudden shift in her body language; a change only a lover would notice.

"Let me think about it," she said, returning her gaze to the night sky.

Hollow words. Dismissive. Causing him to understand just how pivotal this exchange was, that their relationship had traversed the Rubicon. His gut was suddenly laden with despair, making him realize that he was feeling sorry for subliminally knowing they'd been teetering on this precipice for months, yet being unable to acknowledge it.

*Why?*

Well, for several reasons, but mainly because of convenience and—as long as he was being completely candid— because relinquishing his adolescent fantasy had become so difficult.

Wow. Admitting this was horrendous.

*Do I really love her?*

The question hit like two thousand volts, making his ears feel as if they were ringing in the absence of sound.

A moment later, she was softly grasping his hand—a signal she'd established early on.

She whispered, "Why don't I take a shower?"

*Jesus, talk about schizophrenogenic!*

He nodded; his throat too dry and constricted to answer.

*Say something.*

But he was too torn to even open his mouth.

She pushed out of her chaise and drifted into the kitchen taking the empty bento boxes.

A moment later, he carried in the wine bottle and glasses.

# HONOLULU

# CHAPTER 7

ARNOLD SAT BOLT upright on the chaise, his heart rate skyrocketing to one hundred and forty beats per minute the moment his brain registered the caller ID. Holy shit.

*Good news or bad?*

Or was the question even relevant?

*C'mon, dude, answer the freaking phone.*

"Gold and Associates. May I help you?"

"I certainly hope so. I'd like to speak with Mr. Arnold Gold, please," a male voice stated dryly.

"Speaking," he answered in his best serious businessman voice.

"This is Troy Manning, assistant to Mr. Webster Collier of the Larkin Standish law firm. He would like to schedule a meeting with you. How is Friday morning looking?"

*Wow: The Call. The initial contact.*

The opportunity he'd been praying for.

He swallowed, steeling his nerves in an effort to force himself to stick to the plan he'd hammered out. Three weeks ago he'd received a telephone query from a much smaller law firm about a pen-test, but never heard back after the initial conversation. Reason for this failure? No clue, on account of having never heard from them again—leaving huge question marks hovering overhead even after replaying every word he'd

43

uttered during the brief interview.

Exasperating.

Though in the end, he suspected that he simply came across as pathetically too eager—perhaps desperate—for a contract. So, if there was one thing he *could* do differently this time, it would be to do everything possible to ditch the overeager impression.

*How?*

Well, for starters, appear less available.

With eye lids scrunched tight, heart pounding at least three hundred beats per millisecond, he said, "I'm thrilled to meet with Mr. Collier, but unfortunately, I'm completely tied up in our Honolulu offices the rest of this week. Could we possibly push the meeting into next week?"

"Certainly, but perhaps it'd be best if you give me a few options so I can coordinate with Mr. Collier's schedule. I know he's anxious to set this up."

*Perfect.*

"I'm looking at my calendar now, and see that I can move a few meetings around, so can be in Seattle just about any day next week. Depending, of course, on flight availability."

A brief pause, followed by: "In that case, why don't you make flight arrangement, so I know what day you're available, and then I'll schedule the meeting. It may be late afternoon, the exact time, naturally, depending on Mr. Collier's schedule that day. Will this be acceptable?"

Arnold fist-pumped air.

Flight booked, meeting scheduled, Arnold rocked back in his leather chair to decide what to do about Chance. His preference? Bring him. The downside, of course, was that if his luck held and they did land the gig, work would be all-consuming, and he didn't want to neglect Chance.

The other option would be to board him with the sitter he'd lined up for exactly this possibility. Rachael? Not even negotiable. She'd stated, rather emphatically, that her twelve-hour neuro-ICU shifts made caring for Chance impossible. She'd also been super adamant about not staying at his place when he was out of town. Period. Nonnegotiable.

A quick call to the dog sitter confirmed that, indeed, she could care for Chance next week but wanted the specific dates. After he explained the fluidity of the situation, she agreed to leave the duration open-ended. Good. Now, at least, Chance was taken care of. With this major distraction off his mind, he could focus one hundred percent of his attention on prepping for the meeting.

"Good news. Sort of," Arnold told the team as he semi-reclined on the deck chaise again, white ceramic Starbucks mug of hot chocolate on the glass side-table. "I'm scheduled to meet with the Larkin Standish dude next Thursday afternoon." He allowed this blockbuster news to sink in. "I'll be coming into Sea-Tac late Tuesday evening and would like us to meet at my place Thursday morning for a strategy session. Everyone available then? If not, I suppose we could do it Wednesday evening, but I'd really like to use the day to settle in."

"For sure Vihaan and I can make it," Prisha answered for the couple.

"Me too," Lopez added.

"Totally tubular, guys. I'm super hyped. All we have to do now is convince them that we're the best choice for the job, right?" Which, as he said it, sounded stupid and simultaneously sounded like some good team-building shit, so just let it slide. "So let's see where we stand with preparations and update each other on what we've got so far. Prisha, got anything yet on communications?"

*Jesus, calm the fuck down, dude.*

She gave a sarcastic laugh.

"Perfect timing. Just made a big-ass hole in our operating budget. Bought a seriously sick scanner that covers all the usual walkie-talkie channels. Also picked up four Vertel walkie-talkies complete with throat-mic headsets. So our comm needs are officially covered for this and future capers."

"Excellent." Arnold said. "Carlos, anything?"

Lopez cleared his throat.

"That court case you mentioned? I uploaded all the material to our Dropbox a couple hours ago. Seen it yet?"

"Not yet, but I plan on doing that as soon as this is a wrap. Thanks."

"That put me behind on my other research," Lopez added, "but I'm down to the junior partners now. I did a thorough dive on Collier, which I'll post later today."

"Cool," Arnold said. "And let's have a big shout out to Vihaan and Gene for keeping us up to date on our routine work. You dudes've been amazing." He paused to change topics. "Carlos, I'd like you to start scrounging up anything you can on the firm's floor plans. Search for anything with pictures of their offices: advertising, brochures, building permits, architectural sketches...you know the drill. All the usual sources, right?"

"No prob, boss."

Arnold was pleased with the progress.

What was he missing? Anything?

Couldn't think of that might be, so: "Anything else from anyone?"

Silence.

"Okay, then," Arnold said. "Let's keep on keeping on and I'll see you guys next week."

Meeting adjourned, he phoned Mr. Davidson to ask if he was available for dinner Wednesday evening and was surprised to actually have him answer his backline.

"I was not aware you planned on coming to town," Davidson said. "May I ask the reason? More work, I hope."

"Exactly. Our group's being considered for a potential pen-test with Larkin Standish, so I'm being interviewed by Mr. Collier on Thursday. I actually arrive late Tuesday and would love to have dinner with you Wednesday at Nell's if you're available?"

Nell's, a terrific little neighborhood restaurant, was one of his favorites, right behind Flavio's Pizza. Especially because it was in the neighborhood not far from his place, as was Flavio's.

"I am free then, so yes, I look forward to seeing you. Will Rachael be joining us? Shall I include Martina?"

"Unfortunately, Rachael won't be coming on this one..."

*Jesus, if you ever knew"...but, yes, please bring Martina. Hey, I'm super stoked at seeing you guys."*

Dan Calvo, the leasing agent for the building, popped up on Itzhak Mizrahi's caller ID.

*Huh.*

He put the phone to his ear, said, "Hey, Dan, what can I do for you?"

"Uh, Itzhak, this might be nothing, but I just got a call from a guy asking about available office space, which in itself's no biggie—I get these calls all the time—but the interesting twist about this one is, guy starts asking me to send him detailed floor plans. I ask, why not just come walk the space and see it in person? He claims he wants a better read on the space first to see if it meets their needs before wasting my time. As if tours aren't part of my job, you know what I'm saying? Of course I tell him, no problem, I do walk-throughs all the time, after all, that's what I'm here for. But the guy's dead set on eyeballing the schematics first."

After a couple seconds of dead silence, Mizrahi said, "Okay...?"

"See, I started thinking, in light of your warning the other day, the request sounded, you know, a bit fishy, if you see what I mean?"

*Could be. Or could be nothing.*

After filing it away, Mizrahi considered how best to respond.

"Good thinking, Dan. I appreciate you letting me know. What'd you tell him?"

"Couple things," Calvo said conspiratorially in a slightly hushed voice. "I pointed out that the *general* floor plans are already up on the website, but that as for sending detailed drawings of specific floors for lease, I was O-O-T-O till morning but would get back to him the moment I came in tomorrow. I wanted to run this by you before calling him back. How do you want me to handle this?"

"*Are* you out of the office?" Mizrahi asked out of simple curiosity.

"Hell no, I'm here sitting at my desk. I saw no need to fork over any information until I checked with you. Why?"

He'd always assumed that Calvo's intelligence hovered somewhere between a toadstool and the toad perched atop it, but now, maybe he should consider elevating that estimate a half-notch. He considered the leasing agent's words. The man could be right: the request for information might be indicative of the intelligence-gathering phase of a pen-test. Was Collier smart enough to exclude him from any contract negotiations with testers?

*Huh.*

Worth a moment of serious consideration.

"Smart move, Dan. I appreciate it. Let's think this through a moment..."

Including Dan in the decision process should further cement the man's allegiance. For Mizrahi, building and fostering solid loyalties was his cornerstone for maintaining the strong intelligence network essential for proactive security.

"Here's my thought: there're several ways your caller can get his hands on those plans, so I can't think of a valid reason *not* to give him a copy without raising suspicions. Look at it this way: if you're wrong and he's legit, refusing to give them to him could cause you to lose a potential lease, which I don't think you want. But if you're right, and this *is* part of a pen-test, refusing

48

to provide it could tip them that we're onto them. See what I'm saying?"

Probably not, knowing what a dumbshit he was.

"Hey, that makes real good sense, Itzhak. I didn't look at it that way."

*No, of course you didn't.*

"You happen to get his phone number?"

"Matter of fact, I did."

This surprised Mizrahi. Mildly. It raised Calvo off that toadstool another half notch.

"I'll tell you, Dan, we need to see the world from the perverted perspective of these assholes, especially if we want to be able to counter their threats. Okay, let's do this: call him back just as if it's business as usual, get his contact information same as you normally would, then send him a copy of a floor plan, then forward the intel to me. You with me on this?"

"Yup, I'll do exactly as you say."

Mizrahi rode down to Lorna Glass's floor and strode purposefully to her open office door. The head of building security was, as always, solidly in her straining desk chair, frowning at tandem monitors. He rapped on the jamb.

She glanced up; "No need to knock, door's open. What can I do for you?"

She leaned back in the protesting chair, muscular tattooed arms intertwined across her broad chest.

Mizrahi took two steps into the cramped sparse room.

"Want to let you know Dan Calvo just received a request for *detailed* floor plans of available spaces," he said in his conspiratorial tone as if such highly classified intelligence was intended for her ears only.

She screwed her face into a questioning expression, but said nothing, just stared back, hardly blinking.

Simmering dyspepsia began bubbling in the depths of his chest.

*Fucking passive-aggressive twat. What's her point? That she had bigger cojónes?*

He shook his head and cast a fleeting disgusted glance at the rainbow gay-pride flag on the wall.

"You understand the implication, don't you? That the request is very likely part of an intelligence-gathering probe for an impending pen-test?"

She followed his gaze to the flag, then back to him, cocked her head slightly, and waited a beat.

"I'd have to be flatline to not get it, Itzhak. On the other hand, it could be nothing more than a potential renter making a valid request. So what?"

"So *what?*" he echoed, making no attempt to tamp down his incredulity. He paused, blew a theatrically exaggerated sigh. "You really *don't* get it," he said as if dressing down a snotty, petulant adolescent. "I've just given you perfectly good intel of a potential intrusion and you're not the least bit interested? Are you serious or are you just trying to jerk me around?"

She arched her eyebrows.

"And just what, exactly, would you want me to do with this *perfectly good intel?*"

It took a supreme effort to restrain his initial response.

Composure in check, he said, "Let me point out to you, that if it becomes known we were provided credible intel about this attack yet sat back and did nothing to prevent it, we'd look like those fools who ignored all the signs that al-Qaeda was intending to fly pirated planes into the Twin Towers. Is that what you want for a legacy? We need...no, we *have* to be on top of this. What don't you understand about this? It's all about the optics."

She calmly fiddled with one of the many gold piercings peppering her right ear.

"Itzhak, what *you* don't seem to grasp is that so far there's not one scrap of credible information to indicate a vulnerability test is in play. And furthermore, if one is planned, we'll deal with it when it materializes. And as for your heartrending song and dance about our asses being on the chopping block, if, per chance, *your* offices are breached, it's *your* ass out in the cold harsh wind, not mine. After all, you never pass up an opportunity to tell everyone who'll listen that *your* firm's offices are *your* jurisdiction and *yours* alone."

She punctuated this last statement with a *so-there* nod.

*Cunt.*

# HONOLULU

# CHAPTER 8

KICKING IT ON a park bench, his mind wending through
endlessly intersecting paths, eyes lazily tracking Chance as he
sniffed out numerous shrubs along the periphery of the view
spot, Arnold teetered on Stage 1 sleep when James Brown
jarred him fully awake.

*Rachael.*

"Hey there. You and Chance out for your afternoon
break?"

A week—even, two days—ago he might've laughed at
how well she knew their rhythms, but today her question made
him wonder if their daily routines made him, well, boring?

*Was this just one in a list of reasons she was dropping him?*

Just one more item to add to the list of questions churning
his mind.

"Arnold?"

"Sorry. Was distracted, is all. Yeah, we're over at the view
spot, why, what up?"

"Why don't I bring dinner to your place tonight?"

*What?*

He sat upright, and strangled the urge to ask why tonight?

Since returning to her apartment, she'd been sending him
a series of mixed messages characterized by unpredictable
fluctuations from an acute need for intimacy to the need for

distance. Although he'd tried to pin her down as to what she wanted from this death spiral of a relationship, she uncannily weaseled out from underneath the subject every time. For Arnold, this emotional morass was about to cross the intolerable threshold.

"Arnie?"

"Oh, yeah, sure, cool. Distracted by Chance is all," he lied.

"Cool. No need to hurry or cut his break short. Give him plenty of quality nose time, and by the time you get home, I'll probably be out on the back deck reading."

*Home? How the fuck do I interpret that? Or am I just being too picky?*

"Roger that. See you when I see you."

After ringing off, he stared at the phone. Was bringing dinner over a good sign, or a prelude to bad news? A whisp of cotton brushed his heart. *Something* was up. For sure.

*No, don't let her aggravating mixed signals upset you so much.*

Easy enough to tell yourself. Much more difficult to enforce. He blew a long anxiety-laced breath and tried to refocus on Chance, but like one of those barely out-of-reach itches, he couldn't ignore the anxious churning in his gut. Something was up. Just had no idea what it might be. She wanted something.

The moment Arnold blew into the kitchen from the hall, he recognized the white compostable containers from Yohei Sushi—one of his favorite take-out joints—on the counter next to a bottle of Otokoyuma Saki.

*Nice! Hmmm... maybe I'll get lucky later?*

Shit, that niggling anxiety shouldered its way into consciousness again.

*Let it go, dude.*

He passed on through the kitchen, out onto the back deck with its lovely bougainvillea honeysuckle-like perfumed warmth. The ever-present scent from the tiny purple-red paper lantern blossoms was always comforting. Rachael was stretched out on her angled chaise reading her Kindle. Chance trotted straight over to her, the scrape of his paws on the deck catching her attention, for she turned around and glanced at Arnold.

"Oh, you're back," she said, giving Chance a two-handed dose of choobers.

He squelched the urge to ask why such royal treatment and instead said, "Thanks for picking up dinner and the sake," while dumping himself onto his chaise, eyes immediately zeroing in on the sniper spot on the other side of the ravine.

*Jesus, a lifetime ago.*

"Tell me more about this new Seattle job," she asked, powering down her Kindle.

"*Potential* job," he corrected, then went on to recite what little he knew about Larkin Standish and that Mr. Cain was responsible for the referral.

When he wrapped up, Rachael asked, "Why don't Chance and I come with you? After all, since I'm the business manager, this'll give me an opportunity to get a better feel for the company."

Wow, the out-of-nowhere proposition from Miss Nose to The Grindstone, Never Miss a Shift Nurse hit like a blindside left hook. So totally out of character. Making the suggestion, well, suspect…

"What about work?"

"Oh, that?" She said it as if it were no big deal. "Already taken care of."

*No shit? Something was definitely in the works.*

He turned to study her. She was innocently watching the Kindle shut down, radiating that angelic aura that girls seem to hone to a fine edge during early childhood, the look that Daddy always falls for. And this freaking redlined his suspicion meter.

"What's going on? Everything okay?"

She shifted her stare to the back of her hand, as if weighing her answer, then let it drift up to his eyes a moment.

"Auntie Shira called. She's worried about Mom. She's noticed some weird balance issues going on." Her lips pressed into a thin determined line. "She wants me to come home to help her assess the situation."

She locked her eyes onto his now, waiting.

Questions swamped his brain. But above them all floated a strong suspicion that her mother's new health concern, although undoubtedly valid, had just become a convenient parachute. A deception for what would drive the spike through what was left of their relationship. A cold gust of anxiety began whistling through his innards.

*Boom.*

Leaving him in a total zugzwang.

*Fuck it. If this was what it is, then so be it.*

In that instant, he was so exasperated over constantly walking the razor blade of their relationship, he no longer cared. But that particular internal debate would have to wait to be sorted out in the near future, for at the moment he needed to play this out.

Then, he was out of the chaise, heading for the office, calling over his shoulder, "Hang on, let me see if I can get you on my flight."

# CHAPTER 9

## Seattle—Wednesday Morning

AFTER CHOWING DOWN on Starbucks sausage, cheddar, and egg breakfast sandwiches, Arnold, Rachael, and Chance sauntered along East Green Lake Drive North toward the PCC market to pick up enough staples to sustain them until they had more clarity on how long they might be staying, although Arnold was harboring a strong suspicion that they wouldn't be returning to Honolulu in sync.

"We don't need to pick up anything for my lunch," Rachael said offhandedly. "I'll be at Mom's all day."

Rachael and her now-deceased brother Howie had grown up in the family house just two blocks from where Arnold's family—now deceased—had lived.

"Plan on seeing your dad this trip?" Arnold asked, steering Chance away from a shrub.

"I'm sure I will at some point, but for now I just want a better feel for what's going on with Mom."

Although her parents divorced years ago, Rachael had never—as far as he could tell—sided with either one the way so many children in divided families tend to do. Regardless, he'd simply assumed that she'd pitched her tent in her mother's camp because of the bond of Sisterhood in addition to the law of averages. Now that the subject of her dad was fresh in his mind, he realized that Rachael had already tried and convicted him of her father's primary felony: excessive business travel.

*There you go, your Honor: Exhibit A.*

Home again, lunch and dinner in the fridge, Arnold schlepped his box of newly purchased programable key cards, Flipper Zero, and Hak5 Rubber Ducky USB drives downstairs to his specially designed and tricked out basement room.

When constructing his present brutalist cube on the plot where the family's original 1920s Tudor had stood, he'd completely redesigned the original basement room where SAM 1.0's birth had taken place.

The new room was outfitted with a dedicated electrical circuit and separate temperature/humidity controls to one day accommodate a SAM 2.0 clone. The SAM concept began several years ago when Arnold networked three computers together in an attempt to emulate Nate Silver, a dude with an amazing ability to forecast events by complicated probability analysis.

Arnold's network eventually grew to twenty-five fully loaded Dell servers forming a neural network. The present system—SAM 2.0—represented more than four years of dedicated development that was continuing to evolve. SAM did amazing tasks for him; like actively trading his stock portfolio and making cannily accurate predictions.

It'd become an extension of Arnold's persona. Think Alexa meets HAL.

The name SAM was his snide riff on Apple's famous Siri, the AI program first introduced in Beta form on the Apple 4s iPhone. The insider joke was that the name, Siri, was a spinoff from a Department of Defense project at SRI, the Stanford Research Institute. Hacker humor. Guess you needed to be one to fully appreciate it.

SAM 1.0 went up in smoke when Arnold blew up the original Tudor. Weeks after fleeing Seattle, Arnold inked the buyer's agreement for his present two-bedroom Honolulu place. The first thing he did after being handed the house keys was to become a Best Buy frequent flyer, purchasing enough off-the-shelf PCs to build SAM's replacement in the guest bedroom.

Rebuilding SAM was easy in comparison to the first iteration because all he had to do was network enough hardware together to accommodate the software he'd already developed and backed up across three different Cloud storage sites. In no time at all, SAM 1.0 had risen from the ashes—so to speak—and was humming along. At which point, Arnold began tinkering it into SAM 2.0. Then, last fall—as soon as the completely redesigned and rebuilt Seattle house became inhabitable—he'd started to assemble the hardware in the Green Lake for a Seattle SAM clone. Why? To provide a geographically remote back-up to Honolulu SAM. Just in case.

After tucking in at his desk, he began to program one of the newly purchased Rubber Duckies. The ultra-cool thing about these USB drives was that when plugged into a computer, they immediately injected, at superhuman speed, malware that eluded antimalware software by masquerading as nothing more than a few normal keystrokes.

Arnold modified this one to install a chunk of malware in the victim's computer. Once it was embedded, it allowed him to access the machine at will to do just about anything he wanted, including download documents and credentials. It was this capability that made Rubber Duckies a must-have utility tool for any self-respecting pen-tester and would serve as Arnold's go-to secret weapon for stealing access into the Larkin Standish computer network.

He devoted the remainder of the afternoon to working on the SAM 2.0 clone.

"You down there, Sweetie?" Rachael called from the doorway atop the basement stairs.

A quick glance at his watch.

*Wow. Already time to head over to Nell's for dinner with Mr. Davidson and Martina.*

Had totally lost track of time. He eyed his project with a sigh, figured it was, after all, a work in progress, right? That's the thing he loved about this one, no pressure.

"Be right up."

As Arnold was locking the front door, Rachael touched his arm: "Please don't mention my reason for being here, okay?"

Arnold nodded acknowledgement. Rachael eschewed disclosing details of her personal life to anyone, including him. Especially when touching on any subject she believed carried the slightest trace of reflecting badly on her or her family. She obviously felt her mother's potential condition fell into that bin. At least in her eyes, it did. He simply didn't see it that way, but oh well...but this enigmatic secretive aspect was also annoying now that he was gaining more objectivity.

"Rachael, what a pleasant surprise that you are joining us," Davidson said above the white noise of a busy restaurant while they were approaching the table, the four of them waving greetings to one another, the air carrying pleasant suggestions of cooked garlic and pasta water. "Arnold failed to mention you were accompanying him."

"That's because it was a totally last-minute decision," Rachael said, smiling, folding herself into the chair to Arnold's left, then promptly popping the napkin to drape over her lap. "I wasn't sure if I could get my shift covered. Since I'm the business manager, I decided that tagging along would give me a better appreciation for our work. So, Ta da!"

Arnold marveled at how smoothly fabricated the fib flowed, and suspected it wasn't as spontaneous as she made it appear.

Davidson turned to Arnold.

"Speaking of business, congratulations on meeting with Webster Collier tomorrow. That's quite a prestigious job if you were to land it."

"So I understand," then hesitated a moment to collect his wording. "Hey, long as we just touched on that particular subject, I want to ask a favor." Paused another moment. "If we're lucky enough to get it, we'll need a lawyer of record in the off chance, God forbid, one of us is apprehended during the deed. Will you serve as our attorney of record?"

Davidson leaned back in his chair and eyed Arnold with a curious expression.

"Why me? Why not Noah Cain? Or has he already refused?"

*Good question. Why indeed?*

The question had never even brushed consciousness. He began finger-combing his hair, sorting out the answer. In his peripheral vision, he caught Rachael watching him.

"I guess seeings as you're my defense attorney and all…" A shrug. "I dunno…makes sense that way."

Their waitress arrived with their wine and poured a sample glass for Davidson to approve. Davidson went through the nose-in-the-glass sniff routine followed by a sip, a tongue roll, then a final nod of approval.

"Are we ready to order?" she asked.

"Yes, I believe we are," Davidson proclaimed for the group.

As the waitress turned heel, Davidson continued, "Getting back to your question, I need to read the contract to assure myself the group is legally indemnified before I will agree to represent you."

"There you go," Arnold told Rachael. "A perfect example of why he's my lawyer." He picked up his phone and started typing. "I figured you'd say that, so I'm emailing you a draft. It'll be in your office in the morning."

Later that evening, as Arnold and Rachael were accompanying Chance on his routine end-of-day potty break, Rachael took his hand, stopped walking, and looked at him.

"I understand what's concerning Auntie Shira so much."

Arnold decided to listen to the rest of the message before saying a word.

"I'll feel more comfortable if I stay at Mom's while we're here," she said, then quickly added, "I plan on moving some of my clothes over in the morning, right after our business meeting."

*Boom.*

And there it was. Suspicion confirmed.

A series of emotions roman candled though his mind, headlined by profound sadness for her mother's situation. Perhaps the diagnosis hadn't yet formally been made, but that was just a matter of time. Clearly, there was a problem, and Rachael was rightly worried for her, so yeah, he got *that* part. But...to be heartlessly honest about it, there were other ways of dealing with this unfortunate situation than walking away from their relationship. Because he knew in his soul that they were headed down this exact path. The actual diagnosis was irrelevant; it was nothing more than a smoke screen for more serious issues. Relationship-naïve he was, but stupid? Naw, not stupid. First the apartment, now this. Duh! The only question was, what would be her next move?

In the next moment, he was shocked to realize he was feeling sorry for *himself*.

*For himself? Hated to admit it, but yes.*

How freaking self-centered was that!

A tsunami of intense guilt rolled in, as in: what kind of person feels sorry for himself in a situation like this?

Well, what about someone being forced to confront the dissolution of a relationship? For knowing all too well the loneliness he was facing now? For not wanting to lose someone when you can't admit to yourself that it's the best for your mental health and general well-being? All of those issues rolled into one fat emotional enchilada.

Shit, she was staring at him, waiting for a response, but his mind was freaking blank. He simply nodded that he understood. Perhaps understood too much.

"I'm having lunch with Dad tomorrow," she blithely continued, "so don't expect to see me at all tomorrow after the meeting wraps up, okay?"

*See? Case in point.*

Was that a *whew, glad that's over* expression she just flashed?

"Got it," he croaked, returning his attention to Chance.

*What else was there to say?*

# CHAPTER 10

## Seattle—Thursday Morning

"WE DECIDED TO pick up Carlos on the way over as today's contribution to fighting climate change," Prisha told Arnold while crossing the threshold into the great room from his porch with Vihaan and Lopez trailing like baby ducks.

Arnold introduced each team member to Rachael, who, Arnold noticed, seemed to be checking Prisha out. Discreetly, of course, but clearly engaged in that head-to-toe assessment thing that women seem to routinely do. If Rachael's antennae were searching for the slightest vibe of something more than a professional link between them than taking care of business, this should finally drive a stake through the heart of that suspicion.

Not that it made a rat's ass difference at this point. To his surprise, his restless night had left him with a strange fatigue-fueled, emotionally draining, resignation to the slow dissolution of their relationship and his impending bachelordom. And surprisingly, this unanticipated stoicism was also a bit unsettling...as if he were starting to embrace this change as one he was now admitting was for his own good but one he'd been too goddamn spineless to instigate.

He directed the team into the kitchen. The table was generously stocked with an enticing carton of Starbucks pastries and two containers of their black coffee.

After a few minutes of obligatory chitchat and enough time for everyone to devour the pastry with coffee, Arnold kicked off their official agenda.

"I want to thank you guys for the incredible effort you've put into intelligence-gathering these past days while still keeping our nose above water with the bread-and-butter workflow." He applauded them. "All this hard work will pay off once we land the contract."

"You mean, *if* we land the contract, don't you?" Vihaan asked.

Ignoring the jab, Arnold turned to Lopez.

"Any update on the floor plans?"

Lopez shoved the cardboard pastry box to one side and replaced it with an enlarged schematic of the typical floor plan for those floors occupied by Larkin Standish. Although rudimentary, it did provide relevant information by demarcating the exterior walls in relation to non-modifiable internal structures like elevator shafts, stairwells, and toilets. The exact layout of corridors, offices, and various other rooms would vary somewhat for each floor.

Smoothing out the folds in the paper, Lopez said, "Although this only gives us a skeleton for the target floors, we can fill in specifics as they're acquired." He traced his index finger along the building outline, he continued: "As you see, each floor approximates a capital A with core structures like elevator shafts within the horizontal bar." He tapped the rectangular block of shafts with his fingertip. "The north and south stairwells bookend the elevator shafts here and here and to each side of the stairwells is a restroom. Men's room to the north, women's to the south." He glanced at the team. "Questions?"

Not a peep.

He returned to the schematic.

"As we know, the firm is on floors thirty-four to thirty-nine. The only specific detail we know so far is that their reception lobby's on thirty-four, which puts it around here." He tapped the space in the immediate vicinity of the elevator shafts. "With this in mind, it makes sense that this floor contains the bulk of their conference rooms." He glanced at the others as if waiting for any questions. No one asked any. "After a bit of snooping I learned that their law library used to be on thirty-five, but with so much of it online now, I don't know if that's still accurate. That's it for me, guys."

"Nice job, dude," Arnold said, giving him a playful shoulder punch. "We'll fill in the blanks as we learn more. At this point, I'd like you to start searching for whatever documents you can find online. Press releases, motions, whatever you can get your hands on that originated from their offices."

"Why's that?" Rachael asked.

Arnold glanced at Prisha to answer, wanting to showcase her worth to the team.

"By tracking down work from their offices, we can search the metadata to find out what operating system they use. That'll help us find how to get into their network."

Rachael glanced at Arnold, but he didn't know what to make of her expression. He then caught Prisha tracking the subtle non-verbal communication.

After a brief hesitation, Prisha added, "A firm that big might just be running Linux."

Arnold suspected she threw that in as a way to keep the discussion moving.

Lopez said, "Definite possibility, but my money's on Windows."

"Might as well make sure, if we can." Arnold said, glad they weren't getting mired. He glanced at Vihaan. "Any additional word on the head guy, Collier?"

After carefully setting down his coffee cup, Vihaan cleared his throat professorially.

"Not much other than routine information. Born-and-raised Seattleite. Undergrad at Stanford before matriculating UW Law. Married with one sixteen-year-old son, William, a sophomore at Lakeside." He was referring to an academically upper-echelon private school in the city. "That's it for now, at least."

Arnold slapped a high-five with him.

"My man!" He turned to Prisha and asked primarily for the benefit of the group, since he knew the punch line.

"Any update on security and IT support?"

With a sly smile and a slight head bob, she spoke: "We got a fascinating mixed bag. Security for the building's contracted out to a city-wide security company, North Sound Security." Pause. "But get this: the guards who actually work the building are managed by a *building* employee."

She wagged her eyebrows comically.

"Jeez, sounds awkward. Any idea why they run it that way?" Lopez said.

"I'm getting there, but the word I heard is it's supposed to provide more relevant direct oversight. The head of security for the building's one Lorna Glass. Interesting backstory there. She's a retired King County detective. Allegedly." A brief pause. "But back to the general overview. What makes things more confusing is that Larkin Standish maintains their own security managed by an Israeli dude, Itzhak Mizrahi. Legend has it he's ex-Mossad." Laughing, she added, "I mean, that's, like, so cliché. Even got a whiff there's some hinky backstory floating around about that, but it's so deeply buried that I haven't been able to dig up any real facts." Then, almost as an afterthought, Prisha added: "Doubt I ever will, either. But back on point...they have their own IT with a SysAdmin, name of Serge Valchenka, and a couple techs." She scanned their faces. "Get all that?"

"Jesus, girl," Lopez said with a note of awe, "that shit's outlandish. How'd you manage to do all that so fast?"

She just smiled slyly and turned to Arnold. "How you coming with copping their network?"

"Slowly. It's presently a work in progress, but I should have something soon, like, right after we wrap up our in-person recon. At least, I hope to have it by then. I've got a plan presently in the works."

After polishing off every possible pastry crumb and drop of coffee, the other team members split. Once the front door closed behind them, Rachael grabbed her coat from the hall closet and said that she was leaving but would call later. No mention of dinner plans or where she would be spending the night...

Arnold hugged her tightly.

As another wave of sadness soaked his heart.

"Love you, Rach."

After a perfunctory hug, she held him at arm's length and studied his face questioningly.

"I'm sorry about the circumstances, sweetie, but they are what they are. And besides, I can already see that this job's going to consume you. The time will simply fly past."

For a long moment he stood looking at the front door, wondering when, if ever, she would walk back through it again or even if this was one of the last times he would see her. After another fleeting bout of self-pity, he shook his head. The best remedy was to get back to work.

Back in the basement room, he labeled the malware infested Rubber Ducky with a self-stick label that read CONFIDENTIAL.

# CHAPTER 11

## Seattle—Thursday Afternoon

LUCKY PRISHA FOR snagging an ultra-rare curb parking spot along Eighth Avenue. Not only that, but only a couple blocks off James. No fire hydrant, no passenger-load zone, no nothing but an empty space big enough to squeeze the car into.

"Holy shit, maybe I should put down five on a Lotto ticket today," she muttered while backing in.

She shifted into park, pulled a blue DISABLED PERSON placard from the glove box, hung it from the rear-view mirror, negating any worry about paying for parking.

Grinning broadly, Arnold asked, "How the hell did you manage to score one of those puppies? Or is it forged?" hiking a thumb at the handicap card.

"Oh that?" she said with a dismissive wave. "It's Vihaan's, but I do most the driving."

Her husband had been injured in a car accident when the car he'd been driving was t-boned by jerk with multiple DUIs

Prisha, Lopez, and Arnold climbed out of the car into bright sunlight and stood facing west, with a full-on view of their target. For today's little drama, Vihaan was at home slogging through routine work orders. Prisha turned toward Arnold, hands cupping hips, sizing him up.

"Know who you remind me of? Christian Bale in *American Hustle*."

She was wearing an orange Grubhub T-shirt with a Jimmy John's sandwich bag dangling from her right hand.

Arnold chuckled at the image; the scene dredged from memory.

"Loved that flick." Then spread his arms to do a three-sixty. "I take it that you like."

She laughed.

"That padding porks you out a good thirty pounds. With those fake jowls and studio-grade moustache, you could land a role as El Chapo."

"Sounds like an endorsement," he said, bending over to adjust the external knee brace clamped on his right leg.

In addition to his khaki Dockers, he had on an oversized pale blue dress shirt, Blaze wraparounds, blue blazer, backpack, and a Tesla ballcap with the bill pulled down to his glasses. The pièce de resistance: a vintage leather attaché case he'd picked up at an OfficeMax just hours before his flight went wheels-up from Daniel K. Inouye airport.

Lopez didn't need a disguise since he wasn't playing a major role in today's performance.

"You sure you want me as the shill for this?" Prisha asked Arnold. "I mean, why not just drop that sucker right next to the desk and let human nature take its course?"

Shrug adjusting his backpack, Arnold answered.

"Naw, she'd be suspicious of me. Women trust women, so odds are better she'll buy it coming from you."

Prisha hiked a shoulder.

"If you say so."

She turned to scope out their target again: a massive, towering glass and steel office building embedded in the steep hill just beyond an elevated span of I-5.

"All set?" Arnold asked.

They were.

Arnold, Lopez, and Prisha started down the steep north side of Cherry Street toward Fifth Avenue.

As they came out from under the shade of the freeway, Arnold halted for a look at the awe-inspiring building from this novel perspective. Prisha and Lopez pulled alongside to gaze at it too, palms shielding their eyes from the reflecting glare.

"Any reason we're not flying a drone outside their windows as one more way to scope out the floor plans?" Lopez asked.

Arnold said, "Yeah, thought about that, but it's too problematic for a couple reasons. First, we'd have an audience." He threw a nod toward an assortment of tents and tarps on the sidewalk sheltered by the freeway, inhabitants scattered about, some already watching them. "Not sure we want that. Secondly, there's no control spot around here that's worth a damn." Then, tossing another nod at the building, he added: "More importantly, it'd be, like, freaking impossible to keep track of which floor we'd be scoping out. Good thought, though."

"Yo, Carlos," Prisha said, "time's a-wasting."

Lopez resumed walking the steep grade down toward the building. A moment later, Prisha fell in behind, maintaining a respectable separation to sell the impression they weren't together. Arnold gave her a reasonable head start then fell in too, getting into character with an appropriate limp.

Pushing through the heavy glass door, Arnold entered a voluminous high-ceiling lobby of glass walls and glossy granite floors. Dead ahead stood a waist-high wrap-around counter. First impression? An information desk, but then a closer look showed an enclosure around a uniformed guard watching a wall of HD CCTV screens. Not only that, but the dude was freaking *standing*. It suddenly dawned on him: Security Central was strategically positioned to provide the guard an uninterrupted, naked-eye three-hundred-and-sixty-degree view of the entire lobby. Impressive. Challenging.

Off to his right was a free-standing building directory, a granite slab angled at forty-five degrees on a matching pedestal, Prisha already in front of it, as if looking up a name or floor.

He sidled up to her and asked in sotto voce: "Scoped out the security yet?" while also appearing to study the list of names and floor numbers.

"No way to miss it, dude," she answered out the side of her mouth. "Lopez should be in position by now."

She drifted off toward one of several separate banks of elevators, each bank serving a different group of floors.

It took Arnold a moment to realize that she was heading for the bank to the Larkin Standish reception. He fell in a few steps behind her. Seconds later, one of the four cages arrived. As the descending passengers began exiting, Arnold rudely shouldered his way in, thumbed the button for floor thirty-four while Prisha slipped unobtrusively into the opposite corner, turned to face the doors, and folded her hands primly in front of her, a bored expression masking her face.

Arnold watched each of the five other passengers swipe key cards over a black card reader before pressing the button for their floor. All different. Rats. This building took its security freaking seriously. But on second thought, it made perfect sense, given the number of financial and legal firms here. It also dawned on him that the only reason he'd been able to access the Larkin Standish reception floor without a card was that it must be one of the few floors open to the public. A wave of vindication rippled through his chest for having stocked up on blank key cards and a Flipper Zero.

He suppressed a smile.

*Okay, chalk one up for the good guys.*

Moments later, the elevator doors glided noiselessly apart, exposing a tastefully subdued reception lobby befitting a law firm of such illustrious reputed stature. Fully in character now, Arnold and Prisha jostled each other, jockeying for first to the reception desk. Per their plan, Prisha arrived a half step ahead of him, pulled up, shot him a fleeting glare of supreme annoyance, before calmly handing the receptionist the Jimmy John's bag with: "Delivery for Jenkins and Cauthorn."

As the receptionist was skewering Arnold with a tempered-steel glare, Prisha set the sandwich bag squarely in the center of the desk along with the Rubber Ducky beside it.

As per their choreographed diversion, Arnold continued to rudely elbow Prisha aside with a down-the-nose-sneer while loudly announcing, "I'm here for a conference with Drexel Bush."

Flashing a forced smile, the receptionist turned to Prisha: "You were saying?"

"These are for," Prisha checked the cellphone in her hand, "Sue Jenkins and Miles Cauthorn."

The secretary said, "Thank you."

As Prisha started to turn toward the elevators, the receptionist called, "Oh miss, you dropped this," waving the Rubber Ducky at her.

Prisha hesitated for a fractional beat…

"Uh, I just picked that up off the floor, so…"

The receptionist's eyes narrowed into a chastising glare.

"Oh, I guess in that case, you won't mind if I dispose of it thusly," and tossed it under the desk with the hollow *thunk* into what sounded like a metal wastebasket.

Arnold's heart dropped.

*Jesus! That was his best shot. Now what?*

Walk away now, she'll know he was part of the scam. Had to continue his role now. He leaned forward, palms flat on the desktop.

"Do you *mind* answering me now?"

He stole a sideways glance at her monitor. Ah, a Word document running in a legal software package that he recognized from his work at Mr. Cain's firm. He also noticed an RFID key card on a neck lanyard next to her keyboard.

The receptionist skewered him admonishingly for five full

passive-aggressive seconds before she smirked.

"Wrong office, *sir*."

"Oh."

Straightening, he feigned embarrassment, turned, and limped back to the elevator. He stopped, stood to the right of the doors, and mimicked making a call with his phone while actually recording a video of the area. Fake conversation over, he opened his phone's settings, brought up the Wi-Fi, snapped a screen shot of the three strongest signals, one of which bore the title "LarkinStandish Guest." Encased in a free-standing plastic frame on the reception desk was the sign: WI-FI GUEST PASSWORD = LARKIN!STANDISH. He included a nice shot of this too.

He emailed all of that to Lopez, who—according to plan—should be camped out on the landing on one of the stairwells to either side of the elevator shafts. The plan was for Lopez to immediately implant a RAT into the guest network so that Arnold could check it for a possible crossover into one of the firm's private networks. The odds of this panning out were, like, admittedly dream-on low, but to not at least give it a shot would be dereliction of duty. Besides, the results—positive or negative—would give them a quick initial read on the firm's network security. Besides, trying it didn't cost them anything but a few minutes, so why not do it, right?

With his role in the little drama finished, Arnold thumbed the elevator button while casually scoping out the closest stairwell. *Goddamnit!* The door required a key card. Same with the north stairwell. Meaning, Lopez wasn't out there on either one. Well, damn, so much for catching a break on this job. He began to mentally scramble for a fallback scenario.

*What the hell, why not just embed that freaking malware now?*

Just sit down in one of the chairs in reception and do it, right?

*Well, duh, you dumb shit.*

Not without a laptop and a copy of the malware—both of

which were in Lopez's possession. Okay, so much for that bright idea. On to plan B. An elevator arrived.

Arnold exited the cage, glanced around the granite lobby for the separate bank of elevators to the garage. The plan had been for him and Prisha to walk both stairwells from the law firm down to the lobby as a way of surveying the state of the building's security. Obviously, that had been impossible, so the next item on their checklist was to recon the garage. But now, with the stairs no longer an option, their only garage access from inside the building was via this separate bank of elevators. The only other garage entrance was the car ramps off the street. And those were undoubtedly under constant CCTV surveillance too. Goddamn building security was turning out to be way more of a pain in the ass than he had anticipated.

When the doors opened on the A level of the parking garage, Prisha was already there, inspecting a building directory to the right of the doors.

"Well, that exercise just turned to shit," Arnold said, stepping out of the elevator.

She shrugged.

"Exactly the reason we're doing this, dude. Look at the bright side; we just learned a ton."

"True that. Man, that receptionist was something else." He shook his head woefully. "If she's any indication of their security, it's like super tight. She sure as hell's had some serious-ass training on how to recognize and deal with social engineering."

"Agreed."

They meandered down to B level but no further, discovered it to be boringly unremarkable and stereotypic for an office building with floors segregated into public and reserved spaces. Vehicle access from the side streets. Pedestrian access only through the secure stairs or from the lobby elevators. Several signs posted about anywhere one might possibly look warning that the 4th Avenue lobby doors were locked from six PM to six AM, limiting pedestrian access to the single door on Fifth. Again, pretty damn secure building, this one.

They circumvented the red and white-striped barrier-arm guarding the car entrance onto the side street.

"Garage doesn't strike me as being worth a shit on this one," Prisha said. "Whatdaya think?"

Arnold paused briefly to glance back inside the gaping entrance.

"Totally agree."

They began to trudge back up the steep grade of Madison Street toward Eighth Avenue where the car waited.

"You notice almost all floors require an RFID?" Arnold asked, breathing hard.

Prisha just nodded. Both of them short of breath.

"Just stocked up on blank programmables along with a Flipper Zero," he offered between pants.

She tapped his shoulder, motioned him to stop walking, then stood, hands on hips, gasping out a laugh. After finally catching her breath.

"Nice, but you still gotta steal their network, dude. Got a Plan B in your hip pocket, because Plan A's now doing the backstroke right on down the sewer."

After a few deep breaths, he shook his head.

"Haven't given up on Plan A just yet. Have a fallback for sneaking one of those babies in." He was referring to the malware-loaded Rubber Ducky. "That secretary seriously pissed me off with all that haughty righteous-indignation bullshit. That firm's really trained their employees well and it's pissing me off. So, far as I'm concerned, it's now game on."

# CHAPTER 12

## Seattle

"Yes?" Mizrahi barked into the phone.

Serge Valchenka, their System Administrator, or SysAdmin, was the recipient of his irritation.

"We have a security issue, Itzhak."

Mizrahi glanced at the phone in hand, put it back to his ear.

"So why call me?"

"To let you know."

"No, dumbass, I'm asking why *call* me instead of walking the two fucking doors down the hall to my office so you can tell me in person?"

*Lazy propeller-head.*

Two seconds later he heard the click of the connection being dropped. A moment later the gangly dork materialized at the threshold to Mizrahi's small office, arms dangling loosely to his sides as if not knowing precisely what to do with them.

Mizrahi sat back.

"Well? What?"

"I just removed a RAT from our guest network."

Mizrahi sat bolt upright, face dead serious, mind running through scenarios to account for this. All of which spelled trouble.

"How long ago?"

"Just now. That's the reason I called. Considering what you said about a break-in and all...got me thinking..."

Mizrahi raised a just-a-moment hand, narrowing down possibilities. You could never trust what a Russian said unless you pinned the bastards down unequivocally. Even then you never could be completely convinced.

Then, just to be certain he'd heard the information correctly: "You removed this from our *guest* network and not one of our secure ones? Is this right?"

As an Israeli, he believed that all Russians—without exception—lied. That being deceptive was a characteristic that had, over centuries, been bred into their DNA as a perverse example of Darwin's principles. Simply put, the bastards couldn't help themselves. Learning to be deceptive had been a defense mechanism created by necessity.

"That's right, the guest network. Think it has to do with the pen-test?"

Mizrahi surrendered a thoughtful nod.

"Could be...but to my knowledge, no pen-test contract has been signed." He paused, as if evaluating this point in greater detail. "I'll nose around, see what my sources have to say about that. Rest assured, I'll let you know what I learn." Then, with what wavered suspiciously close to a sneer, he returned to his monitor, saying, "*Spasibo tovarishch*," with a distinctly sarcastic edge.

Serge flashed him an *up-yours* look before disappearing from the doorway.

Mizrahi returned a one-finger salute to the empty doorway. The Russian was almost certainly right, but he'd be damned if he'd tell him that.

As Prisha was ferrying Arnold and Lopez back to their respective homes, Arnold phoned Vihaan.

"How's it coming on the personnel backgrounds?"

Vihaan's primary task, besides keeping them as current as possible on grunt work, was to collect as much relevant data on key players as possible.

"Making slow but steady progress. Why?"

With Plan A now fading into distant memory, Arnold was scheming another stab at fast-balling a Rubber Ducky into a Larkin Standish computer. Today's major setback had blown a massive hole in his plans and timeline, forcing him to scramble to make up time if they intended to adhere to their blitzkrieg plan.

"Gotten as far as the accounting department?"

A tentative pause, then: "No…"

"In that case, I'd like you to make a temporary change of priority and have find me the name of whoever's the head of accounting, okay?"

"I'm all over it, boss."

Arnold was opening the front door to his house when his phone started in: Vihaan. That Vihaan! Mr. Always on Top of Things.

He closed the door with his free hand before starting for the kitchen.

"Yo, Vihaan. What up?"

"Got it. Head of accounting's Stephanie Wardell."

He spelled the last name to make sure Arnold had it right.

"Cool! Thanks, dude."

After letting Chance in from the back porch, Arnold spent several minutes giving him a healthy dose of choobers and rabber-de-jabbers while his laptop was booting, mind jetting along now at Mach II rabid bat speed, adding and discarding various wording iterations, tightening sentences into just the right sequence and tone.

Once the computer was fully booted and was ready to go, he formatted an email to Wardell in the Larkin Standish style modeled on his email exchanges with Mr. Collier. Finished with the message, he worked through a series routine stretches to help clear his mind, then refreshed Chance's kitchen and porch water dishes. Next, he formatted a Gold and Associates invoice to make it appear like it was being sent to Wardell from Collier.

The terse message simply read: Please Pay.

Arnold attached a RAT—a Random Access Trojan, a chunk of malware—to the message in such a way that it would embed in the accountant's computer the moment the attachment was moused. After one final inspection for errors, he decided it was good to go, hit Send, and watched it vanish into cyberspace.

*Now what? Nuke a hot chocolate?*

"Three Hearts in A Tangle" started in. He fished his phone from his pocket and checked the ID banner.

"What can I do for you, Mr. Davidson?"

"Good news, son. I just finished reviewing your scope of work, and everything appears to be in order, so I agree to serve as your designated attorney of record."

"Aw man, that's great!" Arnold fist pumped air. "Thank you, sir."

"However, if I may…one word of caution. Just be *very* careful that no team member is apprehended while in the Larkin Standish office. In spite of your Scope of Work, disentangling yourselves legally from a breaking-and-entering charge might prove to be an unwanted expense."

"Got it. Thanks."

After disconnecting, Arnold emailed the team the good news. As he started to slip the phone back into his pocket, Mr. Brown started singing again.

Rachael.

"Hey, Rach, what up?"

"Just wanted you to know I've decided to have dinner at Mom's tonight, so don't expect me, okay?"

Why tag the declaration with "okay?" Didn't sound like a question. Not even remotely. And besides, what if he wasn't "okay" with it? Yeah, that was a tad picky, but he was growing highly sensitive to the seismic shift taking place in their relationship. Or was he just getting paranoid? No way to know for sure, but he seriously doubted it. And besides, what difference did it make? None.

"Okay. Will I see you later, then?"

Her hesitation answered the question before she finally said, "More than likely."

*More than likely? Translation: don't bank on it.*

# CHAPTER 13

## Seattle—6:25 PM

THE TEAM WAS sitting around Arnold's kitchen table scarfing down an ample order of ribs, slaw, and mustard greens that Arnold had Grubhubbed over earlier from Jack's BBQ in the South Lake Union neighborhood, and sweating bottles of Anchor Steam.

The evening's agenda was an in-depth analysis of the various intelligence they'd accumulated with an eye to identifying what additional information might be needed before pulling the trigger their blitzkrieg attack. That was, of course, if they landed the contract.

*Fingers crossed.*

Until now, they'd been concentrating on the ribs and greens with some idle chitchat thrown in, no one seemingly in any rush to ruin a good meal with the diversion of work. Prisha caught Arnold's eye and raised an eyebrow. He returned a slight nod.

She announced, "Okay, kids, recess is over."

The conversation died; however, the eating did not.

"Sorry if you guys already know some of the points I plan to cover, but it's critical for all of us to be operating with the same information," she said, then paused a beat. "Point one:

with the exception of floor thirty-four, all the Larkin Standish floors require a key card to access. In fact, far as we've determined, this applies to pretty much the entire building."

"How do we know this?" Vihaan asked.

The question surprised Arnold. But then it dawned on him: Vihaan was the only team member to have not physically set foot inside the building.

"Because," Lopez answered for her, "the times I was in the elevators alone I tried punching as many buttons as possible and none of them worked. Simple extrapolation..."

Arnold added, "Same thing for the stairwells. You can't get in or out of either one—even the one to the freaking garage—without one. Not only that, but I suspect the cards are company-specific. So let's think about this a moment." He paused. "This means that each card's unique and likely identifies the card holder and the company they're with. Which means that there's a central computer constantly monitoring who's accessing what door at what time of day for the entire building. Day and night." Another pause. "That's one ginormous pain in the ass that we need to factor into our strategy."

"What you're really saying," Lopez remarked blandly, "is we need to steal some keys."

With a smile, Arnold nodded.

"Exactly. I'm on it, dude."

When no one bothered to comment, Arnold asked Lopez, "Find out anything in that guest account?"

After setting down his bottle, Lopez rolled his eyes, "Oh, that," and began wiping his fingers with a crumpled stained paper towel. "The network to nowhere." He gave a forlorn headshake. "Bad news. So I install the RAT, like, as soon as I get your email. Fine, no problem, smooth as silk." Sliding his hand horizontally. "Try it out. That sucker works perfectly; I go straight in. I figure that part's done, so before bothering to implant any fallback access, I take a lunch break and run a chore or two...takes, oh, I dunno, maybe an hour or so, but when I go back, guess what? That RAT's like gone, man…try a couple times, but it's gone."

"What?" Prisha asked.

"Yeah, totally MIA." A beat passed. "What I'm saying is, the only explanation is that their SysOp was onto it, like, insanely instantaneously. Unbelievable." He nodded. "Bottom line? Like you said, that dude Mizrahi's running one goddamn tight-ass ship. A hell of a lot tighter than the other firms we've been working with."

Vihaan shook his head.

"We all knew it'd be a longshot."

Prisha opened her mouth to speak but Arnold cut her off with: "Hold on, let me try this." He was taking a big gamble on account of not yet having checked to see if Stephanie Wardell, Head of Accounting, had swallowed the phishing scam he'd emailed her. The rest of the team watched silently as he typed commands into his laptop, then studied the screen with obvious growing concern. They continued waiting…

Nothing.

"Shit."

He reentered the commands. Again, they all waited.

Slowly shaking his head, he again muttered, "Shit."

"What?" Prisha asked.

Arnold sat back, dabbed a napkin to his lips, then described the fake invoice he'd emailed the Head of Accounting earlier with the RAT attached. A classic phishing scam.

Chalk that up as one more failed attempt at hacking their secure network.

Prisha shook her head mournfully: "Dude, I'm getting the very distinct feeling this job ain't gonna be any cakewalk."

Heavy silence permeated the kitchen.

"So," Prisha finally said to Arnold, "I believe that was plan B. You going to tell us you got a plan C?"

"Unfortunately…" Arnold began massaging the back of his neck, mulling over a fallback position now that his two favorite scams had gone down in flames so quickly in flames.

"Mizrahi's obviously given some serious cybersecurity and social engineering training to those people. Guess you gotta hand it to the dude."

Hated to admit it, but he was developing a fair amount of respect for Mizrahi's work.

No one said a word. Probably because no one has any bright ideas to suggest. This was his problem to solve. Goddamnit.

"Okay," he finally said, throwing up both hands. "I'm still convinced the Rubber Ducky scam's the perfect way to sneak in, but I admit I totally underestimated how tough it'd be…so…what I'm thinking is we give it one more shot, but this time I blow out all the stops and gin up a killer con." Then, addressing Vihaan and Lopez: "Remind me: which one of you's researching court cases?"

"I *was*," Vihaan answered.

"Got any bead on an ongoing one?"

Vihaan shook his head.

"Nope. Hell, I haven't even been able to find a way into those files short of breaking into the court records. And you for sure appreciate would how long that'd take. We don't have the time."

Mr. Davidson's strong warning to not get caught doing anything that would result in legal repercussions began to ring loudly in his mind.

"Yeah, no, that one's out. We can't take the risk. Not for this gig."

Just then, an idea hit.

"Hang on, be right back."

He walked from the kitchen into the living room, phone in hand. He scrolled through his contacts, found her number.

"Kara? Arnold Gold…"

A few minutes later he scooted back into his chair.

"A friend of mine's working on it. She says no problem."

Prisha shot him a dead serious dose of side-eye.

"That the Kara I think it is?"

Arnold shrugged.

"Hey, at the moment we need help, right?"

Prisha rolled her eyes, Lopez and Vihaan sending her questioning looks. She turned to her husband, shook her head: "Nope. And don't even think about asking on the way home."

Arnold was in the process of shoveling in another bite of collard greens when his phone rang.

He dropped his fork and grabbed it: "Hey, girl, whatcha got?" His right hand reached for the mechanical pencil and the note pad. He listened, nodded, jotted a few notes.

"Cool. Thanks…yeah, we can do that…tell you what, I'm in a meeting. Call you tomorrow for sure. Okay, thanks again. Bye."

The moment Arnold disconnected, Lopez said, "Okay, spill. What the fuck's up?"

Arnold explained his plan.

# CHAPTER 14

## Seattle

ARNOLD WALKED THE group out to Prisha's car when he noticed Rachael hiking up the hill from her mother's place.

As Lopez and Vihaan were climbing in, Prisha stopped by the front fender and raised her eyebrows at Arnold.

"You okay?"

He glanced back toward Rachael.

"Yeah, sure, why wouldn't I be?"

Prisha gave a slight nod in Rachael's direction.

"Look, I can sense something going on between you two, and hey, I get it, none of my business, but it is my business to ask if your head's still in the game."

"I'm fine."

"I'm here for you, you find the need to discuss it. I'm here, okay?"

She stepped around the front of the car to the driver's side.

Then Rachael was next to him saying, "Are you ready to take Chance for his walk? If so, I'll go with."

Strolling leisurely toward 80<sup>th</sup>, Arnold said, "Tell me on what's going on."

They paused, giving Chance an opportunity to check out

the base of one particular shrub he never missed when passing this yard.

"Auntie Shira's right. At first, I was worried I was *looking* for things, you know, preconditioned by her concerns? But the more I watch her, the more I believe she's right. Mom's not normal."

*Shit.*

His heart sank for Rachael. He knew that her grandmother had developed multiple sclerosis in her late forties. Plus, her great-grandmother had suffered some undiagnosed neurologic problems too, but in those days, that diagnosis was confirmed only with an autopsy of the brain. Which didn't happen. Although MS didn't have strong genetic links, Rachael had worried that her mother would one day develop the disease. Apparently now…Jesus!

"For example," he asked, hoping that maybe she was wrong. But knew that was unlikely. Not about something this important to her.

"The first thing I noticed was her balance. It's not all that obvious, so it took a while before I could see it, but it's there if you know what to watch for. It's subtle, but present. A little unsteady here, maybe a weave there, but then I began to notice patterns, like weaving to the left, for example."

She stopped, perhaps giving him an opportunity to ask a question, which he didn't, lest it be construed as challenging her judgement.

"I called her internist's office and set up an appointment so we can hopefully get a workup started along with a referral to a neurologist."

Arnold's eyes never wavered from Chance, but his mind cleaved into multiple tangential thoughts. But for some strange reason, focusing on how seamlessly this MS thing was slotting into his predicted exit scenario. Sure, he could be totally off base seeing this new development through the eyes of his expectations but doubted that. Rachael was justifiably alarmed over her mom's balance. Plus it wasn't her nature to fabricate an excuse like this.

Yet it did provide her with the perfect off-ramp. And as much as it hurt to see one more piece of the break-up puzzle clicked solidly into place, he was also feeling deeply sorry for the anxiety and fear she must be experiencing. A perversely ironic thought hit: perhaps the only upside to how his parents died was that it spared them from having to deal with the gut-wrenching health-issue roulette that living brings. One moment they were living, the next moment…

*Jesus, what a perverse thought.*

"—are medications now," Rachael was saying.

Making him suddenly realize he'd totally zoned out.

"There anything I can do to help?" he asked.

She gave his hand a gentle squeeze.

"No, sweetie, but thanks for asking. I just need more clarity, is all."

There was ambiguity in her words, somewhere in between gratitude for his offer and gratitude for her new portal to freedom. There was also her choice of the word *clarity*. As to what, exactly? Her mother? Them? Both? What? He turned to her for a hint, but she was now watching Chance. And this instantly reinforced his growing suspicion that this was more than her mother's unfortunate situation.

A sudden rush of emptiness swept into his gut, making him once again sad for the loneliness he knew was barreling toward him like a freight train.

Back in the kitchen, Arnold checked his email and found a new one from Kara waiting that contained the title of an active King County Court case, the case number, as well as the name of the Larkin Standish attorney representing the client.

*Perfect.*

Exactly the information he'd requested.

With a Sharpie, Arnold printed the lawyer's name in bold

black block letters on a five-by-seven plain manila envelope, slipped in another malware-infected Rubber Ducky, closed and sealed the flap securely, then set the package on the small table to the right of the front door for the morning.

He stood, eyeing the name in block letters, his Hail-Mary fourth-quarter pass. The success of their entire operation now hinged on what happened when it was opened.

# CHAPTER 15

## Seattle—Friday Morning

ARNOLD STEPPED FROM the Uber, made sure he wasn't about to get slammed in the bike lane—all clear—then crossed to the sidewalk and the stately brass doors of the Smith Tower; the uniquely shaped, iconic white Seattle landmark office building. It was home for several law offices, including Mr. Davidson's.

After shouldering his way through a heavy glass and brass door into the white-marble lobby, he moved off to the side, summoned a courier service he knew Mr. Cain's group frequently employed, then watched the bike lane from just inside the door.

Ten minutes later a bearded dude in a Day-Glo chartreuse jersey, black Spandex, cycling shoes, black Smith Engage helmet (LED attached), and calves the size of a VW Beetle screeched to a halt in front.

Before he had a chance to dismount, Arnold was through the doors, heading straight for him calling, "Pick up for Davidson law?"

Dude was straddling a serious-looking flat-black cycle with black, water-resistant back-fender panniers. He paused long enough for a long pull from his water bottle, swiped sweat from his forehead with a Rainbow coalition wrist sweatband, shoved the bottle back into the strut holder.

"Yup."

"Here you go." He handed the messenger the manila envelope with the Hak5 USB inside, along with a crisp five-dollar bill in addition to the tip already added to the app.

The courier checked his phone app—probably to confirm payment—oh, and destination.

Apparently satisfied, he muttered, "Thanks for the extra," while carefully securing the envelope into the right pannier. Then, after a quick forlorn glance up the street he'd just come down, he remounted and rode off.

Arnold watched him pushing hard up the Second Avenue bike lane, perhaps hustling to squeeze in a quick turnaround before a competitor had a chance to ace him out.

*Oh man, if this failed, his trick bag was, like, empty.*

Didn't even want to think about it. After an equally determined assessment of the freaking incline, he started up the same grade the biker was pedaling.

Arnold pushed through the substantial plate-glass door into the voluminous lobby of reflective gray granite, glossy blond wood panels, and recessed LED lighting. Entering from this different entrance caused him to take a moment to sort out which of the four elevator alcoves would whisk him to the Larkin Standish floors.

He was wearing stonewashed 501s, his favorite Def Con 2000 T-shirt, a gray speckled Google beanie, dorky tortoise-shell frames with non-prescription lenses, and a North Face backpack. The *pièce de résistance* to the mega-dork look was sandals with white socks.

Once again, the outfit porked him out a hefty thirty pounds. From his right hand dangled a plastic Amazon Go bag with his newly purchased Flipper Zero. Once in the appropriate elevator alcove, he busied himself with his phone until a cage arrived. A handful of passengers exited, but no one else was there to board, so he let it go.

Mere seconds later a dude with a key card on a neck lanyard came striding purposely into the area, thumbed the call button, then banged it two more times in quick succession.

Perfect.

A chime dinged. The elevator doors opened to an empty cage. The harried dude stepped on, with Arnold right on his heels. A split second later, another passenger, a woman, thrust an arm against the closing doors and darted in. The doors slid back open to the annoyed glare of the first passenger. The dude swiped his card across the card reader above the panel of floor buttons turning a small red LED to green.

Soon as he pressed twenty-six, the green LED reverted to red. The woman then swiped her card across the reader and pressed thirty. Finally, Arnold leaned in and tapped thirty-four for the Larkin Standish reception lobby, which didn't require a key card.

Bummer that neither of them wanted a secure Larking Standish floor, but the odds of lucking out to that degree had been, like, Powerball-winner miniscule.

*Oh well, you get what you get and work with that.*

Arnold shuffled to the back of the cage, pleased that the two other passengers were adhering to the strict face-forward pay-no-attention-to-the-person-beside-you elevator thing.

Exactly what he'd been counting on.

As the cage started up, Arnold slipped his hand into the plastic bag, took hold of the Flipper Zero, sidled a step closer to the dude with the lanyard key, and thumbed the trigger. He got a muted beep that the scanner recorded a signal. The guy shot him an inquisitive what-was-that glance, but Arnold remained impassive, staring straight ahead.

*Beep? What beep?*

The elevator decelerated to a gentle stop on twenty-six. Dude hung an immediate left and vanished. As doors closed again, the female passenger not-so-discretely sidestepped as far from Arnold as possible. Arnold took the hint and backed up, giving her maximal space.

*Some people!*

Try for her card too? Naw, she was way too squirrelly. Best wait for other opportunities. Okay, so he hadn't scored a Larkin Standish key, but he'd at least captured *some* data which, when analyzed, would be a valuable first step in figuring out what information they contained.

Scooting from the cage on thirty, the woman cast a suspiciously cautious glance at him before vanishing into a side hall.

*Seriously?*

Moments later, Arnold exited into the familiar reception lobby, stepped to the side of the elevator doors, planting himself in front of the south stairwell door. He played the iPhone charade again while rescanning the immediate surroundings for surveillance devices, looking for ones he'd missed last time. Saw only the smoked-glass bubble on the ceiling directly above the elevators. That, he believed, probably fed to the building-wide CCTV monitoring system.

But who knew what Mizrahi might have in addition? Couldn't see anything suspicious, but that would be exactly the point, right? Task finished, he repocketed the phone and drifted over to the reception desk.

Glancing up from her monitor, the receptionist asked, "May I help you?"

"Yes. I have an appointment with Mr. Collier. I realize I'm, like, way early, but I totally misjudged the bus schedule, so if it's okay, I'll just park over there and wait."

He pointed to an ensemble of identically upholstered chairs and couch.

"Certainly," she said with a remarkably plastic smile and blindingly white teeth. "I'll let him know you're here. He'll fetch you when he's available."

*Fetch you?*

Arnold settled into the small and uncomfortably hard couch and casually slipped his Surface from the rucksack. Considering the courier had biked here during his amble up from the Smith Tower, the envelope should've been on his target's desk long before now. The only question now was, did the attorney fall for it? Or—come to think of it—was he even in his office today to accept delivery? Or maybe he was in court or off taking a deposition…or maybe sipping a bloody Mary on the beach in Cancun on vacation. Should've checked.

He logged into the guest network and was seamlessly whisked off onto cyberspace. The first order of business: probe the guest network on the remote chance—like, Antarctica remote—of sniffing out a link into the firm's private networks. (The odds he estimated at someplace way south of two percent, but he figured what the hell, he'd be remiss to not try). After that, he would try pinging the Hak5 malware couriered over here from the Smith Tower about thirty minutes ago. And if the lawyer wasn't in Cancun and was actually in the office to accept the envelope, had he opened it? And if so, had the USB been used? And if not, did he have sufficient moxie to recognize it for what it was?

*Jesus, if you really objectively considered all the variables, there were way too many what-if ways for these scams to ever work.*

*But you had to try, right?*

That's exactly why some dipshit in Nairobi coughs out ten million spams on the off chance that all it takes is for just one sucker to bite.

Hold on. Long as he was on the guest network, why not embed a trapdoor just to probe their security again. And if their SysAdmin sniffed out *this* malware, Arnold would know his opposite number was, like, seriously formidable.

With the trapdoor now in the guest network, he pinged the Hak5 and…

Holy shit! It *worked.*

He was now inside one of the firm's secure networks. Suddenly he could hear a mental stopwatch ticking as loudly as the one on *60 Minutes*. Because the moment that lawyer realized the USB was blank, he would know he'd been royally hosed, and if he wasn't brain-dead—a fair assumption seeing as how he was a partner in this firm—their SysAdmin should be going Defcon 5 *toute de suite*. And considering what he'd already quickly learned about this firm's security, it would be only a matter of minutes before his access would vanish. The corollary, of course, was that any backup access he implanted had to be super stealthy or it too would also be wiped out in a blink.

Heart now thundering a flat-out gallop, fingers blurring at warp speed, struggling to push aside the ginormous pressure of sensing the seconds jetting past, he embedded the first trapdoor and then was starting in on a stealthier one when an authoritative male voice called, "Mr. Gold."

Collier. Had to be. Arnold nodded, but never wavered his eyes from the screen nor blinked.

More seconds flew by.

"Mr. Gold," the voice called again, this time closer and more emphatic.

Two more commands, and the second trapdoor would be locked and loaded.

*C'mon, dude, The Man's waiting...*

Arnold hit ENTER, smiled, and glanced up: "Sorry, sir."

And was scoping out a trim, ramrod straight, African American who, to Arnold, appeared younger than his listed age of fifty-seven years. He sported a well-trimmed, short, graying beard and strikingly strange Auschwitz-like sunken eyes. Arnold flashed through several facts: graduated Stanford Law. With honors. Married. One teenage son.

Arnold said, "Sorry, didn't mean to ignore you, but was answering a critical email."

He folded the Surface onto its keyboard, then quickly cramming it into his rucksack while scrambling upright to proffer his hand to the managing partner.

"Mr. Gold, Webster Collier," the lawyer said, giving his hand a quick but gentle shake.

"Glad to meet you, sir."

"We're in a conference room just down the hall," the managing partner said, sweeping the same palm toward a hallway just to the left of the reception desk.

Rats, the conference room was only one door down the hall from the lobby so that limited how much he could scope out. Still, he started memorizing every detail that he could during the short walk, in addition to continuing to scan for obvious surveillance devices. Didn't see any.

The room itself was small and sparsely furnished: one credenza against a wall with a large-screen TV a few feet above, floor to ceiling windows, a conference table barely sufficient to accommodate six, and three other people at the table chitchatting. Their conversation died the moment Arnold and Collier stepped in.

Before taking his chair, Collier introduced Gloria Kim and Elijah Black as members of the Security Committee along with Itzhak Mizrahi, head of security.

*Ah, so that's the Big Kahuna of Security.*

The Israeli had thick black curly hair, well-healed pock marks shotgunned across both cheeks, a dimpled chin, and brown granite pebbles for eyes. Arnold couldn't ignore how blatantly this guy was sizing him up, way more than just in passing. Like, seriously sizing him up. Then again, he *was* their head of security.

But still…Arnold's antennas began vibrating like crazy.

*Keep an eye on that one.*

While settling in, he casually glanced at the credenza and large-screen TV a second time as well as the speaker phone on the top shelf of the credenza, did a double take. A television? For? Ahh yes, for conference calls, of course, and as a computer monitor.

Thought about this. If the TV served as a monitor for conference calls, this necessitated a webcam...he looked more closely.

*Voila!*

There it was. And the speakerphone? Could also serve double duty as a microphone. And there it was, hiding in plain sight: built-in surveillance.

But only if someone chose to use it as such...

# CHAPTER 16

## Seattle

MIZRAHI WATCHED THE disgusting pork chop waddle in like a prize-winning 4-H oinker to a food trough. What a pathetic cliché for a pen-tester. A wannabe, wildly out of his league. Yet, he cautioned himself to not sell the kid short. Competent, effective pen-testers were typically master chameleons sporting oil-slick social engineering skills.

*But this guy?*

He cast a second glance.

*No, no way.*

Then a third look. Huh.

*No, this joker simply couldn't possibly be a serious player...or was he?*

He decided to withhold any conclusion based around a flash first impression and just sit back, observe, listen carefully to what the oinker had to say, and only then solidify an assessment. After all, if the committee asked for his impression, he intended to provide a thoughtful objective estimation.

But right now, he was having considerable problems believing that Gold could be focused on anything more than his lunch menu. The immediate corollary: Gold's company couldn't possibly possess the talents to penetrate a bowel of Jell-

O with a hot spoon.

He relaxed.

"May I get you a cup of coffee or a bottle of water?" Collier asked, directing Arnold to the empty chair at the head of the small conference table.

Otherwise known as the hot seat.

Pulling back his chair, Arnold said, "No, I'm fine, thanks," and dumped his backpack on the floor next to him, settled in, all too aware of the attendees discreetly checking him out, no doubt sizing him up.

After shutting the door, Collier settled in at the opposite end of the table, Mizrahi on his left, the other two to his right.

Once seated, Collier began the discussion.

"The purpose of this meeting, Mr. Gold, is to learn more about the types of security evaluations your company offers. I believe the proper term is penetration-testing." He glanced at Gloria Kim and Elijah Black for any amendments to this statement. They demurred. Collier asked, "What can you tell us about your new service and your company?"

Smiling, Arnold made eye contact with each of the convened, ending with Collier.

"First, thanks for the opportunity to introduce you to our extremely talented team of experts. As you undoubtedly know, we're a boutique IT company that specializes in serving the unique needs of law firms. I believe you're also aware that we only just recently added vulnerability testing to our portfolio of—"

Kim spoke with a noticeable edge to her tone.

"Let me just cut to the chase, Mr. Gold. How many of these tests has your team conducted?"

Arnold caught Kim flash Mizrahi a barely perceptible eye message, which Mizrahi returned with an equally subtle nod of affirmation.

*WTF? You didn't throw out a loaded question like that one unless you for sure knew the answer.*

Donning his best Mr. Earnest face, Arnold leaned forward, forearm on the table.

"Should the committee elect to hire us to conduct a pen-test, it would be our first *official* one." He dangled the titillating unstated implication in front of their imaginations to bat around. "It's worth pointing out that the results of a pen-test shouldn't be thought of as binary. By that, I mean, they shouldn't be seen in terms of success or failure. As you probably know, these tests are used primarily as a tool for *tightening* security." He shrugged. "So it only makes sense that there may be some instances when a test is unable to turn up a security flaw. In those cases the negative result should actually be seen as a positive, right?"

Kim's eyebrows arched in mock surprise.

"You're obviously implying something by emphasizing *official*. How exactly are we to take this, Mr. Gold? That your company's been involved in *unofficial* illegal intrusions?" flashing a shark-like gotcha smile.

Arnold simply spread his hands: Mr. Cool. Although his armpits were actively leaking.

Mizrahi said, "Gloria, I suggest we move on to a more productive topic."

This red-lined Arnold's suspicion meter. Especially after watching their exchange of eye notes. Was this some sort of orchestrated good cop, bad cop schtick? Sure smacked of it. He sneaked quick glance at Black, who seemed to be curiously disengaged from the interview. On the other hand, Collier was looking either impatient but simply hesitant to intervene. Which in itself was interesting. Arnold decided to change the subject.

"What type of pen-test is the committee interested in?"

All eyes snapped to Webster Collier.

After a thoughtful pause, the managing partner said, "That, Mr. Gold, is one of the issues we hope to clear up during this discussion, so this seems to be a good time for you to describe what your company is offering."

"My pleasure." Arnold quickly eyed the group again. "Let's start by asking what you wish to achieve from a pen-test?"

Sitting back in the chair, clasped hands pressed against the edge of the table, Collier sobered.

"We have several objectives in mind, but primarily we want to assure ourselves that our confidential files are well protected. The issue of safeguarding confidential material is a major concern when taken within the context of the staggering increase in cybercrime—in particular ransomware—involving law offices such as ours. This unfortunate trend recently spurred the American Bar Association to encourage its members to reevaluate their security through a variety of measures, one of which is penetration testing." Then, to Mizrahi: "ABA guidance clearly states that such evaluations are to be conducted by an *independent* organization, so I hope you understand that this is not intended as a lack of confidence in your excellent work. Everyone in this firm has the utmost trust in the security you provide."

Mizrahi nodded.

When no one else spoke, Arnold asked, "I assume you have a dedicated IT team?"

Collier nodded for Mizrahi to answer.

"Yes, we do," Mizrahi responded.

"In-house or subcontracted?"

Mizrahi studied him a beat with almost a bemused expression.

"We have an in-house SysAdmin plus two full-time techs but I oversee both our physical security and cybersecurity."

It wasn't the answer itself, but the way he said it, that carried a barely perceptible challenge. As if he relished the idea of Gold and Associates taking a shot at his tempered steel firewalls. Arnold drummedg his fingers on the table, searching for a softball to toss him.

"According to your website, this firm has an impressive number of offices. Does each one manage their own security, or do you oversee it all?"

*Only a village idiot could possibly think he did.*

"Yes, yes, of course, just this one," Mizrahi said as if this was the stupidest question he'd encountered since...well, ever.

"However," Collier quickly added, "by working symbiotically we form a cohesive strategic alliance capable of leveraging exclusive internal referrals as appropriate, forging all participating members into a fully integrated system."

He ended this well-oiled speech with a triumphant smile.

*Bet he's rolled out that collection of gibberish more than once.*

"Do any of your affiliates share or have access to any networks in this office?" Arnold asked for another read on Mizrahi.

"Of course not," Mizrahi answered, as if this was second most stupid question of the interview.

"Smart," Arnold replied, struggling to maintain a straight face.

*Schmuck.*

Then, to Collier: "To answer the original question, we provide comprehensive pen-testing as well as vulnerability assessments. Depending on your needs, you can elect to use either or both, but unless I'm mistaken, you're mainly concerned about your cyber-integrity, right?"

Implying that, obviously, Mizrahi had physical security locked down tighter than a porpoise's blowhole.

Collier seemed puzzled.

"I'm sure Itzhak understands those terms, but I don't, so will you please explain the difference?"

"You bet. A penetration test—or pen-test for short— evaluates your ability to repel various forms of cyberattacks. In other words, we'd try to hack your firm's network and report on our results. On the other hand, in a vulnerability assessment we'd try to physically break into your offices and walk off with relevant material. For example, if you were a Ferrari dealer, we'd try to break into your showroom and drive off with an 812

GTS. See the difference?"

Collier's expression immediately soured as he turned to Kim.

"I'm *not at all* comfortable even thinking of allowing outsiders to try to break into any of our confidential files, whether electronic or paper...regardless of the circumstance including either of these security tests. How do you see it, Gloria?"

Lips pursed, she appeared to consider the question seriously.

"In general, I would tend to agree, but I also realize that our overriding concern is to objectively evaluate our security under real-world conditions...so perhaps this is the risk we must assume if we're to accomplish this goal. In other words, I see the end justifying the means. Now, having said that, this places an even higher importance on selecting a company we can trust completely."

She turned to Arnold.

"But this just raised another question: are these tests analogous to financial audits in that once the initial evaluation has been completed and any corrective measures implemented, should a follow-up evaluation be undertaken? And if so, how frequently do you recommend repeating them?" Before he could answer, she turned to Collier: "Just so we appreciate the full financial impact of embarking on this road."

*Smart lady. Terrific analogy.*

"Great question," Arnold said in full suck-up mode. "The answer depends on our findings. Such things as how many issues are identified and their level of importance. Once the testing has been completed, we provide a detailed report of our findings, good and bad. Once your committee has had ample time to review and digest the report, we can sit down with the committee to discuss the findings and answer your questions. If, for example, we discover a serious vulnerability, then a follow-up *test* might be indicated as soon as corrective measures are implemented. But again, we only make recommendations. What the committee decides to do with these recommendations is totally up to you."

She smiled. "All the more reason to employ someone we trust."

Arnold sensed that he may have scored a point.

Collier asked, "What is the cost of a comprehensive evaluation, Mr. Gold?"

*Oh, man. There it was: the question from hell.*

Low-balling it would certainly make them more cost competitive, but that risked making them look like cheap knockoffs. Too high would price them out of consideration—especially considering their nonexistent track record. Paradoxically, a high price might bestow on them a cachet. After all, Arnold was convinced that 90 percent of a Ferrari's allure was the exclusivity its jaw-detaching price dictated. A freaking conundrum, this one.

They were staring at him now, awaiting an answer. Crunch time.

"By comprehensive—I assume this means both cyber and physical security—that would run close to fifty-five thousand dollars, but can vary, depending on your facilities. If you're interested in a firm quote, I can provide it after inspecting your space. Granted, that *is* expensive, but here's the deal: if we can't break into your network within"—he glanced at the ceiling, tapping his chin with an index finger— "forty-eight hours of signing a contract, we'll do the entire project at no cost."

If he'd pegged Mizrahi correctly, an outlandish challenge like this would be a direct affront to his manhood.

Two seconds of dead silence ensued before Collier asked the group, "Any additional questions for Mr. Gold?"

Arnold could hear only a soft hum of the HVAC from the overhead vent. His gut sank.

Then Collier's chair legs scraped the tile as he pushed back his chair, buttoning his suit coat as he stood, a residual habit

Arnold suspected from years of courtroom appearances. A habit he'd initially noticed from Mr. Cain and Mr. Davidson.

Collier cast a final glance at his colleagues before turning to Arnold.

"Mr. Gold, we certainly appreciate the information. We'll pass along our assessment to the managing partners and be back in touch in a timely manner."

Arnold was up now, pulling a manila envelope from his backpack, his gut not giving him any hint as to how well or badly his pitch went. Could easily go either way.

*Go for it? Take the risk?*

*Why not? Feels like you've got nothing to lose.*

"I'm sorry, last thing I want to do is to come across as pressuring the committee, but is it possible to have a firmer idea how long your decision will take? Reason I ask is we're presently knee-deep in a large Honolulu project, so I need to get back there soon as I wrap up here. But if we have a reasonable shot at the contract, this job would, of course, take precedence."

He ended the statement with an *I'm sorry* shrug and clenched his teeth.

*There! The gambit was played. No going back now.*

His stomach did a series of serious backflips.

Collier glanced at his seated, poker-faced colleagues questioningly. Mizrahi began to fiddle with his phone. Kim shifted position and scrutinized the palm of her right hand. Black just stared blankly at the opposite wall. No one said diddly-squat.

Opening the conference room door with one hand, placing his other hand on Arnold's shoulder, Collier began ushering him from the room.

"We'll have an answer for you within forty-eight hours. That's the best I can do."

*Perfect. A surge of encouragement washed into his heart. At least they didn't flat-out tell him to take a hike.*

Instead of moving, Arnold told the group, "Thank you. We

can work with that. Oh, and by the way, any further discussion should exclude Mr. Mizrahi." Then to the Israeli: "No offense, sir."

"None taken," Mizrahi said, still studying his phone.

Collier cocked his head.

"I don't understand. He is, after all, head of security."

Glancing up from his phone, Mizrahi spoke.

"Precisely. My presence would be a clear conflict of interest. Ideally, Security should be completely blinded to any test to ensure the most realistic assessment possible. I have no problem with that. In fact, I welcome the challenge."

He punctuated the statement with a smug smile.

"Two additional items then," Arnold added. "If you do decide to hire us, we require a signed Scope of Work that would include what you would accept as proof of penetration. For example, in the case of the Ferrari dealership we'd return the car. Think about it so that if you decide to move ahead, we can nail this down in our next meeting." Then, to Mizrahi: "Since you're already involved with this discussion, we might as well determine what you would consider proof of penetration?"

Mizrahi again glanced up from his phone with a shark-like smile.

"Of course..." He began rubbing his upper lip, his shark smile growing more deadly. "A map of our storage network should do the trick."

Arnold nodded.

"That's a good one."

He handed the manila envelope to Collier.

"Here's a model agreement. Share it with the committee, but please don't let *anyone* outside this room know about this discussion. Ideally, these discussions should be completely secret. Soon as I have all the information, I'll tailor the final draft to apply to this office."

Collier raised his index finger.

"I just occurred to me...what if you can't produce either

objective…say, for example, you can't provide the map Itzhak designated, how can we evaluate the effort put into the work?"

"Another great question. We don't submit an invoice until after submitting our report. That report will describe each step taken along with the corresponding results. Since most steps are easily verified, you should have no problem judging our effort. Bear in mind, we maintain an excellent reputation among our present clients. I'll gladly supply a list of contacts if this will help you evaluate us. Although we haven't established a record as far as pen-testing yet, I guarantee we'll provide the same high level of work as we *are* known for."

# CHAPTER 17

## Seattle

MIZRAHI WATCHED THE goofball shake hands with Kim and Black before offering him an outstretched palm. After quickly discarding the porker's mushy grip, he was back anticipating the possible routes that Gold's team might use to try to weasel into to the network. Although, a contract had yet to be signed…

*…or had it?*

Interesting question. One that intrigued Mizrahi, his mind now running with it.

*Could this meeting be nothing but a deception to throw him off? Could Collier be that cunning? Huh.*

He gave the managing partner a quick once-over.

*No, not Mr. Straight and Narrow.*

In spite of this, Collier's enthusiastic body language made it clear to him that the decision was already made, that Larkin Standish would award Gold the pen-test contract. Over the years of scrutinizing Collier closely, he'd decided that once the man made up his mind on a course of action, he effectively steamrolled it straight down the gullets of the Governance Committee—probably one of the reasons he'd been elected to the exalted post of managing partner for so many consecutive years.

Mizrahi heard Collier telling the group, "I'll walk Mr. Gold out but will be back straightaway to tie up a few items."

He led Gold out the conference room door, hand on Gold's shoulder as if they were old drinking buds from the country club instead of potential employer and employee. Far as Mizrahi was concerned, Collier's enthusiastic tone just sealed the deal: no question, Gold and Associates would have the contract.

Kim and Black glanced knowingly at each other before sitting back down, as if they'd reached the same conclusion.

*Now what? Excuse himself?*

No. That would tip everyone that Mizrahi knew the decision was a done deal now. Better to act naive and let them play out their amusing little charade. Mizrahi slipped his phone back into his pocket and returned to sorting through various scenarios and possible points of attack. Their networks were impenetrable, but Gold didn't know that, so he would make a concerted effort.

*Or, were they as impenetrable as he believed?*

A faint specter of vulnerability squirmed through a fissure in his confidence. Just how sophisticated was that nerdy little porker? Without any track record, there was no way to know. Yet, something kept nagging at him. A snippet that Gold had casually dropped into the conversation like an Alka-Seltzer tablet. The not-so-subtle implication that his team had been carrying out unauthorized penetrations. Plural. Which begged the suddenly germane question: was that implied threat nothing but chest-pounding silverback bravado from an overweight wannabe, or was Gold's crew a serious group of battle-hardened hackers?

For that matter, what *did* he know about Gold and Associates? Who were they? And what was Gold's contribution to their work? A mere administrator? A hacker? A wannabe? What? In fact, he knew nothing. And this just became unsettling. Probably best to start working forward by objectively reviewing what few facts—not impressions, but hard cold *facts*—he did know.

Mizrahi thought about this for a moment and came up with a goose egg. He didn't know one thing about their capabilities. In fact, he had no solid evidence that Gold *was* responsible for the malware that the Russian had removed from the guest network. He'd naturally assumed that it was Gold's work simply because it was discovered in close proximity to the security committee's first discussion about conducting a pentest...

After mulling *that* over, he realized that linking the malware to their initial discussion made little sense, for how would Gold know about the committee if he hadn't been contacted?

*But still...mere coincidence?*

Perhaps. Regardless, it seemed too huge a stretch. It was equally possible that Serge just happened to discover the malware during a routine security scan and that it'd been in the guest network for months.

*Was that even possible?*

Objectively, yes. Likely, no. However, the facts were still glaring: 1) he had no idea how long that malware had been there before being discovered; and 2) he had no objective evidence to suggest it was Gold's work.

Yet, his gut kept insisting it was Gold's work. And his gut instincts were seldom wrong.

Assuming it was Gold's work, the question became: did Gold intentionally implant the RAT as a ploy? A straight-up psych-ops mind fuck? A ruse intended to make him believe that he and his team were nothing more than a gaggle of Triple A jokers trying to shoulder their way into the major leagues? An attempt at misdirection?

He began factoring in his impressions of Gold during the meeting. He concluded that no, the man wasn't that clever.

There was, of course, no way to know this for a fact, but if forced to guess, all the indicators suggested that Gold—and, by extrapolation, his team—were nothing but rag-tag rank amateurs.

Yet another wave of self-doubt came bubbling up from the depths...something to do with this logic didn't sit right.

*What?*

Something to do with...the malware...no...what?

He began deconstructing this last thought bit by bit. What could be gained by implanting a ticky-tack chunk of malware on a *public* network? The answer remained the same: nothing.

Yes, exactly. And this was the nettle stinging his logic center.

*Why?*

Well, because the act was either extraordinarily stupid or just egregiously naïve. There was no middle ground here. So which was it: naïveté or stupidity? One thing he *did* know about Gold and his group was that they'd accumulated an excellent reputation within the local legal community for solid IT work. But truthfully, those jobs were nothing but run-of-the-mill bullshit. Updates, installs, occasional maintenance. Yet...there was that notorious Cain ransomware case, and that *did* score a point in Gold's favor.

So where did this leave him?

Nowhere.

Still, his gut kept insisting that Gold couldn't possibly be a serious threat.

# CHAPTER 18

## Seattle

AS COLLIER AND Arnold were strolling through the reception lobby to the elevators, the lawyer said, "I found your presentation extremely informative and outspoken. I also applaud your aplomb when fielding the issue of your lack of pen-testing experience. I believe you demonstrated the integrity that's in harmony with the glowing recommendation Noah Cain lavished on you. I can assure you the committee will have a decision for you within the requested time frame."

Arnold's hopes soared.

"Thank you. I apologize if this causes you any inconvenience, but I'm sure you appreciate how busy work can be sometimes. I have no intention to pressure the committee and apologize if I gave you that impression."

Collier patted Arnold's back.

"No problem. We understand completely."

After thumbing the down button, they exchanged a handshake, Arnold added, "It was a pleasure to meet with your committee and an honor to be allowed the opportunity to describe our services. Please know how excited we all are over the prospect of a possible collaboration with Larkin Standish."

"The pleasure is all ours, Arnold."

With that, Collier did a crisp about-face and began striding straight toward the conference room.

The elevator arrived.

Arnold cast a quick glance at the reception desk and then at the fire door to the stairwell. No one appeared to be watching him, unless, of course, someone had eyes on the feed from the overhead CCTV, which he thought doubtful since this floor allowed public access. He seriously wanted to slip into the stairwell but couldn't. Yet. So he resigned himself to waiting for another opportunity.

Arnold shuffled past three passengers with blank robotic stares and moved to the back of the cage, turned to face the doors, and subtly shuffled two steps to the right for a glimpse at which floors were pressed: the 1$^{st}$ floor button, of course, but yippee, so was twenty-two.

Twelve floors later, he tailgated a tall middle-aged dude out into the hall, stopped, pulled out his phone, and pretended to read a message while scanning the immediate area for security cams. But he could see only the black overhead CCTV bubble. The halls to the right and left were now empty. Perfect.

He ducked into the nearby men's room and found it empty. For added privacy, he slipped into the handicap stall, secured the door, sat on the commode, then got to work. He pulled the Flipper Zero and a blank RFID key card from his rucksack, then quickly cloned the information surreptitiously copied from the unsuspecting passenger onto the blank card.

For a moment, he sat, contemplating the white plastic key in his hand. It would allow him access her floor, but what about the stairwells or the other floors? Only one way to find out, right?

After repacking his equipment and tossing his rucksack over a shoulder, he slipped into the hall, beelined for the north stairwell door and quickly swiped the card across the black reader next to the jamb.

*Yay!*

The little red LED flashed green synchronously with a metallic *clack*. He pushed through the door to step into a tiny square landing, the heavy steel fire door closing itself with a definitive *thunk*, encasing him in a square claustrophobic shaft of zig-zagging stairs with ugly purple railings.

*Cool!*

His first valid key card. Problem was, he would be seriously shocked if it allowed him access to any Standish Larkin floors. With both hands on the tubular railing, he leaned out, glanced up and down, but could see only the bottom of the ascending stairs and one flight of the descending set. This was twenty-two, right? No freaking way was he about to entertain the thought of hiking all the way back up to thirty-four.

Okay back to work. He thumbed the fire door latch. Locked. Okay, one more bit of information. He swiped the key card over the reader. The latch released. Double cool. He'd just accumulated a boxcar of data.

At the elevators again, he pressed the Up button and dialed Lopez.

"Yo, dude, just dropped a backdoor into their network."

He went on to explain the specifics along with the request to jump on it *tout de suite* to implant some redundancy. And then, once that was secure, to work on finding a route into the firm's storage network. ASAP.

"I'm on it, boss."

"And once you find it—as if there was no question he would—begin making a map of it, okay?"

"On it."

# CHAPTER 19

## Seattle

MIZRAHI WATCHED COLLIER almost pimp-roll back into the conference room. Mr. Total Confidence, subtly telegraphing the group a *See?* expression before settling back into the same chair vacated mere minutes ago.

The managing partner leaned forward and eyed the group.

He made no attempt to mask his blatantly obvious enthusiasm and bias.

"Thoughts?"

Everyone exchanged glances.

Kim finally said, "Truthfully, I'm *very* concerned over their complete lack of experience with these tests. If we're serious about the need for one—which I staunchly believe we are—I'd prefer a company with more experience under their belt than what we just heard. Elijah. What are your thoughts?"

Black blinked, designer frames dangling from his left hand, then squeezed the bridge of his nose between his right thumb and forefinger, adding theatrical gravitas to his forthcoming declaration.

"I concur. Wholeheartedly. Given the profound significance of these tests, we must have unfettered confidence that those entrusted with potential access to our highly sensitive records be competent. More importantly, they must also possess impeccable integrity. We have no assurance that such a wet-behind-the-ears company as Gold and Associates can meet our high standards."

Mizrahi watched Kim send him an almost imperceptible nod of agreement, so before any pack-mentality dynamic could begin gathering steam, he interjected: "I realize I'm no longer to be privy to these discussions, but here I am, so I'm going to strongly disagree with both of you on this."

All eyes locked on him.

"I did some research on their work for other law firms and have to admit I'm extremely impressed."

He went on to describe the nasty ransomware that paralyzed Cain's firm and how Gold not only resolved the issue but, in the process, uncovered a junior partner embezzling from the firm; a finding that led to a formal indictment for a case currently pending trial.

As he wrapped up his little speech, Mizrahi surveyed his audience and found it amusing that Elijah Black and Gloria Kim appeared to be shocked at his support of Gold.

*What did they expect? Pushback based on professional jealousy?*

Not a chance.

Truthfully, if the firm intended to conduct a pen-test— which was clearly where Collier was now headed—he would rather deal with Gold's rag-tag pack of buffoons than a pack of battle-hardened veterans armed with a trick bag the size of China.

*Besides, what did he really have to worry about?*

Gold had no idea how well-trained and prepared the firm's employees were at spotting and combating highly sophisticated forms of social engineering as well as practicing excellent cybersecurity techniques—training that Mizrahi made a point of refreshing every five to six months. All because he knew full well that the weakest link to any secure system was the human factor. No, there was no way Gold could penetrate their defenses. Which was precisely why he'd asked for a network map as acceptable proof of penetration. No way could those clowns provide one.

Black seemed to reflect on Mizrahi's words for a moment, then nodded.

"Itzhak's clearly the most qualified person among us to evaluate their work. If he's convinced that they're sufficiently qualified to conduct these tests, then I bow to his judgement. Now, having said that, I also believe we shouldn't totally turn a blind eye to their lack of experience in such matters. Accordingly, I propose we limit our exposure by splitting the tests into two separate contracts and that we proceed by approving only the cybersecurity assessment. If their work meets our high standards, only then do we move ahead with the second phase."

Black punctuated this last with questioning eyebrows.

Before Kim could even start to respond, Collier jumped on it: "That's an excellent suggestion, Elijah. I propose we adopt said strategy. Gloria?"

Gloria Kim gave with a resigned shrug.

"In that case, I'd have to agree."

She didn't sound all that sold on the plan.

"Itzhak?"

"I admit, splitting the proposal is brilliant," he said, struggling to maintain a straight face. "You have my vote."

Collier beamed.

"Well then. I'm pleased the group's reached a consensus so seamlessly and rapidly. I'll present our recommendations to the exec committee this afternoon. Hopefully they'll have a decision for us straightaway so I can let Mr. Gold know our decision."

Following another passenger out of the elevator onto floor forty-two—two levels above Larkin Standish—Arnold cut left to the north stairwell door, ran the cloned key card over the reader and watched the LED flash green. He pushed into the concrete and steel stairwell, letting the heavy fire door swing shut on its own, enclosing the concrete and steel shaft in echoing silent air that carried a distinct hint of bone-dry cement.

*Did Security notice him dart straight from the elevator to the stairwell?*

The other passenger had flashed him a suspicious eye while exiting.

*Maybe, but so what?*

Regardless, better get on with the test.

He tried the key card on the reader, but as he suspected, the lock didn't release. Okay, so it was looking like the key would allow him to enter either stairwell from any floor but would only allow him to enter the specific floor assigned to the card holder. Made perfect security sense.

He started down the stairs, pausing at the next fire door to try the card again. No dice. Same with the Larkin Standish floors. Turned out that the key card proved ineffective on all floors but thirty; the same floor his unsuspecting victim had exited on, thus confirming his suspicion.

He grabbed an elevator back to the lobby, his mind now scuttling through schemes for swiping at *least* one key card from the firm, but as many others as he could.

# CHAPTER 20

## Seattle

MIZRAHI LEANED BACK in his desk chair, tapping a Bic against his teeth, working through a plan, the office door closed for privacy and to ensure his thoughts would not be interrupted.

In spite of no longer being privy to further pen-test discussions, he was positive that Webster Collier would ram the decision to hire Gold's team straight down the naïve throats of the firm's hierarchy. Meaning that Gold's team might start work on the pen-test within days. The only remaining question was how soon would they be sufficiently prepared to attempt it? And when they were, what approach would they try? Certainly not a direct assault on the firewall. They should realize that would be a complete waste of time.

Which brought him straight back to the malware in the guest network.

*What the hell was that all about?*

Who embedded it? Gold? If so, why even bother with such a ridiculous act? What could that possibly gain him? Access? Even that didn't make sense because, being a public network, it would be completely isolated from their critical infrastructure. He should know that. But if they were lame enough to not realize it, then he had nothing to worry about.

Still...

Round and round he went, growing increasingly frustrated over the puzzle. If it had been Gold, he had to have had a reason and if so, why was he missing it?

Did Gold embed it simply to test their security: to see if they could find and removed it? That was the only possibility that made one atom of sense. If so, then Gold should have seen how quickly it'd been neutralized. And this should give him an inkling of what he would be up against. This brought him a slight degree of comfort.

But...what if Gold intentionally embedded the malware as an attempt to sell a bumbling Columbo act? Then what? Well, if that were the case, then he was confronting a more formidable adversary.

*Could that be?*

Two very opposite possibilities: stupid vs smart. Which was it?

He began tapping the ballpoint on a notepad, breaking down his conundrum to essentials. The most fundamental question being, who was Gold? And his group? He drew a blank. And this dearth of fact was disturbing. He began jotting down what few facts he *did* know. The company had an office here and in Honolulu. The company was relatively new. They provided IT services to small law firms. They had yet to conduct a pen-test. *Officially*. That was the pathetic total. Four facts. Not much.

But the one item that wouldn't stop nagging him: the word *officially*. What did that choice of words mean to imply?

As much as this haunted him, there was no way to know or find out. He simply needed to press on. Which brought him straight back to the question of whether the RAT was Gold's work. Without his fingerprints on it, again there was no way to know. But regardless of naiveté or stupidity, it made no sense for *anyone* to expend the time and energy it required without a reason. Could a small group such as Gold's afford to devote that much time to a project they hadn't yet been contracted for? Mizrahi thought hard about it…then realized the RAT had definitely been discovered *before* Gold's interview. And this, he decided, was the strongest argument against that little fucker or one of his minions planting it.

A wave of relief rinsed his mind, for he could now focus on what Gold's strategy and tactics might be for hacking the network. Now clear-headed, he suspected Gold would likely start with the easiest approach: social engineering. Although the employees were well trained, he had the least control over the human factor: a harried secretary knee-deep in work receives a benign-sounding call and mistakenly divulges sensitive information; a paralegal opens a legitimate appearing email that infects the entire network.

These ever-present risks were precisely why he spent so much time training everyone—from Collier to the mailroom clerk—on how to spot and foil sophisticated scams. Although Serge and his techs did an adequate job of managing their firewalls untouched, it was Mizrahi's responsibility to make certain that the human factor was equally impenetrable. This was why he'd been so delighted when the alert receptionist recognized and foiled the Hak5 trick.

Starting now, he would funnel one hundred percent of his effort into shoring up what he could without letting Collier realize that he knew a pen-test was imminent.

Yeah, the more he thought about it, the more convinced he was that they were ready to defend against the testers. That goofy porkchop had no inkling of the meat grinder he would be walking into. Of this, he was confident.

His next step was to prime his techs to be ultra-vigilant for attempts to breach the firewall. If he could keep that intact for the next ten or so days, the entire threat would blow over. In the meantime, he should do whatever possible to harden access to the server room. Good, he now had a plan.

Mizrahi left his desk, dropped down a flight to Collier's office, knocked on the open door.

"May I have a word?"

Collier glanced over the tops of his readers and nodded.

"Certainly. Door open or closed?"

Mizrahi softly shut the door but kept his hand on the knob, signaling this would be brief.

"I understand the need to keep me blind to any future discussion about pen-testing, but I feel compelled to make one comment."

Removing the glasses, Collier leaned back in his chair and began to tap his lower lip with a stem.

"Yes?"

"I believe that in spite of their purported lack of experience, Gold's team is fully capable of competently conducting the test if that's the direction committee decides to go." A nod of affirmation for his own statement, believing it added a nice touch of sincerity to his contrived song-and-dance. Kim had whispered in his ear that Collier had presented the proposal to the Governing Committee yesterday shortly after the security committee met. "That's all. Thanks for your time, Mr. Collier, I'll not mention this subject again."

He cracked the door, preparing to leave.

Casually slipping back on his glasses, Collier said, "I'll take that under advisement. But Itzhak, please understand that I took Gold's words to heart. We will not speak on this subject again. Is this understood?"

The door fully open now, he backed up a step and nodded.

"Yes, sir, I understand perfectly."

Mr. Admonished.

Out the door, Mizrahi began a beeline for Serge's cubicle, now convinced that within the next forty-eight hours Collier would have the signed Gold and Associates contract on the books in accounting.

*Perfect, absolutely perfect.*

Serge's large cubicle shared a desk with two techs who worked different shifts, their chairs back-to-back, desks facing opposite directions. The fucking Russian was gone, but John Nusbaum was slouched in front of his monitor robotically typing commands. Mizrahi could hear rap seeping from the fool's earphones.

"Anything?" Mizrahi asked Nusbaum in a volume that would override the noise.

Nusbaum jumped, spun around.

"Huh?" slipping off the black Logitechs.

"Anything?"

"Naw. Quiet as the Titanic."

"Good. Let's keep it that way. My sources now tell me a pen-test *is* in the works, so stay hypervigilant, especially on the firewalls."

Nusbaum cast him a blasé look before clamping his earphones back on.

Fucker.

Settled in his office again, Mizrahi phoned one of the firm's field investigators. From now until the pen-test went down, he wanted to know every time that squirrelly little porker so much as blew his nose.

# CHAPTER 21

## Seattle

ARNOLD DRIFTED TO the right of the lobby doors, out of the pedestrian flow, and into sufficient shade to read his screen. He rang Prisha.

"I'm outside now," he told her. "Where're you?"

A large noisy dump truck was rumbling past, forcing him to plug his free ear.

"Luxuriating on a bench in front of the *pubic* library. You completely done-done or what?"

In spite of the usual traffic cacophony and harsh hiss of air brakes, he caught her play on words and laughed.

"Yeah, done-done. Not only that, but I'm seriously starving. What say we grab lunch at Dog in the Park?"

Dog in the Park was a cool little hot-dog stand nestled in a corner of Westlake Park, one of his favorite quickie downtown good-eats spots.

"Sounds like a definite wiener, dude. Am on the sunny side of Fourth. Head on over and we can compare notes as we walk."

He was already at the corner, heading in her direction.

"On my way."

"I feel pretty good that my pitch scored a point or two," Arnold told her on the southeast corner of Fourth and Pike, waiting for the light to go green.

"Like, what's that mean, exactly?"

He explained Collier's proposed strategy of splitting the contracts into two successive elements, cybersecurity and physical security, adding: "I'm optimistic we have a very good shot at the cybersecurity part. Do that, then we're a lock for the second phase, right? I mean, we pretty much have the first part already."

The light turned green, and they stepped into the crosswalk, Prisha untypically silent. Arnold glanced at her profile but could read nothing.

"What I'm saying," Arnold continued, "is, we need to keep pushing, like full-court-press pushing, with the recon. Yeah, I know, it's still a gamble, but…"

Another glance. Still no reaction. Which seemed, well, decidedly out of character.

Perhaps feeling his stare, she glanced back.

"Yeah, obviously. So, what's the problem, dude? You're weirding on me."

"Moi?" He thought about it. Yeah, the girl had a valid point. He began rummaging through the cubbyholes of consciousness, searching for words to express the wariness worming through his brainstem. Nothing surfaced, so he settled for: "It's Mizrahi…I don't know…dude creeps me, is all."

"Like how? What'd he do?"

More mental mining, then: "Nothing. Just the opposite…the guy was, like, *way* too supportive. I mean suspiciously supportive." Shook his head. "Makes me seriously twitchy."

She appeared to consider this. "Suspiciously supportive? Like…is that a problem?"

As they started past the Arc'teryx window, a very cool windbreaker snagged his attention. He pulled up for another look. Hmmm…didn't really need a new coat but it was completely cool…

"Dude?"

They started walking again.

"He was supporting us when I sort of expected him to claim we're too wet behind the ears or…" He stopped and threw up his hands, "I don't know…it's just weird, him *pushing* for us. Just freaked me, know what I'm saying?"

"Dude. What difference does it make if he supports us?"

Arnold rolled that one around a moment.

"Dude's definitely up to something."

"Up to something?"

Arnold stopped and turned to her.

"What are you, little miss echo? Stop that. Yes, up to something, like setting a *trap*."

Prisha nodded, then nodded again.

"Yeah, a definite possibility, being up to something…I mean us being a direct challenge to his security system, that's understandable…"

Arnold shook his head.

They queued up, side by side, behind three people waiting to order, silent, Arnold still fretting the issue to death.

Prisha elbowed him.

"I get your point, dude, but like, so what? The cyber part's already a lock, soooo the big deal is what, exactly? We can't lose."

She was right, of course. But it still didn't lessen the Mizrahi storm clouds he sensed brewing. Something wasn't right about it, and being unable to identify exactly what that was, continued to be distracting. He needed to be able to focus.

She nudged him again.

"It's clear you're worried, but the point is, you don't need to be. What's the worst that can happen?"

*Was she serious?*

"The worst? We don't get contracted for any of it."

"Yeah, so? We keep trolling for the next job. In the

meanwhile, we keep on keeping on. That's all we can do."

He gently took hold of her arm, so she'd look at him.

"No, you still don't get it. This isn't just any job. This is Larkin Standish and—"

"Yeah-yeah-yeah, everyone's watching and yada-yada-yada. No, I *get* it, dude." She studied him a bit longer. "But you think you had a good interview and that should mean something."

When he said nothing, she continued: "Say we get the cyber portion, since that sounds promising. Again, what's the worst that can happen?" It really wasn't a question. "We bank the fee and, boom, our first successful pen-test's on our résumé. Word'll get out and we'll look like champs. What's so wrong with that?" She shrugged. "Nothing, far as I can see; absolutely nothing. In fact, all I see's upside. Or what am I missing?"

He shook his head, then finger combed his hair, still working on it...

"Naw, you're right about that..."

"But?"

He shook his head.

"Don't know about you, but this gig's become more than a simple pen-test for me. It's going to validate who we are as a company." Suddenly there it was. He raked his hair again, molding the thought into words. "When Mizrahi started supporting us, it's like he was saying we're nothing but bush-league losers instead of a valid threat. In other words, if he helps grease the skids so we get this gig it makes his life a lot easier. See? It's insulting. And *that's* what's *really* pissing me off."

"So?" Prisha spread her hands. "Think about that," tapping her temple with an index finger. "If that's true, good, 'cause it's telling me he's concerned about us. And if that's the case, I'm totally amped. Makes me want to find out what it is he's so worried about, so I can exploit it. Hey, we're miles ahead of him already, dude, so just focus on our mission. Just focus."

*Right again.*

But Mizrahi was still making him nervous.

He simply changed the subject: "Update me on security."

"You didn't happen to check out that in-your-face booth right in the middle of the lobby, did ya? The one with the wall of monitors and the guard?" She barked a short cynical snort. "I mean, is that a statement or what?"

"Yeah, subtle it ain't." Then added: "Guess that's the point."

"I walk straight up to the counter, ask the dude if they're hiring. Without so much as one slight eye deviation from the monitors, he side-mouths a number to call then promptly cuts me off, like, he's not going to get sucked into a distraction. I mean, that dude's either totally in the zone or's making a supreme effort to give me that impression, as if I'm the diversion in some bizarre *Ocean's 11* plot to take over the building. Or maybe he's just super paranoid about being under the microscope by *their* head of security. Regardless, you gotta admit they're certainly making it known how super tight their security is."

They moved up to the counter, the stand doing brisk business on such a lovely spring day.

Prisha said, "I'll head back over this afternoon, see if their three-eleven shift's equally intense. Long as I'm there, I'll see what other security items I can sniff out, but from what I've seen so far, the cyber portion's going to be easier than any entry'll be. That's for damn sure."

Arnold wagged his head.

"True that. And you're doing an amazing job. I'm shocked at what you have."

A shrug.

"No biggie. Used the library Wi-Fi to do some research on North Sound while you were wrapping up. That's one ginormous firm. Apparently, they do security for several downtown buildings. I've got no idea how many guards they must have on the payroll."

"What can I get you?" asked the young Asian male working the counter. A similarly aged Asian male was furiously grilling butterflied wieners, opened buns, and chopped veggies. Arnold was convinced that their secret ingredient was the veggie-flavored salted grill oil that soaked the buns.

Prisha ordered a Seattle Dog that featured cream cheese and caramelized veggies on a toasted bun. She also grabbed a Diet Coke from the ice bin crammed with assorted drinks pushed up against the counter. Arnold went for an all-beef large with caramelized veggies and bottled water. Orders paid for, they moved to the side of the counter to watch the grill master do his magic, masterfully butterflying wieners in one fluid slice without amputating a finger, then pressing the cut side flat against the hot grill, then flipping a pile of diced veggies with the spatula: a fascinating spectacle of methodical, efficient wizardry. When their dogs were almost cooked, two butterflied buns were toasted on the grill of seasoned oil.

Dogs and drinks in hand, they lucked out and snagged a highly prized table just as another couple was vacating it.

Settled in and ready to eat, Prisha said, "Check this out," and pulled the newly purchased scanner from her backpack, plunked it on the small bistro table, flicked on the power. Though the signal was weak and scratchy from this far away, they could hear episodic radio chatter between security guards.

"Is that them?" Arnold asked in astonishment.

"Yep."

"Jesus, Prisha." He shook his head in awe. "That shit's off the hook."

Mouth closed, jaws chomping like crazy, she simply tapped her closed lips. A moment later, she washed down the mouthful with a sip of Coke.

"*Man*, I love these things." She paused for another pull of Coke. "This scanner's so freaking easy a brain-dead kindergartner could operate it."

Arnold shook his head in amusement. Just another

example to justify his decision to hire her over Rachael's objections. Exactly what those objections were remained a mystery. Perhaps Martina had been right when she suggested that they were based in jealousy. In spite of giving her no reason to be.

"Hold on. Does this mean you know what kind of radios they're using?" he asked, more awestruck.

She flashed a white beaming smile.

"Yes indeed, Kemosabe. Take a wild-ass guess."

He laughed.

"Haven't a clue."

Her smile widened.

"Nothing fancy, just plain old FRS hand-helds."

Meaning Family Radio Service. Inexpensive walkie-talkies bought from Amazon or other common retailers. He laughed again, even more amazed at how much crucial information she was accumulating in so few days.

"You know this because?"

"Because they're transmitting on 462 and 467 MHz." Her wide trademark smile reappeared. "No, they're not scrambled or masked, meaning we're now officially tapped directly into their comm link. I mean, you can't get any better than this, dude."

She was now full-on beaming.

"You're right. We can't. How cool is that." He shook his head in disbelief. "Makes you wonder why a security service like North Sound doesn't go to greater lengths to protect communications?"

She shrugged.

"Could be a ton of reasons, you think about it."

He did. For a beat. Then nodded.

"I guess it simplifies things when personnel are moved from building to building to cover staffing holes that crop up...vacations or call in sick. Probably keeps them from messing up radio settings."

*Jesus, you're thinking like a boss now.*

Which gave him pause. For like a millisecond or so. But pause, nonetheless.

Then: "Still, I *am* surprised that a security company isn't concerned about this."

"Yeah, but it's not like they're guarding JP Morgan or Air Force One. They're just keeping eyes out for problems, then call the cops when something hinky starts."

Arnold nodded.

"Good point."

Prisha set down her half-finished hot dog, used a paper towel to degrease her fingers, and dialed her phone.

A moment later: "Hey hon, want me to pick up something for dinner on the way back? ... Okay. By the way, why don't you see what you can dredge up on Itzhak Mizrahi...yeah, that's right, head of security at Larkin Standish."

After she rang off, Arnold said, "Good idea. Thanks for thinking of it."

She gave him a dose of weird-eye.

"What's up, dude? And don't give me your deer-in-the-headlights bewildered look. You know exactly what I mean...between you and Rachael?"

*What could he say? Well, how about the truth.*

"I'm not sure I know," he answered softly, with a woeful head wag.

Prisha studied him a beat before saying in an equally soft voice, "Well, if you want to talk it over, I'm here for you, dude."

Arnold wadded up the little paper tray on which the hot dog had been served and glanced around for the compost bin.

"We'd better get back to work."

# CHAPTER 22

## Seattle

BACK HOME, ARNOLD phoned Rachael before setting out with Chance for their afternoon break. Figured on stopping by the PCC to pick up something for dinner from the deli counter. Always a staple of his shopping.

"I'm glad you called, sweetie. I was going to update you earlier, but time just seemed to somehow slip away, so no, don't plan on me for dinner. I'll eat here and spend the night. Auntie Shira will be joining us." She added, "I hope you don't mind," in what sounded suspiciously like a gratuitous afterthought.

Yeah, in fact he *did* mind. Which shocked him to admit even if just to himself. Made him feel, well, more than a bit slimy on account of it wasn't the sort of emotional response to be proud of. After all, why resent her spending the night with her mother? She and her mom were being thrown into a totally shitty situation over which they had zero control.

"Arnold?"

"Okay, yeah-yeah, talk to you when I talk to you."

He disconnected the call.

Standing in the kitchen staring blankly out the window, he began to dissect the reason for his resentment. What did this say

132

about *him*? What kind of person would begrudge a decision to support her poor frightened mother in such a stressful time? A total asshole, that's who. Is this what he wanted to be? He felt ashamed of himself.

On the other hand...

In the wake of the shock of self-incrimination and loathing, another possibility began to peek around the corner into consciousness: what if her decision to stay there was not so much about daughterly devotion to her mom's plight but just one more minuscule side-step toward extracting herself from the relationship? String enough of these teensy-weensy withdrawals together and you eventually have a functionally dissolved relationship months in the making.

Yeah, this felt right. She would vociferously deny it of course, but...yeah...

So which was it: an act of pure devotion or another small move toward dissolution?

*How about both?*

*Jesus.*

He grabbed the leash and halter and went looking for Chance.

As Chance meandered from shrub to shrub as they made their way to PCC, Arnold couldn't stop ruminating over his total blindness to Rachael's insidious emotional detachment these past months.

No one sentinel event marked a definitive beginning; at least not that he could see even with the brilliant clarity of retrospect, but there was an inflection point. And, if forced to timestamp it, he would bet it kick-started with those additional days in Seattle on the heels of the ransomware gig.

*How had he missed it?*

He halted, the leash snapping taut. Chance glanced over his shoulder, gave a doggie shrug, and returned to sniffing a tree trunk. Well, that was on account of each of them seeing his delay through very different filters. He believed those few days were essential; she saw them as what, frivolous? Perhaps not frivolous, but certainly unnecessary. So, what did that say about them as a couple? After all, every couple has different views day to day. The trick was to prevent these trivial disagreements from driving a spike through the heart of a relationship. Unless…

*Did she ever love him? Or—more shockingly—did he truly love her?*

*Wow.*

A prickly sensation started scintillating up and down his body like a tacky row of blinking neon arrows simulating motion.

Chance tugged the leash again with another over-the-shoulder glance. Getting no response, he resumed exploring shrubbery.

Do I love her?

*Of course I do.*

Really?

*What other explanation is there?*

Interesting question. Especially in light of a niggling skepticism that—as long as he was being brutally honest—had been kissing the periphery of his consciousness for a time now without cracking through. It went like this: she was the first girl he'd ever had a "crush" on.

*Yeah, a crush…as embarrassing as that sounded.*

And in a strange sort of way, that sophomoric emotional commitment seemed to compel him to make his adolescent fantasy of her being "his girl" come true. A goal driven more by hormones than rational thought.

*Seriously, dude?*

Jesus, seemed as if today was morphing into the Large Hadron Collider of pertinent—perhaps embarrassing—self-reflections.

*Well, hell, break it down, dude.*

As difficult as that might be.

To be savagely honest, what interests did they *mutually* share?

Football? Well, minimally.

The stock market? Naw.

Nursing. Nope.

His business? Definitely not. Her job with the company had been—again, in total truth—a Hail Mary relationship Band-Aid.

In spite of subliminally knowing all these things on an individual basis, combining them into one conscious revelation hit with what felt like a thirty-amp jolt.

But it didn't stop there. Nope. A kaleidoscope of swirling questions began to snap into logical sequence, forcing him to confront his ongoing denial of the various events of these past months: Her reaction to the few extra days spent in Seattle. Her unjustified resentment of his business travel. Her unilateral decision to return to her apartment. Taken one by one in real time, each one simply bounced off his reality center. But now, taken in ensemble, they telegraphed an unequivocally clear message: Rachael—his adolescent Dream Girl—was nowhere close to a soulmate.

*Soulmate? Jesus, just freaking gag me.*

Arnold swallowed hard and blinked away a budding tear.

*Fuck!*

Face it, dude, you don't really love her. You've always been in love with the fantasy of what you wanted her to be.

In reality, that was it. Period.

Chance tugged on the leash again, more persistently now, staring at him from over his shoulder.

*C'mon, Dad, let's get moving.*

Back at the kitchen table, Arnold forced himself to concentrate on deciphering the information contained in the key cards cloned from the unsuspecting elevator passengers. When comparing the numbers embedded on them, only one set of values varied. There could be limited reasons for this, most likely it determined what floor the computer allowed the holder to access. Only Larkin Standish employees, for example, could access their floors via either elevator or stairwell.

Leaning back in the chair, he played with the various riffs on how to leverage this into an advantage when breaking into the law firm. Several ideas popped to mind, all of which he jotted down for further analysis. Right now, this was just a brainstorming session.

Fifteen minutes later, he decided that he'd generated enough ideas to put together a rough plan of attack. But before devoting serious effort to it, he should verify his suspicion about the meaning of the unique number set. And the only way to do that was to swipe a few more key cards; ideally, from Larkin Standish personnel. Better yet—*yeah, in your wildest dream*—Mizrahi's.

Fingers interlaced across the back of his head, Arnold arched his back: his favorite stretch after long periods of intense laptop work.

Three Hearts in a Tangle began.

Jesus, seen thirty? Already?

Since scarfing down lunch, he'd been so focused on formulating attack details that tracking time hadn't rippled his awareness. But this sort of total immersion was worth every second, for it was not only productive but was also an absolute distraction from the Rachael thing.

Without checking caller ID he raised the iPhone to his ear.

"Hello."

"Arnold Gold?"

"Yes?"

"Good evening. Webster Collier here. I have some good news. The executive committee would like to explore your Scope of Work in greater detail. Can you to meet me in my office at nine tomorrow morning to discuss a few items?"

*Yes!*

Arnold's heartbeat hit a thundering gallop. He sucked a deep breath, cautioned himself to temper his excitement.

"I'd be delighted, sir."

"Excellent. Please email me your updated SOW ASAP so we may review it fully by then. We've only gone over your general template."

*Perfect.*

Modifying the template was one of the tasks he'd finished earlier.

"I'll send it the moment I hang up, sir."

"Good. Alright then, we look forward to a more in-depth discussion in the morning. In the meantime, have a pleasant evening."

Totally pumped, Arnold called Rachael, Prisha, and Lopez with the fist-pumping news, uncorked a bottle of Rutherford cab, then buckled Chance into his halter. The wine could breathe during their tour of the neighbors' shrubs.

This good news was almost too good to wrap his head around. Gold and Associates was about to land their first honest-to-God pen-test. With a high-profile company too. He wanted to do *something* to uncork the joy and relief bubbling inside like a shaken bottle of champagne, but nothing blossomed to mind.

*Wait, not so fast. Think.*

Assume they sign the contract tomorrow. Was the team anywhere close to being ready to breach the firm's physical security? Not even close. Among other things, he needed to steal at least one—preferably more—keys from Larkin Standish employees.

*How the hell was he going to pull that rabbit out of the hat?*

# CHAPTER 23

## Seattle

AS WITH THEIR prior meeting, Webster Collier greeted Arnold in the reception area. But unlike their prior meeting, the managing partner led him to the south stairwell door, opened it with a lanyard key card, then held it open for Arnold.

As Collier led Arnold up the first flight of stairs, he said apologetically, "Whenever possible I try to walk the stairs. It saves electricity, of course, but I primarily do it for the exercise since I spend too many hours at my desk or at a conference table."

They reached floor thirty-five but Collier continued up the next flight to the thirty-six landing where again he swiped his key card across the reader unlocking the fire door. As he was leading him into the firm's inner sanctum, Arnold continued to memorize as many details as possible. As with the other floors, the only obvious surveillance camera was the ever-present smoked-glass ceiling bubble directly above the elevator alcove.

"This way," Collier said, continuing along an angled hall to their left.

Instead of entering a conference room, Collier ushered him into an office of minimalist unremarkable furniture: a dark walnut desk with a matching credenza, two three-drawer matching file cabinets, two visitor chairs, and a stunning northwest panorama of the downtown business district. Arnold's eyes immediately zeroed in on a sterling-silver framed photo of an attractive woman approximately Collier's age beside his single computer monitor. Presumably his wife.

"Please," Collier said, motioning with his hand toward the visitor chairs facing each other; a modification, Arnold suspected, from their usual orientation facing the desk.

As Arnold dropped into one, Collier closed the office door, then folded himself into the other. Once settled, Collier picked up a manila folder strategically positioned on the edge of his desk and handed it to Arnold.

"Since the proposed testing represents your company's first, shall we say *formal*, foray into pen-testing, the partners elected to move forward with a conservative sequential approach. We propose to hire your team for the cybersecurity portion of the test only, but if all goes well and we're comfortable with your competency—and I hope you excuse that word, but it's the only one that readily comes to mind—we'll be in a much better position to decide on whether to commit to the second phase." He clasped his hands together and sat back in his chair. "I hope this proposed two-phased modification is satisfactory to you."

*Satisfactory? Hell, overjoyed was more like it.*

*Be cool, dude.*

Arnold nodded thoughtfully, struggling to keep the joy tugging the corners of his mouth from breaking through to an over-the-moon silly grin.

"Sir, your approach sounds very prudent. To be honest, if I were in your shoes, I'd probably take exactly the same approach. Yes, we're delighted to be given this opportunity to prove ourselves to you and the committee."

*Jesus, dude, can your nose get any browner?*

Meeting over, back on the sidewalk, Arnold phoned Rachael.

"Do me a favor, will you?"

He was fighting to cork his bubbling excitement.

"Depends on what it is."

"Notify the group that we just inked the cybersecurity part of the project. I have the contract in hand."

"Wow! That's amazing," she said, sounding surprisingly amped. "I know how much this job means to you."

"But in addition, we need to set up a brainstorming session like ASAP. The entire team...I mean, like today, soon as possible. Have time to arrange that?"

*Sure as hell hoped so, on account of his brain was zipping along, swamped with details, all of which needed to be nailed down, like, immediately if not sooner.*

"Yeah, I can do that. How soon and where do you want to hold it?"

Hmmm...he glanced around. Naw, not downtown. Not around the kitchen table again either. Sure, they *could* do it there, but he wanted to mix things up a little, if for no other reason than to keep their interest stoked. A glance at the cloudless pale blue sky pushing one of their first 70-degree days of the year. Perfect for an outdoor venue. Hmmm....

"Tell you what, seeing how it's such a beautiful day, why don't we do a lunch meeting over at the Highliner, that pub over at Fishermen's Terminal? It's, like, super close to Prisha and Vihaan's place. You up for that?"

"Great suggestion. That means Chance can come with me."

The Highliner had a cool little patio with umbrella tables where dogs were welcome.

"Perfect."

# CHAPTER 24

## Seattle

FISHERMEN'S TERMINAL—A venerable Seattle landmark—consisted of a congested moorage serving more than two hundred and fifty fishing and pleasure craft and features a handful of retail, restaurants, and other commercial shops. It gained some national notoriety several years ago as the home of the fishing boat featured in the TV series *Deadliest Catch*.

The group scrunched two tables together, then settled in, Chance prone on the gray concrete diplomatically equidistant between Arnold and Rachael.

As soon as the waiter sashayed from the table with their orders, Arnold kicked off the meeting.

"Our first item on the agenda is to decide when to give the Larkin Standish committee the map of their network." Before anyone could speak, he raised a hold-on-a-minute finger. "The answer might not be as straightforward as you think." He allowed a few thought-provoking seconds for this to percolate. "It was brilliant for Mizrahi to designate a network map as proof of penetration, right? I mean, think about it. How can Mr. Collier verify its accuracy unless...?"

He waited a few beats for this chunk of logic to seep in.

Prisha got it first.

"Fuck me! Only way they can is by running it past Mizrahi."

"Exactly. And the moment that happens, dude's going to know he's been had and that we're probably teeing up for an office creep, right? I mean he gets another mondo advantage, right?" A woeful headshake, then: "This whole gig's been contaminated since the get-go."

"So what're you saying is," Prisha continued, "hold off? For what? I'm not sure I see the logic in that."

Arnold lowered his head, eying her. "You seriously believe we're ready to do the creep now? I don't." After a beat. "We haven't even finalized our strategy."

Glances were exchanged all around, everyone waiting to see who would stick their neck out.

Lopez jumped in.

"Well, duh, the longer we take to prepare, the more prepared we'll be, so theoretically the better our chances and blah-blah-blah. But don't forget there's a flip side to this. If I'm Mizrahi and some no-name hack-ass pen-tester maps my crown jewel in a couple hours, I'd be, like, super-crazy insane, man. First thing I'd do is start combing every known access port inch by fucking inch. What I'm saying is, they're going to be crawling all over that network. Do we really want to risk having them shut down our access?"

Prisha jumped in.

"Right now, we only have the one trapdoor. What I think the boss is saying is we take whatever time's needed to build in some redundancy before we say word one to Collier. That should only take us, I dunno...twenty-four, thirty-six hours tops?" Then, to Arnold; "Right?"

Arnold nodded.

"Yeah, at the outside. Could be sooner." Then, to Lopez: "What do you think? How solid are we once Mizrahi's team gets going on this? As you said, they'll be crazy pissed, getting aced like this."

Lopez started raking his lower lip with his teeth, working

through the problem, gave a quick nod.

"For sure they'll nail the decoys, like, instantly. Big question is, will that satisfy them? Maybe, maybe not." He shrugged. "No way to know. But our ace in the hole, the one totally up for grabs, is that hole in the case-management software. I'm super suspicious that the moment they know we're in, they'll realize they didn't update that one, and go ahead and patch it. Once that door's sealed up, we're back to square one. I didn't find any other updates they've neglected."

The entry point Arnold had exploited to access the network was a "zero-day vulnerability" that was known to reside in the firm's legal case-management software. He'd recognized the app when he glanced at a monitor on his way to the conference room the first day. Zero-day vulnerabilities are holes in software that the developers had yet to patch with an update.

The group fell silent, waiting for Arnold to decide; the weight of this decision was now dragging him down.

*Management! Jesus.*

"Oh, man, I don't know…" he muttered, massaging his temple. "Play our hand now, we make the greatest impact, right? I mean, like, within hours of giving us the nod we blow right in. That's got to catch their attention. And we're talking about very influential lawyers here, right? After all, we *are* trying to use this job to break into this line of work…"

"I realize I'm only the business manager," Rachael said, "but my two cents is to establish a backup access point soon as possible, then break it to them they've been had. I mean, really, what do you have to lose? It's inevitable Mizrahi's going to find out about it, so why not just go for it."

The group silently exchanged glances.

*She was right.*

Prisha said, "Know what? To me everything comes down to whether we think our roughed-out phase-two plans are good enough to do the creep *now*. Assuming, of course, we iron out a couple of minor points. Personally, I think they are. Okay, I admit we can always tweak the contingency plans for potential issues that *might* crop up, but hell, realistically, just about anything can and we can't possibly predict every single one, because that's just the way these things play. Shit happens. We simply need to believe we're good enough to react and adjust as needed. What I'm saying: I don't see a good reason to *not* call Collier right now, this minute. I mean, what can we *really* lose? Huh? We've already proven our point. We hacked their network. I mean…"

She scanned their faces. No one seemed to disagree.

She added, "And I agree with Rachael that Mizrahi's gonna know sooner or later. So really, what's the big deal about playing our cards now? We just gotta be better at getting around him than he is at catching us." She threw up her hands. "Tell me if I'm wrong."

"Naw, you're right," Arnold said, "except for one thing. We can't risk Mizrahi knowing until we have at least *one* additional trapdoor embedded. Especially if we plan to shut down their eyes. Agreed?"

Lopez said, "Hey, my laptop's in the car. If you want, I can start working it now."

His eyebrows raised in anticipation.

Arnold nodded at Lopez, who almost catapulted from his chair and headed out to the parking lot.

Arnold scanned the group one final time.

"So that's it, call Mr. Collier now?" He held up his phone.

Prisha shrugged.

"Don't see why not. However, there *is* one thing we need to discuss while Lopez's working." She paused for a sip of water. "I know this is *way* premature, but I think we need to consider it. A brief pause. "Collier and the committee are gonna want to know the particulars on how we did it. How much should we actually disclose? I mean, I don't want to risk getting someone's ass caught in the wringer."

"Good point," Arnold said. "Actually, I was thinking the

same thing on the way over. It's simpler to just attribute it to human error and leave it at that. Even in the final report. After all, we don't know exactly which attempt got us in, right?" Although Arnold was pretty sure the RAT-infected USB he'd put in the manila envelope to be couriered over from the Smith Tower was what did the trick.

Lopez: "I like it."

Arnold looked at Prisha and Vihaan. Both remained silent. "Okay then."

Upon reaching Collier's secretary on the phone, Arnold left a message for him to return the call ASAP, that he had an important development to discuss.

Collier wasn't able to return the call until late afternoon.

After exchanging perfunctory greetings, Arnold dropped The Bomb: "Have the map of your secure network for you…you know, the evidence Mr. Mizrahi designated as proof of penetration. I can deliver it to your office personally whenever it's convenient for you, just let me know."

Several seconds of stunned silence echoed over the connection.

Then: "How soon can you be here?"

There was a clear note of concern in his voice.

"Soon as Uber can bring me. I'll call one now if you'd like," Arnold said, struggling to muzzle overwhelming glee from his voice.

No one likes a gloater Especially when discussing an issue this critical.

At the curb, awaiting his ride, Arnold began to worry.

Just how well prepared *were* they? Good enough to break into a heavily guarded office?

It was one thing to hack a network where the overwhelming amount of work was done with your butt planted in front of a monitor, keyboarding commands, where if one strategy blew up, big deal, you simply pull another trick from your bag until you finally hit pay dirt.

But sneaking through a high-security building full of guards who know to expect you would be a hell of a lot trickier. One mistake, game over.

No second chances.

# CHAPTER 25

## Seattle

COLLIER CAME BARRELING through reception from the north stairwell, face etched in deep concern.

Without breaking stride or uttering one word, he motioned Arnold to follow, leading him through the familiar hall to yet another small conference room with a rectangular table, six chairs, and a few framed unremarkable motel-room photos of nondescript landscapes on a wall. However, the room did offer a stunning view.

Closing the door, Collier said, "Have a seat."

All business. He then scraped out a chair for himself but continued to stand. No offered water this time.

Arnold plunked his attaché case on the table, pulled a chair from the table, folded into it. Collier continued to stare blankly at him.

*Dude's freaking out.*

Collier remained motionless behind his chair, lips pursed, mind apparently grinding through serious gears, none of which, Arnold guessed, were good. After a headshake, he finally settled into the chair, methodically interlaced his fingers, and leveled his gaze on Arnold.

"If what you say is true, that you were able to map our

147

network so...quickly...I'm stunned..." He seemed to think about these last words. "No, I amend that. Astounded is more apt. I'm astounded that you defeated our security to begin with, and then, apparently so easily." Pause. "I assume you brought the map." He held out his palm. "May I please have it?"

"Yes, of course."

Arnold rotated his attaché case so that the hinges were facing Collier, popped the latches, and opened the top, blocking the lawyer's view of its contents. Pretending to rummage through its contents in search of the map, Arnold aimed Flipper Zero at the lawyer's key card, thumbed the trigger and heard the corresponding beep.

*Jesus, did he hear it?*

"Ah, here we go," Arnold said, handing him a USB drive containing the Larkin Standish LAN network map.

He promptly snapped the attaché case locks and said a silent prayer that he copped another key card. An important one at that.

Collier held up the thumb drive, studying it, turning it slowly this way and that.

*Debating its fate?*

Arnold would bet on it. If the dude was as clever as Arnold suspected, he was struggling with how to verify the map without tipping Mizrahi. Which was, of course, impossible.

"Mr. Collier, hope I'm not out of line by making a suggestion, but I suspect you're stressing about the bind you're in. You need to confirm its validity, but to do that you need to run it by Mr. Mizrahi. And the moment you do, he'll be expecting us to try a break-in. Am I correct?"

Before Collier could reply, Arnold added, "But consider this: what if he doesn't catch us..."

He simply let that hang.

Collier seemed to toss this around for several moments before the chair scraped and he was up, saying, "I'll be back soon as I can."

He was out the door, flash drive in hand.

Ten minutes later he was back with an even more perplexed expression. Calmly, almost gently, he shut the door, took hold of his chair, and eyed Arnold suspiciously.

"How did you hack us so quickly?"

*Oh boy, here we go. Well, what'd I expect?*

*Cartwheels? Shrieks of joy?*

The last thing Arnold wanted was rat out a secretary or partner. But strictly speaking, he couldn't be absolutely certain which scam ultimately ended up embedding the RAT in the laser printer....well, this wasn't exactly true. He was pretty sure it was the lawyer. But he neither wanted to finger the poor dude nor disclose their method. And besides, Mizrahi knew somebody messed up. And, was now undoubtedly going completely apeshit. Once the malware had embedded, Arnold was able to migrate to the legal software with the known zero-day vulnerability and let Lopez know to map the network. And now, they had built in some redundancies, so were in better shape than at lunchtime.

Arnold shrugged.

"Nothing fancy. We simply exploited a known hole in some software you're using." He spread his hands. "It's *that* easy."

*Well, sort of close to the truth.*

Glancing away, Collier shook his head in either disgust or a slow burn, hard to tell. Arnold didn't blame the man. Reality can be a real bitch to confront sometimes.

A moment later, with a resigned exhale, Collier folded into his chair and began to absentmindedly drum his fingers on the table, then shook his head again.

"I had no idea... I assumed..." Another headshake. Exasperated. "Now, more than ever, obviously," he said, having reined in his emotions, "we need to complete the rest of the evaluation. To say today is a revelation is a gross understatement."

Waiting patiently for Collier to finish, Arnold decided that if Mizrahi found himself with a brand-new butthole on account this, he wouldn't be all *that* broken up over it.

Collier: "I suspect I know the answer to this next question but feel obliged to ask. Since the test is no longer blinded, should we delay the second phase until conditions normalize?"

A logical, valid question. Luckily Arnold had anticipated it.

"I suggest we stick to the plan and press ahead. Here's why: say we're caught in the act. We always have the option of repeating the test a month or so later when Mizrahi least expects it. Remember, we don't bill for a failed test. On the other hand, *if* we're successful…"

He let that one hang, too.

Eyebrows raised, Collier nodded thoughtfully.

"That makes a great deal of sense. In that case, proceed as you see fit. But I have another question: how do you protect yourselves if building security or SPD catches you during entry? Before you can reach our offices."

"Ahh, perfect segue into my next topic. We all carry our individualized copy of the SOW as our Get Out of Jail Free card."

Collier smiled, as if being exposed to a completely new aspect of life.

"Ah yes, the SOW."

"Which brings me to my next topic: I need you to designate what you'll accept as proof of entry. Any suggestions?"

Collier glanced away for a moment, then shook his head.

"Nothing comes to mind. Have you any suggestions?"

Arnold scanned the office for inspiration.

"Let's start with a floor or a room. What comes to mind?"

Collier massaged his chin for a moment, then shook his head in apparent frustration.

"I should've anticipated this question but…how about my office?"

"Yeah, that works." Arnold glanced around again for inspiration, then walked over to the desk and picked up the silver framed picture.

"How about I take a selfie like this," he said, holding it next to his face. "Does this work for you?"

"That's perfect," Collier said with a smile, apparently relieved to have this issue settled.

"Okay, so now all we need to do is write this into the agreement."

Arnold pulled two copies of the SOW from his attaché case and filled in this requirement in a blank section on both forms, then passed them to Collier.

"Here you go. Feel free to change the wording to whatever you feel is appropriate. Once it's worded to your satisfaction, sign and date both copies, keep one for yourself and I'll take the other, and we're good to go."

"When do you anticipate you'll conduct the intrusion?" Collier asked, handing Arnold a business size manila envelope containing his signed copy of the SOW.

Arnold wagged a finger at him.

"No one, not even you, can know that. But honestly, it'll most likely be sometime in the next three weeks. Which, by the way, raises an important point. From now until we wrap this up, you should be available to answer your cell during off hours. You okay with that?"

The lawyer frowned. "Because?"

"In case we're apprehended."

He nodded.

"Right."

As Arnold was slipping the envelope into the attaché case, preparing to leave.

"You didn't happen to mention this meeting to Mr. Mizrahi, did you?"

Collier frowned.

"I didn't mention that we were actually meeting...but the

151

moment I handed him the thumb drive he knew. Why?"

"You're right, he did...but please don't mention this discussion to anyone including the members of the security committee. Although I'm sure he assumes we're moving to phase two now, he doesn't know when that might happen, and I don't want him to have any hints."

Frowning, Collier said, "I see a potential problem. Once the governance committee decided to prioritize a security evaluation, I've been pushing this project hard and providing them with regular updates. If I suddenly stop mentioning it, won't that in itself be construed as a sign of moving ahead with it?"

Arnold shrugged.

"Perhaps. But as we said, Mizrahi has to know it's in the works now. He just doesn't know exactly when it'll happen, right?"

"Fair enough, but out of curiosity, if you're caught, how soon would you suggest it should be repeated?"

Boy, that's a tough one, especially given their lack of experience...but considering...

"That all depends on how close we come to a successful entry. Once we've submitted our final report and your committee's had sufficient time to digest it, you and I can discuss the next steps. Make sense?"

"Yes, it does. But I'm still reeling from how rapidly you broke into our network."

*Yeah? Just wait for Act II.*

# CHAPTER 26

## Seattle

TILTING BACK IN his chair, ankle over knee, eyes glued to his twenty-seven-inch monitor, Mizrahi watched Collier escort Gold to the elevators and then shake the squirrelly little cocksucker's hand before the cage swallowed him. Well, that confirmed it: the Security Committee had greenlighted the second phase. It was now game on.

As Collier pirouetted, then marched purposefully from the elevators, Mizrahi began reviewing his list of additional security measures to ensure that Gold's team didn't get within a floor of their offices.

Preferably Security would nail the little turd before he made it halfway across the lobby.

Lucky for him, Gold had been stupid enough to disclose that he couldn't stay in town long, which—if true—suggested their attack would probably go down as early as the next few days, depending on how much planning they required. Mizrahi fully intended to shut them down so instantaneously their heads would twist their necks into pretzels.

*Hmmm...how many days would it take for those jokers to cobble together an operable plan of attack?*

Bare minimum, forty-eight hours? Longer? Probably. Or,

153

had those little bastards done some preliminary planning? He considered that possibility but decided the probability was remote. Only a seasoned team might waste time on detailed preliminary planning before having a contract in hand. And even then, who could afford that luxury? Very few. And rank amateurs? Under the direction of that joker? He shook his head. NFW.

Then again…how much of an amateur was that little shit?

To underestimate an opponent is to court disaster.

The problem was, he still knew next to nothing about Gold or his group. Hell, none of his contacts around town knew anything useful about them either. Yet for some unsettling reason, Gold's group had somehow weaseled their way through the firewall in mere hours. And thus far Serge and his techs were drawing a blank at identifying their point of entry. That they'd been in and out without leaving a footprint was certainly disconcerting as well as raising questions about their experience and abilities. And this ambiguity was now growing increasingly irritating, pissing him off mightily.

Mizrahi stormed over to Serge Valchenka's cubicle and stood at the entrance taking in the sight. Case in point: fucking Russian slouched forward, back to him, headphones clamped over ears, eyes glued to his two Samsung monitors; on the right, straight-up heterosexual porn; on the left, a network scan scrolling past. Absolutely no concern at having been one-upped by a rank amateur.

Mizrahi shook his head in complete disgust. Yet the Russian did manage to complete his work. Halfway decent work, at that. Plus he clocked in every day and had done so even through the COVID crisis. Truth be told, he was reliable…so really, other than letting Gold breeze straight into their secure network….

But *that* was unforgivable.

Mizrahi was just about to bang on the frosted-glass partition when a thought slithered along his spine.

*Could he be grossly underestimating Gold?*

Was it possible that the little shithead was more battle-seasoned than he assumed?

Was it possible that Gold had been tipped off about Collier's interest in him *prior* to being contacted, giving him time for a head start on preparing an attack? That would go a long way in explaining the alacrity with which it had gone down…but how likely was it for a fledgling company to devote so many resources to a job they'd yet to secure? Huh. It was something to consider, as unlikely as it was. Had Collier somehow found out about Gold and spoken to him prior to proposing him to the committee? No way to know.

Besides, all these hypotheticals were off point. The point was that he needed to focus on thwarting a break-in he knew was imminent. Now. Today. Perhaps even as soon as this evening. After all, there had to be a goddamn good explanation for how unbelievably fast those little fuckheads had mapped his network. The more he considered this, the more he convinced himself that Gold had had a head start. The fucker.

Forcing himself to accept that he'd underestimated Gold was, in itself, humiliating, pissing him off even more.

He realized he was angrily pumping both fists. Stopped, glanced around, embarrassed at his outward display of rage. Had anyone seen it? Didn't appear so. In hopes of squelching his simmering anger, he flicked his hands as if flinging off water. Didn't help. Instead, he stared at his palms, visualizing his intense rage radiating from his fingertips like blood-red laser sabers capable of slicing that little fucker into…

Not only Gold, but this fucking Russian mindlessly eying porn while Gold and his minions were skipping *tra la la la la* straight through their firewall to map their network. Gross incompetence. If anyone should be held accountable for this egregious failure, it was the Russian bastard. Mizrahi mustered every available ounce of self-control to keep from smashing the Russian's five o'clock shadow through the goddamn OLED screen.

*Want to taste pussy? Here!*

Mizrahi stepped back from the cubicle entrance and inhaled a deep flared-nostrils breath, cradled it in his lungs for several seconds, then repeated the exercise until he was comfortable with the fact that now, more than ever, he needed Comrade Valchenka's full cooperation. After running both palms over his black hair, he gulped one final deep breath.

*Calm enough?*

Yes. Then knuckled the smoked glass of the cubicle. Loudly.

A massive butt spasm almost launched Serge into orbit. He swiveled his head toward Mizrahi. A second of confusion shot across his eyes before the image apparently registered.

Slipping off his headphones, he began stammering, "Yo, Itzhak, I still don't see how—"

"Gold's group's apparently been green-lighted for a physical entry," he announced accusingly.

*You need him now. This is not the time...*

Valchenka swallowed, hesitated, then nodded.

"Your sources have any indication when?"

When? Unable to resist, Mizrahi cocked his head in mock amazement.

"When?" A glare. "It's not *scheduled*. These things aren't *scheduled*." He gave a disgusted headshake. "However, some intel hints that it'll be soon. Perhaps even as soon as tonight."

Valchenka stared back, mouth half open, as if awaiting additional instructions.

Mizrahi wasted five more seconds glaring at the incompetent before turning heel to sound the alarm to the rest of the team.

Mizrahi slapped Lorna Glass' open office door before gliding into her small, cramped space, his slow burn over the Russian finally fluttering down to a tolerable level.

Flashing obvious annoyance at being interrupted, she said into the phone, "Call you right back," before carefully setting the iPhone on the battered gray desk. "Just come right on in, Itzhak.

She didn't try to mask the sarcasm.

Mizrahi chose the high road by ignoring the barb. At the moment, her help was far too critical to get picky.

Dropping his voice to a highly confidential level.

"Recent intelligence indicates that Gold's Red Team will be attempting to break into our offices within the next ten to fourteen days." Then, after a brief dramatic pause: "My personal analysis of the situation suggests the attack is likely to occur within the next forty-eight hours with an increasing probability toward the forty-eight-hour edge of that window."

Which was nothing more than gut instinct. But given the neck-snapping speed with which Gold's team had been able to blow through their firewall, he fully expected the little bastard to attempt to maintain full-on blitzkrieg momentum. Not only that, but he was now convinced that the little fuckwad *had* been conducting preliminary work prior to the initial meeting. Which left the interesting but irritatingly unanswered question: how did he know he was being considered for the job *before* anyone on the security committee had even heard of him?

"So noted," Glass said blandly. "That it?"

*So noted? That it? Ungrateful cunt.*

He glanced away, struggling to deny her the pleasure of seeing his simmering irritation. First Serge, now her. Why were those tasked with protecting this building so blasé about fulfilling the job they were hired for?

"No, that's not *it*, Glass. I have pictures of our target for you to distribute to your team."

He'd surreptitiously captured numerous images of Gold standing in the elevator alcove after meeting with Collier and the group. Once again, he commended himself for such canniness of forethought. No way could Gold, an amateur, anticipate the force of his adversary. It was one thing to exploit a vulnerability in software; hell, several websites listed those. It was quite another matter to go mano-a-mano against trained security guards.

"Fine," she said, effectively terminating the impromptu update before swiveling her chair back to its original position and picking up her iPhone.

At the door, Mizrahi paused briefly to glare at her back.

*Cunt.*

Mizrahi's phone rang at 7:35 that evening.

After checking the caller ID, he swiped accept: "Go."

"Just emailed a few *candid* shots of your new friend," said Turner, one of the firm's two investigators.

"And?"

"I've got news for you, Itzhak. The pics you've been plastering throughout the building are nothing but garbage. He was disguised. He's actually, oh I'm guessing…thirty pounds lighter and ain't got no bum knee neither. You've been had."

Mizrahi's anger flared again. He made no attempt to smooth the acute anger from his voice.

"Bullshit I've been *had*. If I didn't realize he was disguised, I wouldn't have ordered you to surveil him, now, would I?"

"I'm just saying…" Turner put a shrug into his voice. "Check your inbox."

And with that, Turner clicked off.

Mizrahi studied the pictures with hate-filled eyes.

*Think you're such a smart sonofabitch, don't you Gold? We'll see about that.*

# CHAPTER 27

## Seattle

AFTER LETTING CHANCE into the back yard for his morning potty break, Arnold powered up his laptop and while it was booting, he poured a mug of black freshly brewed Kona blend brought straight from Honolulu. He settled into the kitchen table to savor the first aromatic sips. Perfect. He turned to the computer and typed in the commands to access the trapdoor embedded in the Larkin Standish email server.

No response.

Interesting. A typo? He carefully reentered the commands. Nope, still no go.

*Uh-oh.*

Kaput. Most likely discovered and removed. Wow. That played out, like, crazy quick. Although he'd figured the RAT would be removed eventually, he didn't imagine it would be *this* neck-snapping.

*Double wow and a serious bummer.*

But what about the others? The more cleverly embedded trapdoors, squirreled away as backups in case this happened? He typed another string of commands, and...

Bingo. He was inside the network.

*Whew!*

But solemn realization quickly snuffed out the golden glow of relief: this was another poignant example of just how tight the law firm's cybersecurity was.

*Would this also serve as a harbinger of what to expect during this next phase?*

If so, this Mizrahi dude was no slouch.

Ninety minutes later Arnold pushed through a heavy glass door into the cavernous granite lobby, cut left, and beelined for the appropriate elevator bank to whisk him to floor forty-one.

Other than a Mariners ball cap with the bill pulled low to shield his face from the ever-present CCTV cameras, he wore no disguise.

*What was the point?*

Mizrahi undoubtedly knew that a pen-test was in the works. Which left him two options: try to be sneaky, which risked drawing more attention, or simply blow into the building and then quickly shake their ability to track him despite the building-wide CCTV coverage. Odds were, even if the two security services were working collaboratively, they didn't have sufficient manpower to scour the entire building. The trick, of course, would be to remain hidden until they gave up.

On the ride up, he lucked out by using his Flipper Zero to surreptitiously snag yet another key card.

*You can never have too many.*

The moment the elevator doors slid open on floor forty-one, he dodged to the north stairwell, used a cloned key card to unlock the heavy door, shouldered it open and scurried down to the fortieth-floor landing, paused to inspect his claustrophobic confines. He stood on a small concrete rectangle within a larger concrete shaft of white walls and stairways with purple-painted metal tubular railings that switched back and forth on each other to and from the adjacent levels.

On each switchback wall was an eye-level reflective red EXIT sign with knee-level arrows pointing to the next descending flight. A vague, weirdly out-of-context scent of Lysol ghosted the still, dead air.

Glancing up the ascending stairs, a black spot seized his attention. Arnold did a double take.

*No shit? Seriously?*

Security cameras in the stairwells? Jesus, one more freaking complication to factor in.

He thought about this, searching for a way to play it to his team's advantage. And he zeroed in on the sheer numbers involved. With more than seventy floors, if each one had a camera in both stairwells and each elevator alcove, that alone totaled way more than two hundred and seventy video feeds. And this wasn't factoring in all the other feeds from more important locations such as the lobby and garage. Holy shit, the grand total of CCTV feeds for the whole enchilada was mindboggling. No way they could monitor every single one in real time, right?

*Right.*

Unless...they incorporated a few simple prioritizing tactics, some chip-shot tricks like making the stairwell and elevator alcove feeds motion-activated.

*Uh-huh.*

That alone would simplify the process significantly. No doubt each feed was recorded digitally and stored for a time, meaning any segment—say the forty-first-floor north stairwell—could be retrieved and reviewed after the fact.

Worse yet, he had no clue how sophisticated their system might or might not be.

*Did their computers incorporate AI?*

For example, facial recognition?

*Wouldn't that be a bitch!*

Naw, that might be cost-prohibitive to install into a system this old. Or would it?

*No idea.*

But the one thing he *did* know for sure was he'd damn well

better get to work, or he'd be freaking toast.

He selected the key card cloned from Collier, swiped it across the reader and immediately heard the satisfying *click* of the lock disengage.

*Yippee-ki-yay!*

He now knew he could access all Larking Standish floors.

Assuming Mizrahi didn't somehow figure out what he just did.

*Probably prudent to get the hell off this landing. Like pronto.*

He quickly descended to the thirty-second floor, used a different key to enter the main hall, then rode an elevator back down to the lobby.

Mizrahi's cellphone showed an incoming call from Lorna Glass.

He answered with: "What?"

A two-second pause followed.

Then: "Just out of curiosity, Itzhak; were you born an asshole or is this characteristic one you've actively cultivated over the years?"

He raised a middle finger to the mental image.

"What's your point, Glass?"

"We just picked up a curiously weird incident in the north stairwell maybe, oh, thirty minutes ago. We suspect it might have to do with your new BFF."

"What was it?" he asked, frowning.

Concerned. It was one thing to suspect a pen-test in the works, quite another to hear that it might actually be unfurling. If, in fact, it was.

She described how a video surveillance officer had picked up a suspicious male matching Gold's description blow through the lobby, heading straight for a specific bank of elevators. So what? People do that all day long. Well, two things of note: the subject matched Gold's description and he took extraordinary care to minimize his exposure to the CCTV.

After exiting onto floor forty-one, he abruptly entered the

nearest stairwell whereupon he descended several flights, only to catch an elevator back to the lobby and promptly exited the building. His route essentially consisted of one big loop, which was the reason for labeling the activity decidedly suspicious. Had she viewed the actual footage? Absolutely. And although it required a major effort to piece together all segments, every second of his time inside the building had been reconstructed into one coherent segment of CCTV footage.

When she finished her narration, he asked, "And this took place thirty minutes ago? Why have you waited until just now to inform me of this? Why didn't you let me know immediately?"

This time Glass waited a solid five seconds before responding.

"For fuck's sake, Itzhak…look, you want to know about this shit or not? Just tell me if I'm *bothering* you and I'll spare us both the pain of any further charade of collegial collaboration."

He swatted away her sarcasm in spite of being alone in his office.

"You *suspect* it was Gold, or you're convinced it was?"

"Tell you what, Itzhak: if you have the cojones to challenge me without ever laying eyes on the footage, fine, we're done here."

When he didn't answer, she added, "Thought so. But if you still have doubts, then, by all means, drag your sorry ass down here and reach your own goddamn conclusion before we erase this footage."

The line clicked dead.

While passing the Russian's cubicle, Mizrahi yelled, "Yo, *Tovarich*, back in a few. Stay hyper vigilant, things are heating up."

Serge flipped him off in absentia.

# CHAPTER 28

## Seattle

THE TEAM, IN full-meeting mode, packed in around Arnold's kitchen table devouring an order of Charlie Vergo's Rendezvous ribs that Arnold had FedExed overnight from Memphis. The order included generous portions of their famous mustard slaw and baked beans, along with a bottle of their killer BBQ sauce. A roll of paper towels stood on end in the center of the table.

Arnold intended the meal to team-build while continuing to hone and critically hash over their impending attack plan, searching for potential weaknesses or flaws that could be resolved now instead of on the fly.

So far, they had yet to identify even one issue, which Arnold found disconcerting as hell. There were *always* glitches that popped up during even the best-planned schemes and this fact made him a firm believer that repetitious mental preparation and rehearsal helped you minimize having to resolve unforeseen problems on the fly.

Adding to his self-inflicted pressure was being in-your-face aware that several prominent local law firms were scrutinizing them. Fornicate the pooch on this gig they could kiss pen-testing in Seattle *hasta la vista*.

*Well, there was always Honolulu, but with most of the crew living here...*

"Anything new on security?" Arnold asked Prisha.

Prisha held up a hold-on finger, wiping sauce from her fingers with a crumpled grease-stained paper towel before washing down the last bite with a long pull of Anchor Steam.

After dumping the soiled wad next to her equally stained paper plate, she said, "Couple things. First, I picked up some interesting chatter on security's comm channel." She retrieved the same crumpled stained paper towel to dab her lips. "From what I gather, their turnover's pretty high. Rumor has it they burn through guards double the rate of industry standards."

"Have any idea why?" Lopez asked.

"Yeah, I do. Started nosing around as much as possible without raising too much suspicion." She flashed Lopez a bright girly-girl smile. "Walked up to the guard in that booth in the lobby and chatted him up under the guise of looking for work." She batted her long eyelashes. "Dude's just standing there—I mean no chair for him to sit on, so when you're manning that station, you're up every second of the shift—just standing and staring at a bank of CCTVs. Maybe that's why he had no truck bullshitting with me. Come to think of it, dude might've even appreciated the company." She threw in a *whatever* shrug. "But apparently, they're always on the sniff for warm bodies."

She paused for another sip of beer.

"During their busiest work hours those guys are glued to those video feeds instead of out poking noses into vulnerable spots like the garage. That bank of videos is just for the lobby, the garage, and the lobby level of the stairwells. The building-wide videos feed into the security office, wherever that is. I couldn't gin up a way of asking that without coming across as suspicious, but considering the astronomical number of cameras they have, you gotta believe there's no way for all of 'em to be monitored in real time. Which makes me think they're fed to the cloud—probably AWS or some shit like that—until someone wants to check a segment. But no way's that volume-stored forever." A quick pause. "Point is, those shifts have gotta be totally brain-numbing. I'm thinking that's the main reason for the high turnover."

"That's some interesting shit, but what's your point?" Lopez asked.

"That we need to think about a way to use this as an advantage."

They were all ears now; the ribs having been forgotten.

"Like?" Lopez asked.

"I'm getting there. From six in the morning till six in the evening during the work week, the four banks of elevator serve all floors including those accessible to the public. Which, we all know, is just a handful."

"How about an example of one," Lopez asked.

"Pretty much exactly what you'd expect. A title insurance company, Larkin Standish's reception lobby, those sorts of things. But from six in the evening till six weekday mornings *every* floor in that building requires key card access. Got that?"

She studied the group again, then repeated the information for emphasis. In other words, since the actual creep would take place at night, they needed key cards to reach any floor regardless of using an elevator or stairwell. Everyone seemed glued to her words.

"From six PM. to six AM, building security runs random patrols through the lobby and random floors, with the garage being an exception. It's patrolled throughout the twenty-four hours, also at random.

"Now the good news," she continued. "Security uses non-encrypted handhelds for all communication. There are repeaters on every floor to ensure solid copy no matter where you are. Which makes listening in, like, crazy-easy even in a stairwell."

Lopez applauded.

"You da bomb, girl," he said in a Cheech and Chong voice. "What's the bad news?"

Prisha held up a just-a-moment finger while polishing off a generous bite of mustard slaw.

"Bad news is they're well aware a pen-test's in the works. They've been seriously chatting it up. They not only know to expect a creep but are expecting it within the next forty-eight. I mean, go fuckin' figure, dudes. It's like someone with a direct pipeline into mission control's been feeding them our playbook."

With a woeful headshake, Arnold stated: "Mizrahi."

He believed that Collier had remained tight-lipped about it, so perhaps as he'd suspected, an abrupt radio silence from the security committee tipped him to what was coming.

*Yeah, but to narrow it down to the next forty-eight?*

That shit was off the hook. No, it made more sense to suspect that Collier's office was bugged. But really, it made no difference. The snake had slithered out from under the rock, and they just needed to roll with it. On the other hand, if Collier's office *was* bugged…Arnold filed that nugget away for future consideration.

Arnold to Prisha: "You don't happen to have any recordings of those conversations, do you?"

An ear-to-ear shit-eating grin sprouted across her face.

"Yeah. Why?"

"Bless you, my child," he said, moving his right hand in a priestly gesture. "Just make sure they're securely stored. That's good to have in our hip pocket, in case we're busted. And if not? Still killer information to put in our final report. I mean, here you go…in spite of Security knowing we're coming in, they don't catch us, right?"

He laughed at the thought, then snuck a glimpse of Rachael. Since his heads-up about this potential gig, Prisha's contributions to preparing for it were huge; a point he hoped didn't fly past Rachael unnoticed. Especially after being so strongly opposed to hiring her. Prisha's performance not only vindicated his decision to bring her on board but also for being second in command.

"Wow, great work, girl," Arnold said. "Anything else?"

She shook her head while picking up another rib.

"Nope."

"How about the firm's internal security?"

Prisha shook her head, ready to start in on the rib.

"Still working that. Only thing we know for sure is Mizrahi runs that show, and the impression I'm getting is, his style's sorta a Putin-Xi Jinping blend." Then, perhaps to offload the conversation to someone else so she could start in on the rib, she asked pointedly, "How you coming on your end of the deal?"

Meaning, breaking into the network.

Since she knew the answer, Arnold assumed she was asking for the others' benefit.

"Everyone knows our initial RAT's gone, right?"

They nodded in unison but were back to chowing down.

Vihaan quickly added, "But our two trapdoors are still good. I checked before coming over."

"Which takes us to our next item," Arnold said to Lopez. "Now that you've had time to nose around the network in more detail, what'd you find out about the others?"

Meaning, their other networks.

Lopez set down his fork.

"A lot, actually. They run three. The guest network, of course. Then there's one for routine in-house workflow. Then, there's the one for networking all the peripherals: printers, routers, et cetera. I'm presently picking through a few servers, searching for good spots to squirrel away a few extra access points, just in case. About fifteen minutes before coming over, I ran across a server that controls their in-house video surveillance." With a laugh, he turned to Arnold and asked, "Know anything about that?"

Stunned, Arnold almost choked on a pickle. Coughing, he shook his head.

"Nope, nada. The few times I've been anyplace other than

the lobby I've made a point of keeping an eye out for cameras but have only seen large-screen TVs and speakerphones in most conference rooms."

"Well, it's there," Lopez said with a broad smile. "And it's super extensive. We're talking video feeds of all the halls and conference rooms."

"And audio?" Arnold asked, flashing again on the conference rooms. Every damn one of those TVs undoubtedly had a built-in webcam and perhaps even a microphone, so the speakerphones might be irrelevant for surveillance. He felt like fist-thumping his forehead. Same thing for, say, Collier's desktop monitor. Christ, Mizrahi probably knew every juicy chunk of gossip floating around that firm.

"Uh-huh," Lopez grunted.

"And Collier's office?"

"Dunno, haven't got that far. Been tied up with a few higher-priority items, like embedding backup back doors and such. Figured that was something worthwhile pursuing. Now, unless Mizrahi's techs find and remove them, we can take down their eyes any damn time we please."

"Wow," Arnold said, reaching across the table to high five him. "Insanely coo-well, dude."

"Yes, tiz, but keep in mind," Lopez warned, "moment we shut it down, Mizrahi'll know we're on our way in."

Lopez's remark generated sobber nods from everyone.

Arnold: "That's why we use it only as our nuclear option."

He was about to start gnawing a rib when Prisha asked, "How you doing on the key cards, boss?"

With a sly smile, Arnold dropped the rib on his paper plate and started to suck sauce from his fingertips.

"So far so good. I've cloned a couple cards from other companies," he said, leaving the conclusion floating.

"Yeah, so?" Prisha prompted with an inquisitive smile.

This would be news to her too.

With a shit-eating grin: "I coped codes off two Larkin

169

Standish cards." He paused, letting the suspense build. "The receptionist's and Collier's. But the one I *really really* am dying to snag"—his hands clenched into tight fist— "is Mizrahi's. Just haven't been able to come up with a slick way to do it." Then, almost as an afterthought: "But ain't giving up."

"An ultimate cool idea," Vihaan said, "but the problem I see with it, soon's he sees his name access a secure area, the gig's up. At least with other keys, we can probably operate under his radar a bit longer before they tumble to the fact we're inside the wire."

"I don't agree. Remember, unless Mizrahi has a sweet deal with building security, how's he going to even know his card's been used? And even if, say it's used to enter a Larkin Standish floor…what's the big deal, right? I mean he's in and out of those doors the whole freaking day." Arnold waved the rib he'd been gnawing. He paused a beat. "Okay, so, next topic: it's time to finalize our plan, dudes. It's crunch time."

He scanned their faces. They all gave him their full attention.

"I know we've hammered this out enough times to vomit, but the OCD side of me needs to be assured we've beat it so dead that we haven't overlooked something obvious. So, humor me, okay?"

They were all locked onto him like a Sidewinder missile.

"The break-in involves two phases." Then a pause for emphasis. "To minimize the risk of apprehension, only Prisha and I will enter the building."

They all nodded.

"To ensure optimal radio communication, you guys," Arnold said, pointing to Lopez and Vihaan, "will be situated above the freeway at a spot with a direct line of sight to the building, hopefully as close as possible. Lopez will be monitoring North Sound's radio traffic while Vihaan will be watching the videos from Larkin Standish's internal surveillance. From the time we enter the building until we're back out, Lopez will be ready to shut down their feed *if* we need to, but we hold this only as a last-ditch necessity. To repeat, we play that card *only* to save our ass. In other words, get in, get out without a footprint. That, dudes, would be pure elegance."

Again, scanned their faces. Total seriousness.

"Any issues? Thoughts?"

Glances were exchanged, but no one said diddly.

Finally, Prisha spoke.

"Yeah, we're good."

# CHAPTER 29

A PETITE WOMAN in all black—including the ski mask covering her face and short platinum-blond hair—sat cross-legged on a triangular patch of weed-infested ivy that, for years, had been choking this neglected embankment. Her back rested against the bark of an aged cedar, the low branches producing a dense island of shadows in a lake of harsh mercury-vapor streetlight that camouflaged her and her prized 35mm digital Nikon 200mm fast lens amongst the bushes. It was an ideal spot providing an unobstructed view straight across the narrow winding road to Arnold Gold's front door.

Waiting patiently in squid-ink shadows, mind in a meditative Zen-like zone, her auditory, visual, and proprioceptive senses remained hyper-receptive to the merest suggestion of a potential threat. Minutes were incrementing slowly into the deepening night. She'd been planted like this for more than ninety minutes now, patiently executing her handsomely reimbursed duty as a Larkin Standish investigator.

Gold's front door suddenly opened and three laughing people—two men and one woman—sauntered into the mild night air, the porch and streetlights providing adequate illumination for the ultra-fast lens to clearly capture their faces.

She began whirring off a rapid sequence of images as the

three drifted casually to a car curbed one property north of Gold's modernist cube. She continued until the last person— the driver—pulled that door shut, then swung the lens back to the target's front door. But it was now closed.

Satisfied with having just fulfilled her objective, she stood, swatted dirt from her black pants, then ruffled the patch of compressed ivy and weeds back into some semblance of typical disarray before melding through a series of dense shadows to disappear as unobtrusively as she'd arrived.

Arnold, Rachael, and Chance reentered the kitchen after finishing the pooch's evening stroll, Arnold rewarding Chance with his end-of-day Greenies, then opening the French door so he could proudly trot—treat in mouth—onto the back porch. Arnold walked over to the counter to pop the stopper from a previously opened bottle of Rutherford cab and began pouring their glasses. Since arriving, their days had been too hectic for a relaxed meaningful conversation, so he eagerly looked forward to a lull this evening as a time to reconnect.

He handed Rachael a glass.

"So, what's going on, sweetie?"

With a sigh, she sank into the chair across the table from his usual spot and leveled a deeply pensive stare into her cabernet. She remained like this for perhaps three seconds before glancing back up at him.

He slid into his usual kitchen chair, waiting, listening.

"Mom, of course," she said with a sad headshake, her eyes wandering off for a long moment before making their way back to him. "Auntie Shira's right. She has a definite limp now...and is showing a few balance issues. Not all the time, and certainly not profound, but they're clearly there if you know what you're looking for..." Another headshake, another sigh, a muttered, "Shit."

Arnold slowly set his glass on the table, clasped his hands together, and waited, a vaporous premonition warning of the impact of the impending conversation. The precise effect remained enigmatic, yet its looming specter hovered heavily overhead, usurping his consciousness. It would be bad news, he realized without any foundation. Just knew...

*Well dude, you knew this was coming—you've been anticipating it for a while now.*

Heavy silence engulfed the room like a kelp-laden fishing net, each disappearing second darkening his foreboding mental storm clouds.

After what seemed like for-freaking-ever, Rachael spoke again.

"Of course we'll get a complete work-up by a neurologist who specializes in MS, but chances are she's got the serious form, the one that's progressive..."

She glanced at the ceiling before meeting his eyes again, then hesitated for one more beat. "Did I tell you that her mom probably had MS? But the diagnosis was never confirmed? After all, in those days there wasn't much that could be done, and imaging was..."

Arnold nodded.

"Yeah, you've mentioned it."

*Numerous times.*

"Uh-huh," she said, more to herself than him. More time sludged past. "There's no documented direct genetic link, but women in families with cases are statistically more likely to have the disease..."

This was beginning to sound more like laying the groundwork—a justification—than stating a medical fact. He continued to silently watch her squirm.

She swallowed, clearly on the cusp of saying something important, but glanced away again. His suspicion meter redlined. Her eyes gravitated back to her wine glass, the cerebral gears imaginably audible from inside her skull. Grappling with...?

For words. No doubt.

Arnold waited, each passing silent second darkening and solidifying his premonition, tightening his knotted gut. Yeah, this was their evening to reconnect alright. Just not the way he'd imagined. On the other hand...if his dark cloud of suspicions panned out as he assumed it would, would things be all *that* bad?

Rachael said, "You realize what this means, don't you?"

The question was sufficiently vague for Arnold to not show his cards. Let her either call or raise. He remained deadpan.

"Her symptoms will only get worse over time, you realize," she added dogmatically now, gaining strength and verging on condescending.

Before he could stop himself, he blurted.

"Don't they have some pretty good drugs for that?"

After blinking, she refocused on him as if suddenly realizing he was still across the table.

"Yes, but those don't actually *cure* it...they just delay the inevitable for the type I think she has. So if you stop them, or there's like a supply-chain issue, or...but they all have some nasty side effects, especially with your immune system."

Her eyes wandered back to her untouched glass of wine.

He felt compelled to offer *something* positive—after all, this was her *mother*.

"But they're developing new treatments all the time..." he offered lamely.

*Jesus, how disingenuous.*

Rachael batted away the comment.

"That's not the point, sweetie."

*Enough.*

"Okay then, what is the point?"

*Oh, c'mon, dude, you know damn well what it is. You just want her to be the one...*

Still side-eyeing him, she finally took her first sip of wine. His gut clenched in anticipation.

"I can't expect Auntie Shira to take care of *every*thing."

"Okay..."

"As her daughter, I have an obligation to look after her."

Strike one!

An audibly deep inhale, followed by crisp words delivered with the decisive punch of a Tomahawk missile.

"I've made a few inquiries. There are scads of jobs available here."

*And there it was.*

Then again, this moment had been hovering in his subconsciousness for weeks as he'd helplessly watched it approach. For months instead of weeks, if he were being truly honest. Ever since her precipitous unilateral decision to migrate back to her apartment little signs had been pointing to this moment. But he suspected that until now she had no idea how to package the message. Well, the bow and the wrapping were off now as he numbly waited for the rest of it.

"Arnold, I hope you understand, but I need to move back in with Mom in order to look after her properly."

*Boom.*

Give the girl an A-plus for originality. But in truth, she'd simply seized a twist of fate to justify what had been brewing in her for months. Still, he supposed couching it in terms of her mother's suspected diagnosis felt kinder than rolling out the clichéd, "It's me, not you," excuse. (Although he'd never been clobbered by that one. Probably because she was his first real girlfriend...) And as long as he was being completely truthful, *finally* uncorking the genie after the months of waiting came as a gonzo relief, for at least now he could begin grappling with the reality of dealing with it.

A tidal wave of silence flooded the room.

Arnold began to berate himself for having put up with so many of her noxious personality traits for so long simply because he didn't have the balls to confront them. Why? Because he was too afraid of losing her. Why? Because he simply would rather put up with the aggravations than be completely alone again. Well, what had that strategy gotten him? Nada.

"—after all, we do have a house here," she said. "I don't see why you can't simply spend the majority of your time here instead of over on the island." Pause. "Don't misunderstand, sweetie, I *love* Honolulu, but I also *really* miss being near what little family I have left."

Her last words snapped him back from self-incrimination.

Staring at her now, back into the conversation, he asked, "*We?*" incredulously.

"What?"

"You just said, '*We* have a house here.'"

She stared back with a puzzled expression.

"Correct me if I'm wrong, but you unilaterally decided to move out because you claimed you needed, quote, your own space, right?" He pressed ahead: "Because you wanted to be *you*, to find yourself, enjoy your independence, whatever..." He gave a dismissive wave. "But now you mention that *we* have a house here? Help me out here because I'm having a huge problem reconciling your actions with words. Mind explaining that one?"

She sent him a very concerned expression.

"I thought..."

Weeks of unconscious agonizing abruptly broke surface, flooding him with previously ignored realities of their relationship: her selfish demands, intolerance, and unrelenting criticisms. All of which came crashing down on him like a collapsing concrete overpass.

"You thought what? That I'd become a full-time resident here so I could be your on-call friend with benefits?"

*Wow, that was a little harsh, wasn't it? Yeah, maybe. But did it matter? No, not really.*

The outcome would ultimately be the same.

"No, that's not at all what I was thinking," she said, suddenly appearing gravely offended, complete with a palm to her chest.

He nodded, more to himself than to her, then wiped his

face and sucked an incisor.

"Look, Rach, here's the deal. I *love* Seattle. After all, I've lived here most of my life. And to be perfectly honest, we both know I ended up in Honolulu not from any burning desire to live there, but simply because circumstances dictated it. Sure, I just sort of stumbled onto that particular place, but know what? I love it now. I love the house, love the island lifestyle, love the walks Chance and I take. Gulick's Deli. On and on. I love the whole enchilada. Why would I ever want to move back here full-time?"

Mouth open, she set down her wine, her face glowing with genuine shock.

"I thought you said you loved me?"

He locked eyes with her.

"Right. I did. But, Rach, just to be clear, it sounds to me like you've already made the decision to move back here regardless of what I do, right?"

She hesitated.

"Yes, I guess maybe...*but* you do understand, don't you, my primary responsibility's now to Mom."

"In other words, I don't factor into your decision at all."

Another brief hesitation.

"No. That's not fair at all and you know it."

"No, I don't know it." He glanced up, then back at her. "Oh, c'mon Rach. You'd already decided to make this move before the wheels even left the tarmac."

Another headshake, this time accompanied by a hand wave.

"You're blowing this way out of proportion. Tell me what difference it makes if you live here instead of there? Because I don't see what that could possibly be."

He just looked at her.

After a moment of silence, she gave a short, resigned sigh.

"Alright, I know you prefer living there, so if you don't want to move back, I can live with you when you're here...just not full time's all."

*Seriously? For real?*

"No Rach, that's not what's happening. Too many things have changed over these past few months. Once I finish this job, I'm heading back and don't plan to stay here longer than a few weeks at a time depending on the season."

# CHAPTER 30

## Seattle

PISSED DIDN'T APPROACH describing Mizrahi's present emotional state; his anger hovered fractionally below the threshold for head-exploding fury.

Though ninety-nine percent of it was lasered on Gold for such unabashed chutzpah in pulling off such a flagrantly—in retrospect—bogus disguise, one percent of it, he grudgingly had to admit, flew right back on himself for not having been the least bit suspicious.

And that, more than anything, was what was *really* pissing him off. He did, however, derive a sliver of solace in knowing that the little shit remained clueless that both security teams now had accurate photographs of him plastered all over their work areas. The bastard would not get away with that shit again. Ever. Not only that, but everyone working in security knew that Gold's team was on the cusp of a pen-test.

Mizrahi had also pointedly informed the troops that, if possible, he wanted to be present when that smug little bastard was captured. Because that's exactly where his little pen-test foray was headed.

Mizrahi paced his confined office, rehashing security measures. He would love to have the time to conduct a refresher course on social-engineering countermeasures for those employees most likely to encounter Gold's team but couldn't risk tipping Collier that he knew that a physical entry was in play.

In fact, he was loath to do anything that might pique Collier's interest in their security above his recent uncomfortable level. Their internal video surveillance, for example. God forbid that was ever exposed. After all, look what happened to Nixon once the Oval Office recording system became known. Perfect example of a colossal clusterfuck. Or Trump's call with Roethlisberger. No, it was best to just hunker down and do everything possible to harden internal security without anyone outside of his team knowing what was being done.

The problem was, he couldn't see anything to improve. And that bothered him.

Slightly.


"I want everyone to make sure your radio's completely charged and locked on the right comm channel, okay?"

Arnold made a show of following his own instruction.

When they all were done double-checking their gear, he asked, "Everyone good?"

They responded in the affirmative.

They were in Arnold's kitchen going through final preparations for the break-in only hours away. They were also chowing down on killer pastramis on rye that Arnold had scored at George's Sausage and Delicatessen on Madison, a jewel of a store he'd only learned about after asking a grocery clerk why no one seemed to stock liverwurst anymore.

"Okay, now I want us to verify that our radios are set for VOX and that we can all copy each other," Arnold said, holding his up. "I'll go first. Everyone's radio on?"

VOX—Voice Operated Transmission—allowed for hands-free operation. Prisha had purchased wrap-around-style throat microphones for their headsets that could pick up barely whispered words. Her choice of equipment served as another prime example of her worth as his associate.

One by one, each team member conducted a confirmatory radio check before powering off their equipment to preserve battery life. Arnold crossed off one more item from his checklist in his quest to verify every possible safeguard to eliminate a stupid *Jesus, I should've* mind-fart from derailing the actual caper.

Arnold had two more items he wanted to verify.

He carefully arranged his sets of key cards on the table in three parallel rows of four cards each, then asked Prisha: "Have your cards organized to your satisfaction?"

"They are," she replied, pointing to them. Following Arnold's example, hers were arranged on the table in mirror-image order.

Both of them would be carrying three separate copies of the cards cloned from four unsuspecting people: Collier, the Larkin Standish receptionist, and the two employees from other firms. Admittedly this much redundancy was overkill, but hey, you never know....each set of cards was color-coded by a band of Day-Glo tape: pink for Collier, yellow for the receptionist, etc. to avoid confusion should a situation suddenly degenerate into hyperventilation mode.

Arnold carefully scanned both sets, then with a satisfied nod, said, "Check."

He crossed off the second-to-last item from the list.

"Next item," he continued, "I assume each of us has a copy of their SOW with them?"

Each team member—regardless of whether they would be in the building or not—would carry the document filled out with their legal name, test date, and Webster Collier's name and contact information. It would confirm the legitimacy of their actions should—God forbid—police or security guards apprehend them during the break-in.

All four confirmed having their copy with them.

"All right then, let's do it." Arnold held his hand above the center of the table, each team member resting their hand atop his. Arnold said, "Okay, on three. One, two, three."

"Go team!" they shouted, just like the Seahawks do in the moments before kickoff.

Arnold texted Mr. Davidson that the break-in would be that night.

# CHAPTER 31

## Seattle—2:31 PM

ARNOLD SAUNTERED INTO the lobby wearing a pair of well-worn 501s, a black, gold, and white UW Huskies hoodie, gray Adidas kicks, a frayed NY Yankees cap, and a black Fjallraven backpack. An additional prop (and nice touch) was the wrap-around Stevie Wonder glints, topped off with a long white probing cane. A security guard approached seconds after Arnold set foot in the cavernous lobby.

"May I help you, sir?" the guard asked, lightly touching Arnold's left bicep.

The ultimate test of his disguise, he knew. He was counting on Prisha and Lopez monitoring the guards' radio chatter to alert him if his cover ended up blown. His gut knotted.

*Could he keep his cool?*

"Yes, thank you, I appreciate the assistance," Arnold said, turning his head toward the gravelly voice. "I need the elevator for floor fifty-one."

His research for this part of the creep included memorizing which floors didn't require a key card to access.

Gently grasping his left biceps, the guard guided Arnold—playing his well-practiced blind-man schtick—across the glossy gray granite to the bank of elevators serving the correct segment for floor fifty-one. A ding announced an elevator arriving seconds later. The guard led Arnold into the cage while asking another rider to push floor fifty-one for him. Arnold thanked the guard profusely, then turned to watch the doors glide shut.

So far, so good.

The moment the elevator doors closed, the security guard pulled the radio from his belt holster.

"Be advised that Gold just entered the building disguised as a blind person. He's on elevator eleven heading up to the fifty-first floor as we speak. Suspect is wearing jeans, a Husky sweatshirt, and a Yankees cap."

Mizrahi grabbed his radio and thumbed transmit.

"Copy that."

Then was up out of his chair, pacing the small office, a surge of adrenaline pulsing moments of raw delight through his arteries. He now held a huge tactical advantage over Gold's bush-league assault on his territory. To hell with any pie-in-the-sky idealistic theory that a blind test was the only accurate way to assess the effectiveness of security.

After all, one of the most integral components for maintaining tight security was the acquisition of real-time, precision intelligence.

*You can't prevent a security breach if you're made aware of it five minutes after the fact, but you can protect against it if you're notified five minutes before.*

Case in point: the Ukrainians' defense against the larger, better-equipped Russian military throughout the first year of the war. A result clearly attributable to having access to superior real-time intelligence sources plus live visual satellite feeds and tapping into on-going communications.

But defending against Gold's attack shouldn't be the only way to use this intel. There should be a way of leveraging it for political advantage. Mizrahi thought this over for a moment. Nothing came to mind. Update Collier and his committee that those assholes just entered the building? That should indeed impress them.

*Wouldn't it? Hmmm....*

Although it would certainly be an impressive demonstration of his security prowess, it would also carry the risk of sparking awkward questions.

*No, it would be best to simply go about his work quietly until he grabbed Gold by the scruff of his neck like the runt piglet he was, then hold him up for the governing powers to see.*

He stopped at the Russian's cubicle.

"Be advised, Gold's now on the premises."

Valchenka responded with a quick bored glance before returning to his monitor.

Mizrahi stayed at the cubicle entrance pondering whether there was anything else to do at this point. Nothing came to mind other than to begin patrolling his territory on foot, looking for potential points of ingress in spite of knowing that the only options were the two stairwells and three elevators.

But, he had to do something.

# CHAPTER 32

## Seattle

AS THE ELEVATOR was about to ascend, Arnold checked out the glowing floor buttons. Forty-three and fifty-one were glowing.

*Perfect.*

The cage rapidly decelerated to a stop at the forty-third floor. Soon as the doors parted, the two other passengers stepped out almost in lockstep and turned right, leaving Arnold alone. Before the door were even closed again, he had his copy of the Larkin Standish secretary's card out of his pocket and swiped across the reader. The LED flashed green. He pressed fifty. The button glowed.

Then the elevator was moving upward. Working as quickly as possible, he slipped off the shades, collapsed his cane, and crammed them into the rucksack. He was throwing it back over his shoulder as the doors parted on fifty.

Arnold was through the doors before they completely opened, cut left into a side hall, moving as quickly as possible out of the ceiling CCTV field of coverage.

Now in a long hall with doors to either side—some closed, others open—he stopped and whispered: "Mother," using Prisha's code name. "Am on fifty."

She responded immediately.

"You're blown, but they have you going to fifty-one."

*Shit.*

"Roger that."

Shaking his head in frustration, Arnold glanced at the long hall of office doors leading to who knew where.

*Wow. Those dudes were, like seriously on top of their game.*

He'd been in the lobby for what, all of two minutes? If that.

*And the disguise? Forget it. Well, shit, no time to dwell on it.*

He needed to figure out a way to wrestle with his present mess without getting busted. After all, everyone involved knew this potential existed, right? Wasn't this precisely why they'd game-planned for different contingencies?

True.

*But having his cover blown within seconds of entering the building? Man, that was like seriously messed up. So, now what? Didn't plan on this one, did you!*

Arnold's heart started sledgehammering his chest like a lunatic, making it difficult to think straight. Freaking Mizrahi. Dude must know every word he and Collier ever uttered, what with the entire office wired for sound and video. Jesus, that snake. Arnold ran his fingers through his hair while sucking down a long deep breath. Well, he knew one thing for damn sure: both security services had eyes on just about every square inch of this building. Well, only the elevator alcoves and stairwells, but still...

He began sorting through options, quickly zeroed in on one, reassessed it, decided...

He radioed: "Team, go to plan B. Roger?"

Then he remembered to check the hallway for anyone watching or listening. Jesus, too late for that now. Luckily, the hall was empty.

Each team member keyed their radio to indicate *message received.*

He sprinted for the men's room, again trying to minimize

his CCTV exposure. Happily the room was empty, so he ducked into a stall, dug into the rucksack, exchanged the sweatshirt for a white shirt, rep tie, and slightly rumpled black blazer. For all the damn good it might do.

He crammed the sweatshirt into the backpack, took a few more deep calming breaths, then rinsed and dried his face with a wad of paper towels, checked himself in the mirror for paper flakes. Nope, clear. He took another moment to mentally get his shit together, cracked the door, burned another beat watching and listening for anyone approaching. Nope. Graveyard quiet. Almost too quiet.

*Don't start going all paranoid on me, dude. Still a loooong day ahead.*

He readied a copy of the Larkin Standish secretary's key card and double-checked to make sure he had the correct one before shooting to the north stairwell. He blew through the fire door, then streaked down the stairs on a freaking beeline for the lobby.

On the forty-fifth floor landing he caught a sound. And froze.

What the hell? Cocked his head to the right, listening hard.

*Yeah, there!*

A footstep?

There. Again. A faint scuff reverberating through the raw concrete shaft. Arnold cocked his head left a tiny bit, listening, scouring the heavy stillness for more clues...

There. Again. Footsteps.

*Shit, coming up the freaking stairs. Now what?*

He glanced up to the stairs he'd just descended. But that was a complete waste of time on account of all he could see was the bottom of the next zig zagging flight, those ugly purple railings, and the claustrophobic square shaft.

*Okay, so...go up?*

*No? Yes?*

Yo, dude, do something. Can't go down. So...

189

Carefully, soundlessly, both feet solidly on the landing, he fumbled a key card from his pocket, checked: a freaking Collier clone. Goddamnit. Pulled one from his left pocket. Good, the secretary's card again.

He waved it over the reader, heard the gratifying metallic *clack* of the lock and stepped into the main hall. He turned and carefully reseated the fire door as quietly as possible in spite of knowing full well that the overhead CCTV was panning down on him. Couldn't suppress a nervous giggle while squelching the smart-ass urge to glance directly at it and bow. Better yet, flip them off. But knew better than to push it.

Head down—for all the good it might do—he raced to the south stairwell fire door knowing that he was being recorded, but also knowing they couldn't have live eyes on every freaking video feed one hundred percent of the time, right? Which might just buy him a few extra seconds, max.

Then he was jetting as safely as possible downstairs, quickly acquiring a rhythmic flow, right hand gliding atop the cool tubular metal, two stairs at a pop, hitting a landing, pivoting one-eighty, then on down to the next turn, covering a dizzying zig-zagging descent until, *boom*, lobby level and his first unlocked door. He burst into the expansive granite-and-glass lobby, streaking straight out through a heavy plate-glass door, on across the planter bordered forecourt and into the pedestrian flow along the sidewalk.

He stopped, stood still, chest heaving with gasps, heart pounding, lids squinting against the acute brightness, mind struggling to coral random zinging fragments of thought into some semblance of coherence while trying to uncoil bowstring nerves.

*Freaking Mizrahi. Goddamn pen-testing. Not fun and games all the time.*

But exciting. For sure.

Ten minutes later, having trudged up the long steep hill he

rounded a corner to see the others, butts up against the passenger side of Prisha's gray Camry, side by side like birds on a power line. They were shooting the shit, soaking in the killer city view, waiting for him. They'd lucked out earlier when Prisha happened across a rare empty parking spot on Columbia Street. A feat that Lopez had assured them was an auspicious omen.

*Yeah, right. So far that was panning out for shit.*

With a nod of recognition, Prisha called: "Bummer, huh dude," as a stone statement.

Arnold just shook his head, too winded to answer. Damn incline. A real monster.

Ten minutes later, as Arnold was changing clothes—for all the good that would do, but you've got to try, right?

Prisha started back downhill toward the building. For this trip his only disguise would be a generic ballcap and a different set of designer shades. Enough of the blind-man shit. That didn't fool them one bit.

Arnold slung a backpack strap over his shoulder, tossed a few parting words to Vihaan and Lopez, then started back down to their target knowing full well that Mizrahi wasn't going to make this one any easier than the last. He just needed to stay one step ahead of the bastard, was all.

*Yeah, but easier said than done.*

# CHAPTER 33

## Seattle

"WELL?" LORNA GLASS asked Mizrahi as she sauntered into his inner sanctum, the firm's security center.

He'd summoned her ten minutes ago.

*Ten minutes, goddamnit!*

Just one more thing to piss him off today, of all days.

"How can you possibly lose a rank amateur?" he demanded. "You should goddamn well know he was never intending to go to fifty-one. Where the fuck *is he?*"

Eyeing him with her arms crossed, alarmingly relaxed, she spoke simply.

"How should I know?"

Mizrahi recoiled.

"You *should* know because you're the one in possession of every video feed of every goddamn elevator alcove and stairwell in the fucking building. It's your job to have that intel for me by now." He slammed his white knuckled fist against his palm. "We're"—he pointed to her and them himself—"under attack, Glass."

Glass calmly leaned her ample weight against a four-high filing cabinet, sending him her well-honed deadeye look of indifference, allowing him to stew for one, two, three seconds until speaking.

"We did *our* job, Itzhak. We alerted *you* to his presence."

Her tone was in impeccable harmony with her flat disinterested expression.

*What!*

While scrambling for an appropriately scathing rebuttal, an intense ache suddenly grabbed his attention.

*Shit.*

From his jaw, his molars ground out a not-so-pretty rendition of tetanus. He quickly jutted his mandible forward as if clearing his ear canals, then quickly tried to cover for it by rocking an index finger in his right ear. Did she notice?

He hated that the moment for a comeback remark was gone, leaving her with the upper hand. But from a more pragmatic perspective, the present situation probably necessitated a more collegial approach. After all, the more eyes he could focus on monitoring halls and elevators, the better it served his needs. And she was, in fact, providing this service. At that moment, his overriding concern was: Where in this monstrous building was that squirely little shit?

*Gold had to be here someplace, goddamn it.*

Probably Gold was holed up somewhere: a bathroom, storage locker, stairwell…but given the sheer enormity of the interior, there was no practical way to systematically scour every possible recess. For him, however, the only square footage of any importance was that leased by the firm. The rest of this shithole was simply irrelevant.

*Well, not entirely.*

He was, in fact, counting on Glass' guards to provide an early-warning indicator of Gold's proximity.

Mizrahi scratched the back of his head; a purposefully designed disarming distraction reserved specifically for situations like this, when intentionally pivoting unapologetically to a different topic.

"Are you convinced that it was Gold you saw on the video?"

he asked as innocuously as possible.

She nodded.

"That is our impression."

Mizrahi feigned serious contemplation, as if just handed words from atop the summit.

"Did *you*," he said, motioning benignly to her, "actually confirm this impression or are you accepting the word of one of your guards?"

He was attempting to gently shepherd her away from their more contentious tone of a moment ago while simultaneously stroking her ego by making it sound as if he actually gave a shit about what she thought.

"No, Itzhak, *I* didn't inspect the actual footage, but we can certainly do that now if that'll make you feel any better."

He savored a flash of downy-warm comfort on the off chance that maybe, just maybe the Arnold Gold sighting was little more than a wrong interpretation of a two-dimensional image, that a slim possibility existed for the little shit to be nowhere even close to the building, that his present four-alarm heartburn was for naught.

*Don't think that way. That would only delay the inevitable. Get this over with. Today.*

He nodded. And he was slightly buoyed by knowing that, for the moment, Glass' crew was supporting him. But, for some mysterious reason, he caught the unmistakable whisper that her support might be beginning to wane.

*Why would that be?*

After all, they were allied against a common enemy.

*Weren't they?*

Good question. They *should* be.

After studying her a moment, he asked, "What's to say you didn't have the guard tell me it was Gold just to fuck with me? What's to say he didn't purposely tell us the wrong floor?"

Without so much as a flinch, she shot back—shot him inquisitively raised eyebrows.

"And what's to say that your comms aren't being monitored?"

That stopped him. Cold.

*Was that possible? Seriously doubted it, but...*

He realized that he was massaging his temple and immediately dropped his hand.

*Did she notice this too?*

"That could explain a lot," she added in a slightly softer tone, as if to help him understand.

With a scoff, he batted away the demeaning suggestion, incensed that she actually thought that he might miss such a nuanced slight.

"Just remember, if that little bastard somehow does manage to infiltrate our offices, *everyone's* jobs are on the line. I suggest you call in every extra body you can and then conduct a systematic search of every square foot of space that you're charged with protecting."

She appeared to consider his words but then blew a nicotine-scented laugh in his face, muzzled it briefly, then started laughing again.

"I can't believe you're actually serious about that, but it sure looks like it."

She wiped a nascent tear from the corner of her eye, then did another lousy job of stifling a lesser laugh.

He glared back.

She raised both hands in mock surrender.

"Hey, Itzhak, I just can't understand why you're so vehemently opposed to a pen-test. Look at it this way: it might help you tighten security."

Before he could reply, she added, "You're going to get two possible outcomes, both of which I see as positive. First—and I guess from your view—the best one is, they can't find a way to break in. Period. The second is they somehow *do* sneak past the gates." She gave a little hand wave. "I know that's intolerable to imagine, but here's the thing: say that happens. That case, you'll find out how they did it and fix the problem. What's wrong with that if it helps you tighten security even more? Huh? Seriously." She spread her hands.

Had to admit, that sounded…logical. But however logical, her simplistic analysis was overridden by any penetration being intolerable.

"You don't get it, Glass. I'm not going to allow some bush-league shitheads to make a fool out of me by sneaking past my defenses. I'm charged with protecting these offices."

"Even if by doing it they just might possibly uncover a security flaw?" She quickly added, "Unlikely as that is."

"There is no security flaw. Unless, of course, you consider the human factor and that's not something I, nor anyone else, can ever control or be totally confident about."

At least toss her that bone.

She shrugged.

"If you say so. Hey, look, Itzhak, what if—for the sake of argument—in the process they *do* find something you could, uh, improve. Wouldn't that be worth the heartburn this appears to be causing you? After all, this isn't a break-in with malicious intent. It's intended to simply evaluate the overall security of your firm. True or not true?"

"No, that's not true at all. Yes"—he threw in a nod—"in general, a pen-test is typically intended for that purpose, but this one's different. That's not the primary intent."

Glass recrossed her arms and redistributed her weight, as if settling in for a longer than anticipated discussion.

"Go on," she encouraged.

Mizrahi glanced away, weighing how much to divulge. His default preference? Disclose nothing. Not to anyone. But in this case, a little disclosure might help lock down her support.

Pounding the side of his fist into his palm nervously, he glanced sideways again, debating one more moment before finally saying, "This one isn't about checking off a box, or verifying that Larkin Standish meets a compliance requirement,

Glass. And it sure as hell isn't a simple friendly assessment of the security I've worked so hard to build. It's about making me look bad in Collier's eyes."

*There. Enough said.*

"To make you look bad?" she said, withdrawing in apparent amazement. "Please tell me you're joking." Then, after a beat: "No, you're dead serious, aren't you." She shook her head. "I don't know about that, Itzhak. Everyone in this building knows what a tight ship you're running up here."

"Tight ship?" Mizrahi's posture straightened. "What's that supposed to mean? What are you saying?"

He stood, pushing away the chair with the back of his knees.

"Whoa," she replied, palms flared out. "I'm not trying to say anything other than pure fact. People have the impression your security's, uh, fully optimized up here."

"People? What people?" he said, slipping in an accusing edge into his tone.

She momentarily puffed her cheeks, apparently choosing her next words carefully.

"I don't know, man, it's just an expression. All I'm saying's don't take it so personally; know what I mean?"

"No, I don't know what you mean. You think I'm massaging a couple of steel balls around in my hand? Is that it?"

"*What?*" Her face scrunched in confusion, the *Caine Mutiny* reference blowing right over her head.

"Then let me explain." He cleared his throat and straightened his posture. "I've made a few enemies over the years for no other reason than I take my job seriously. And what do I get in return? Enemies. Now those enemies want to humiliate me, and this is their one chance." He raised his chin indignantly. "I won't allow them the pleasure."

As he spoke, he realized how emphatic these words sounded. Almost embarrassingly so. The last thing he wanted was for Glass—or anyone, for that matter—to interpret his well-intended appropriately-directed discipline as some sort of Captain Queeg character flaw. A reference she'd obliquely and, apparently unwittingly, alluded to.

She backed away a step with a suspicious eye flicker, hands raised again.

"I get it, Itzhak. Really, I do, but perhaps it might be a good idea to back off a little and take a more, uh, objective overview of this before it does a major number on you."

He simply stared her down, dumbfounded.

*Back off? Look at it more objectively?*

"What I'm saying," she continued, "is maybe you're taking this, I don't know, a bit too seriously? Too personally? I mean, far as I can tell this job is everything to you."

*Where the hell was she going with this?*

"Was that a question?"

"No, just a simple statement. Hey look, you don't have a wife or family, as I remember. Yes?"

Each word from her mouth stoked his anger.

*How dare she.*

"Let's get something straight, Glass. Just because I intend to fulfill my job obligations and fulfil it well, you're accusing me of what exactly?" His hands were now bricks of white knuckles, but he felt powerless to stop. "You've lost me in your steaming pile of psychobabble horseshit."

She shrugged.

"Fine. I'm sorry I wasted your time."

She turned to leave the cramped space.

Couldn't believe how stupid the bitch was in proclaiming that his words were an overreaction.

*An overreaction to what? To some punks trying to violate his space? Well, fuck her and her high and mighty display of righteousness.*

Except for...he *did* need her help with this...

Rocking his head side to side, he cleared his throat and paid particular attention to tempering his next words.

"My team will concentrate on seeing to it that those testers do not step foot on any of our floors. After all, Glass, *we* are the primary target." This, he punctuated with an affirmative sniff. "However, let me give *you* a word of advice: you and your crew will look like rock stars if you're able to nail those little shits *before* they get within two floors of my offices. Why are you so blind to this fact? I'm simply trying to help *you*."

She nodded.

"I know, Itzhak, I know, but tell me this…how the hell did they weasel into your network so quickly?"

She flashed a smug grin.

This caught him completely flat footed.

*She knew. How the hell did she find out?*

Had one of his treacherous techs leaked it? Or did she simply make a lucky guess? No, there had to be a spy in his ranks. Of this he was now certain.

He thrust a pointed finger at her.

"That, Glass, is pure horseshit."

But he realized his face betrayed the truth.

She shrugged, a Cheshire-cat grin tugging the corners of her mouth.

He stifled an almost overwhelming urge to bitch-slap that blatant arrogance off her face.

*Goddamnit, he would humiliate her.*

Once this pen-test was finished, he would hand property management a detailed after-action report detailing her incompetence, so searing that she would be removed from the building forever. But, for today, though…

With a dismissive wave, he sat back down and swiveled his chair to face his office's grimy single window, ignoring her now: meeting over, the result obvious. Given Building Security's incompetence, the responsibility for protecting his law offices now rested entirely upon his shoulders. Meaning, he needed to bear down and produce a more proactive defense.

Again, he considered notifying Collier of a break-in in progress. Again, he recalculated. No. Doing that carried too much downside risk. For if by some incredible stroke of good fortune that little shit actually *did* succeed, he would look incompetent. After all, if he knew the attack was in progress…

*Wait. What about…*

He was up again, strutting into Valchenka's cubicle, waving a hand to catch the Russian's attention.

Slipping off his earphones, Serge turned toward him but with eyes averted.

"When did you last check network integrity?"

"Why do you want to know?"

Mizrahi made a hurry-up motion with his hands.

"Just answer the fucking question."

Frowning, Valchenka leaned back in his chair while digging his little finger into his right ear.

"There is no issue."

"That doesn't answer my question."

"Fine. I'm running a full system scan right now. That's exactly what I was doing when you interrupted. Why? What's going on?"

"Because I know we're under attack and I'm worried that they might also have penetrated our firewall," he answered as calmly as possible.

"I see."

Mizrahi waited for a more enthusiastic response, but Valchenka simply slipped his Logitechs back on and swiveled around to face the monitor, fingers poised above the keyboard, eyes scanning the screen.

*Fucking Russian.*

# CHAPTER 34

## Seattle

EARLY EVENING. ARNOLD and Rachael were out in the patio of Duke's Seafood—a Green Lake dining staple of his—enjoying fresh-out-of-the-fryer fish and chips with extra vinegar and tartar sauce. A nearby tall pyramidal-shaped heat lamp radiated sufficient warmth for comfortable alfresco dining in what otherwise would be air too chilly.

Since their confrontation the other night, a somewhat tense yet superficial veil of peace had shrouded their few hours together. To confuse matters, Rachael had dropped two subtle remarks hinting of a possible reconciliation. That gave him pause, forcing him to objectively calculate the net emotional balance of their relationship. And in doing this, it shocked him to confront the fact that the comfort he enjoyed by her filling a vacuum in his life simply wasn't worth its exhausting emotional cost. Once this sobering realization hit, there was no way to ignore it. Hard as it would be, he simply needed to walk away from the toxicity of their chemistry.

But brute pragmatism triggered a nagging concern: Rachael was their business manager.

*How the hell would he navigate this minefield?*

Or would it even be a problem? Yeah, no doubt it would.

*And it presented a huge complication for him to deal with. Gonzo huge. And now he was struggling to submerge the issue until the pen-test was a wrap.*

"What do you think happened?" Rachael asked Arnold.

"Couple things," he said, pausing to paper-napkin away a smear of tartar sauce from his upper lip. "We know from their radio chatter they've known about the pen-test for days. I'm pretty sure they didn't get that from Mr. Collier, so I'm guessing Mizrahi's got ears in the Security Committee. What I haven't been able to determine is how they ended up with accurate pictures of me."

He neglected mentioning that he suspected Mizrahi had eyes and ears over just about every inch of those offices.

"That's easy enough. Mizrahi knows your name. He could've just put someone with a camera outside your house." She paused to sip her Diet Coke. "So what's plan B?"

Arnold burned a moment dislodging a chunk of cod from between his incisors.

"We're, like, fully committed now. No way we're not going back in tomorrow."

"Gutsy." She appeared to roll this around in her head while dipping a fry in tartar sauce, then popping it into her mouth. "Real gutsy."

"So, where're you staying tonight?" he asked to gauge whether their faceoff the other night actually sunk in or simply glanced off her reality center. New boundaries needed to be established. This floating in limbo had to end.

She studied her fries a moment before looking at him...

"After dinner, I'll run over to Mom's for a bit, but plan on coming over after she's in bed for the night." And then, as an afterthought: "If that's okay."

When he didn't answer immediately her eyes wandered to his face.

"I know how unhappy you are with this situation, sweetie, but you need to understand how torn I am. I feel a real obligation to her but also don't want this to drive a wedge through what we have."

*No, apparently the message didn't penetrate.*

"What exactly *do* we have, Rach?"

Her head cocked questioningly.

"We have a lot together, sweetie. We're good, you and me. We're a team. I don't want to lose that."

There it was: the statement from hell. Whatever he said now was guaranteed to be accidentally or purposefully misinterpreted. He dropped the hunk of fish he was holding on the tub of fries, then began to methodically degrease his fingers with a paper napkin, forging his menagerie of blazing thoughts into one firm coherent explanation of just how radically their relationship was different now. Carefully, he set the crumpled oil-stained napkin atop the basket of congealing fry grease, each move buying another fractional second to collate his words.

"Agreed. We have had our moments, Rachael, but you have to admit they've been wildly inconsistent."

She forced a smile.

"Every couple's relationship has ups and downs and inconsistencies, sweetie. That's just the nature of relationships."

He hand-signaled a time out.

She sat back with arched eyebrows.

Elbows on the table, hands clasped, he looked her in the eyes.

"Listen to me, Rach. This is seriously important."

She furrowed her brows.

"I always listen to you."

He waved his hands.

"Stop it, okay? Just listen."

"Okay."

She set her hands in her lap and ditched the furrowed brow for the Miss Innocence look.

"We have two separate but inextricably intertwined issues going on, so let's not scramble them together, okay?"

"If you say so."

He shot her a hard look.

*Enough of that shit.*

Waited a beat for that message to process, then: "Look, I get it. She's your mother. I *get* that her illness is a major priority for you. That's *not* the issue with us, so let's put that to rest and move on to what is."

"Which is?"

"*Us.* As a couple." Pause. "You were smart enough to realize that something is fundamentally out of sync with us. And in retrospect, I realize that's probably why you never could commit to us."

She raised both hands for him to pause, but then dropped them into her lap.

"I assume you're referring to your marriage proposal," she said as an emotionless statement of fact.

"Yeah, in part, but not entirely."

She squinted at him with a slight head tilt.

"What exactly does that change, Arnie? We're *us*," she said, pointing from him to herself and back.

He scoffed. A massive neuronal short-circuit blew, triggering his brain's Blue Screen of Death. He visualized bright little sparks spewing from the vertex of his head like a cerebral Roman candle.

"Christ, Rach, if you'd committed to us in some tangible way, it would've changed *everything*. At least for me it would've. As it is, we nurdle along in our own separate lives without so much as a hint of commitment from you. Nada. Hey, in retrospect, you never did show any. So, yeah, things *are* changed between us now. Dramatically."

With pursed lips, she appeared to contemplate his words a beat.

"But you see how Mr. Davidson and Martina live…how they live apart but still love each other. And you're just fine with that." She spread her hands. "What's the difference? Let's use that as our model."

Another scoff.

"You *are* joking, I hope. Right?"

*Nope, didn't look like it.*

"Wow," he said, and wiped his face. "I can't believe you're serious." Then, after a nod, he said: "Okay, let's parse that out. First of all, they *were* married. And although you can say that's simply a symbolic scrap of legal paper, for them it was tangible evidence of mutual emotional commitment. It was only after they were living together day to day that they discovered there were too many basic functional discrepancies to continue being under the same roof. So yes, they divorced, but only to salvage *them* as a couple. They're still emotionally, spiritually, and for all I know, still sexually deeply committed to each other. Us? Other than the occasional sex when you're horny…"

He let that hang. He'd driven home his point.

*What else was there to say?*

He sat motionless, staring blankly at his congealing fish and chips, aware of the snippets of waxing and waning chatter from nearby tables intermixed with the unrelenting background ebb and flow of traffic, then the unmistakable pulsating grinding wheels of a passing skateboarder.

After what seemed like forever, she said, "Sounds like you just handed me an ultimatum."

He glanced up, surprised.

"An ultimatum? No, not at all. It was a simple statement of fact."

A tingling sensation began radiating from the depths of his chest on out through his arteries, pulsing the stark realization that he was perching on the threshold of the moment he'd been dreading for weeks in spite of knowing it was advancing inextricably toward him, the moment just before you plunge headfirst off the high dive. It was time she clearly got his message.

He swallowed hard., "Your decision to move out without

so much as one word of discussion provoked a seismic shift in *us*. At least it did for me. In essence, it said my feelings about it were so irrelevant that you couldn't be bothered to hear them. You even said as much, although not so bluntly...it was something to the effect that you did it for *you*." He raised a palm. "Don't. I'm not finished." A pause, a breath. "For me that was a massive wake-up call. And now, with this thing with your mom, it's the same wine in a different bottle. There is no *us* in how you plan your future. Your decisions involve only you. My role is nothing more than an afterthought."

There was more to say, but figured this was enough.

"Goddamn it, Arnold, you're being way too unfair about this. I have no control over Mom's present issues. It's being forced on all of us."

He glanced at a passing Tesla, dark gray, like Davidson's.

*Why can't you say it, dude? Don't allow this to degenerate into a debate.*

Still eyeing the passing traffic, he shook his head regretfully.

*C'mon dude, man up.*

He wallowed again, the annoying weightless tingling sensation zinging through him intensifying. Part of life was having to face unavoidable ugly events. Truly *unavoidable* ones. Like having no option but to accept his parents' cold-blooded murder or live with the fantasy that they're still alive but somehow just not available to him. Right now, at this moment, he was facing another.

He shook his head.

"I can't do this anymore, Rach."

"Can't do what?"

When he didn't answer, she said, "What are you saying? That you don't love me anymore?"

Zugzwang.

"Yeah, basically, if you choose to put it in those words."

Shockingly, a breeze of relief began whistling through him.

Not happiness.
Not sorrow.
Just simple relief, as if he were fifty pounds lighter.

# CHAPTER 35

## Seattle

ARNOLD AND RACHAEL shuffled in silence back to her mother's place, having said no more words than what was essential. Nor had either touched their food again. He'd simply paid the bill, pushed back from the table, and they started the trudge back to their respective homes, each one stewing in private thoughts.

They stood awkwardly on her mother's front porch until Arnold haltingly leaned in to give her an unreciprocated peck on the cheek, followed by a simple "Good night."

She just nodded, turned, and vanished inside.

So much for having dreamed of a future together. For a moment, he stood staring at the locked front door, grappling unsuccessfully with the implications of what just transpired. Rachael was his first and only "girlfriend."

What do I do now? How will this affect work? Would they ever see each other again?

Jesus, dummy, she's our business manager.

A gazillion questions kept vying for answers he neither had nor wished to address yet. His complete loss of what to do now shocked him. He harbored a nagging suspicion that he should "do *something*" but what that might be, was completely elusive.

Capping this confusion was the weighty feeling of being utterly drained and emotionally busted.

He began to trudge slowly back home, simply dropping one foot then the other, knowing that as of this moment his life was emptier. Well, except for Chance. Thank God for him.

What was she thinking? Did she miss him? Had she ever loved him?

He had no idea. And the more he thought about this, the more he realized he really didn't know her at all. Which was pathetic, because what did that say about him? Then again, the more he focused on the answer, the more he realized just how closed and guarded she was. But none of this made him feel any better. In fact, it just deepened his depression.

As was his typical escape hatch for emotional quagmires, he gravitated to focusing on simple pragmatic issues. Like, would the business force them to see each other?

Well, not necessarily. That one was totally up for grabs... wasn't it? Like, what exactly did this mean? Business meetings, for one thing. She was, after all, their business manager. Yes, but those meetings were virtual. He would make sure to keep it that way, especially now that Gold and Associates really *did* have employees in both cities.

But the real issue was, would they see each other during the times when he was here? For the sake of friendship?

*Naw, that would be officially awkward.*

And just how would that work? Text her for a dinner date? Doubtful. Very doubtful. And the thought of her being with another guy...Jesus. He didn't want to think about it.

*And besides, did he really want to be around her now? What kind of mind games would that do to him?*

Jesus, life had suddenly turned infinitely more complex and obscure.

Which raised an interesting question: had he been better off before confronting her, when they were still limping along in, what for him, had been an emotionally damaged relationship?

No. He was definitely better off having come clean. On the other hand, he knew it would require time to process such an abrupt and meaningful change. As it was, his mind was almost pretzeling itself into semi-shutdown. He continued to plod step by stop, now more than ever in need of giving Chance a heavy dose of choobers and rabber-de-jabbers.

After taking Chance on his evening potty stroll, Arnold microwaved a hot chocolate, then immersed himself in an MS Teams call with Gene Ito to discuss their Honolulu workload. Then, he spent another forty-five minutes reviewing SAM's performance since his last check, then initiated another routine security probe. All quiet on the Western Front.

Too quiet. The house seemed too empty. He submerged this thought by turning his attention to whether to promote Gene to be their first and only Honolulu associate. Dude did excellent work and there was little doubt they could use him there, especially during times when Arnold was here. It would also allow him more latitude to come over more often, especially during the prime spring and summer months.

For a fleeting moment he rehashed Rachael's suggestion of relocating his primary residence here.

*But why? Certainly, not for her.*

Their relationship was irreparably blown. Which brought the acute sense of loss roaring back, echoing in the hollowness of his new life. Had he been too harsh? Too intolerant? After all, she was just looking after her mother. Couldn't fault her for that...

*Whoa... you're losing sight of the primary issue, dude.*

The fatal flaw to their relationship, he knew, was that the elemental bonds between couples never truly existed, that the only element that had kept him attached to her was, in reality, the fulfillment of his adolescent fantasy rather than true commonality of interests and emotional interweaving. The thing they did share—fundamental ethical values—was critical, of course, but insufficient in itself to sustain the effort required to grind out a day-to-day existence together.

And since he was being completely truthful, he and Rachael were thrust together by one pivotal event: her brother's murder. If his best friend were still alive, he and Rachael never would've linked up. That was the harsh reality.

*How did he not see this before now? How could he have invested so much emotional currency in a relationship that he should've known wouldn't go the distance?*

It was a ridiculous question, of course. His pursuit of her hadn't been rational.

He laughed at that inkling.

But it made him rethink the issue of making Seattle his home base again. Was he categorically rejecting the idea as an unthinking reaction to her suggestion? Or was his heart really in Honolulu now?

*Could he even be objective about this now? Jesus.*

No, he'd made the right decision: he really *did* prefer spending the majority of his time there. And although this rebuilt house was light-years away from the old family Tudor architecturally, there was no way to exorcise the historical baggage haunting the plot.

Time to move on.

Hard as it was to do this, he had, in fact, taken his first step. And this realization swamped him with gratitude for possessing the strength to change and to grow.

The Arnold of, say, six months ago, never could've done this.

No question that this abrupt loss of companionship and its subsequent return to the loneliness of living alone would be an emotionally difficult adjustment, but he had no other option now, and at the moment, the best antidote was to channel every volt of energy he could muster into the pen-test.

# CHAPTER 36

## Seattle

ARNOLD HAD ON a pair of well-worn stonewashed jeans, muted light-gray sweatshirt, gray-and-black Adidas Ultraboosts, and a black ballcap with an embroidered red Tesla T above the bill.

Not a disguise (since that proved to be shockingly ineffective), just functional clothing for what he hoped would be a very functional and productive day.

He transferred Chance's water and food dishes from the kitchen to the back porch. Rachael had assured him—as their business manager, he assumed—that she would periodically drop by during the day to check on him since she was only two blocks away.

She'd offered this service as if it were no big deal. Which he found slightly suspicious, given their hyper-sensitive circumstances. Although he had to admit, being able to rely on her in this situation was nice. And for a brief moment he fantasized about what it might be like if they rekindled their relationship. He promptly jettisoned the thought. This, he suspected, wouldn't be the only internal debate on this subject he would endure during the ensuing months....

He led Chance out onto the back porch, squatted on his

haunches, held the pooch's head gently in his hands, and got face to face.

"Daddy has to go. Chance stays. Daddy will be back."

The same three phrases he routinely told him before leaving, regardless of how long he intended to be away.

Chance's flaps drooped, but he knew that Arnold never failed to return. They were pack.

Arnold pushed through the side gate to the sidewalk to wait for Prisha to roll by for him.

Arnold cut an abrupt right, slipping through the wide cavernous maw of the parking garage, scooting around the white-and-red-striped boom blocking the vehicle exit, crossing over a series of yellow lines defining the thirty-minutes parking stalls, moving toward the elevator bank.

Just before reaching it, he cut right to push through the heavy steel fire door into the stairwell. He stopped to listen, the faint odor of oil and car emissions lingering in his sinuses.

*What're you listening for, dude?*

*Don't start getting all paranoid and shit on me already.*

He shook his head, then began climbing the stairs to the lobby.

The rationale for entering through the garage went like this: security might not be paying as much attention to garage foot traffic as they were to the lobby during business hours. But what did he know about security protocols here? For all he knew, they could just as easily be applying the exact opposite strategy, especially since there were no garage doors. At the door to the lobby, he paused to catch his breath and mentally rehash the next move, then physically enacted it three times. Ready?

*Yeah, probably.*

He shook his hands as if that would stop them from tingling, sucked a deep breath, cracked the door just wide enough to see straight across the narrow hall to the closest elevator bank. And waited.

Heard the ding of a cage arriving. In one fluid move, was out of the stairway, jetting straight across the short span of hall and through the opening doors, minimizing his exposure to the CCTV. Three other passengers piled in behind him, forcing him to shuffle to the rear of the cage while keeping one eye on the panel of floor buttons. Cool, he totally lucked out. This bank of elevators served a segment of floors directly above the firm. Couldn't ask for a more perfect ride.

As the doors slid shut, Arnold said, "Excuse me," and reached past a passenger to nonchalantly swipe a key card over the reader then thumbed fifty-two.

*Please work.*

His luck held. The button glowed. He withdrew his arm but kept the card in hand.

Stifling a smile, he shuffled behind the others again, making himself inconspicuous. They ascended in silence; well, except for the deafening pounding of his heart.

*Could they hear it? Jesus, and this was only the overture to Act One. The really dicey part was yet to come.*

The cage glided smoothly to a stop. The doors noiselessly parted.

Darting quickly out of the cage, he turned left, waved the key card over the black wall reader, heard the click of the lock, slipped into the fifty-second floor north stairwell and let the door swing shut on its own as he descended down to fifty.

Reached the landing and stopped to catch his breath and listen. Other than his pounding, racing pulse, heard only heavy graveyard stillness. He took in his immediate surroundings, more out of nervousness than need. Yeah, no one else in sight.

He carefully exchanged the key card for the Larkin Standish secretary's, then double-checked to make that it was correct. One more nervous glance around before he unlocked the fire door, slipped into the hall, and darted into the men's room. Thankfully the two lavatories flanked the elevator shafts.

A quick check confirmed that both stalls were empty.

Sighing in relief, he entered the closest one, locked the door, whispered, "Mother, have a copy?"

"Copy," Prisha's answer came through his earbud loud and clear.

*Whew!*

What a relief to know they could communicate so clearly inside the concrete-and-steel building and that his throat mic picked up his barely whispered voice.

"Location?" he asked.

"South stairwell. Fifty-one."

"Roger."

He nodded to himself. So far, so good.

"Uncle, Son, copy?" Son was Lopez's code name.

They confirmed solid copy. Another huge relief. For now.

With the essentials taken care of, Arnold stepped from the stall to look for a camera or any other monitoring device.

*Yeah, sure, the probability was, like, zero that the building would have any in the johns, but you never knew unless you checked, right? Didn't see any.*

Satisfied with his privacy he pushed back into the stall, locked the door and slipped off his rucksack. He dropped heavily onto the commode and checked the time, in spite of being good at subconsciously tracking a reasonable estimate.

*Damn. No mystery here; showtime was, like, freaking eons from now.*

Not that this should come as any jaw-dropping revelation, for he'd known that this particular stretch would be butt-numbingly long and boring. Regardless, it totally sucked to be facing a gazillion minutes that would creep past with the speed of a narcotized sloth.

With a sigh, he dug his Surface from the rucksack, booted up, logged into the Internet to check a stock price, then opened his chess program.

*Hmmm…might as well play the Sicilian Defense.*

# CHAPTER 37

## Seattle

A DISEMBODIED VOICE broke the squelch on Mizrahi's radio.

"Itzhak. We just saw your boy hop an elevator."

The high-quality FM transmission allowed him to easily recognize Glass's tenor. He thumbed transmit.

"Just now?"

"Couple minutes ago."

*The fuck?*

"And you're just now telling me? Minutes later?"

Mizrahi heard five seconds of dead silence.

Then: "The tech couldn't be absolutely certain it's him, so before he started pounding the big red alarm button, he wanted me to confirm his impression. I'm standing here in front of the screen now and concur that the image is highly *suggestive* of, but not conclusive for, your man."

Mizrahi drummed his fingers on the desk.

*What were the odds?*

"Okay. Keep it on screen. I'm on my way."

He glanced at his watch while awaiting the elevator: 1:45 PM.

*Was she serious? A pen-test in the early afternoon? NFW.*

Or...could Gold be staging his team inside the building for an assault later tonight after most offices cleared out? Hmmm...the more he considered this, the more likely it seemed. In fact, that's exactly how he would do it.

*Was Gold that smart?*

Mizrahi rolled into the monitoring room as if suddenly bestowed with command of the entire building instead of just the Larkin Standish floors. Glass stood directly behind the right shoulder of her seated female minion—tatted-up, ratty bottle-blond ponytail, obscenely studded from ear to ear with piercings—studying a high-def color image on a twenty-seven-inch Dell monitor.

"I'm here. Show me what you have," he ordered.

With a nod at the screen, Glass stepped aside so he could position himself directly behind the minion with a straight-on view of the screen: a freeze-frame of a male in mid-stride, moving right to left directly toward an open elevator door.

He could've come from either the north stairwell or from the T-junction of the short elevator hall with the rest of the lobby, but the single frame gave Mizrahi no indication as to which. The image would show the subject's face if not for the bill of his ballcap; precisely the reason he was wearing it like that. Yet, enough of a vibe radiated from the image to pique Mizrahi's suspicion. Highly pique. Perhaps it was the combination of the seemingly purposeful stride in concert with the hinted sideways glance—one frozen fractional second—that slowly solidified his suspicion into a conviction.

He studied the image for five additional seconds before being convinced that figure *was* in fact Gold. Had to be.

"Go ahead, back it up a few frames," he ordered.

Glass nodded to her assistant who, with a mouse click on a blue line across the bottom of the video strip, moved the video segment back two seconds, then rolled the scene in slow motion. If you knew exactly where to look at the right top of the frame, you could see the mystery person pivot just enough to assume that he'd come from the garage stairwell. However, the fish-eye lens distortion toward the image periphery made an *incontrovertible* conclusion impossible. Nonetheless...

Mizrahi straightened, massaging his chin thoughtfully.

*What now? Compliment her and her team for catching this?*

He tossed that around a moment, decided that although she was probably correct, there was no point in emboldening her. As it was, the bitch was already too full of herself. Mizrahi shook his head.

"Glass, are you messing with me? There's no way to positively identify him. Not with his face obscured like that."

"Perhaps not," she said, never taking her eyes from the screen, "but watch again, Itzhak."

She nudged her assistant.

The assistant replayed the scene once more in slow motion.

Again Mizrahi shook his head.

"I still don't see what all the hoopla's about."

She eyed him, as if sizing up an opponent.

"Look *closely*." Then, to her assistant: "Okay, Shelia, take him through it one more time, but this time slow it even more."

Shelia rewound the segment to a point ten seconds before the subject actually stepped from the stairwell onto the glistening gray granite floor.

Tapping a specific area on the screen with a ballpoint pen, Glass said, "Look closely. You'll see the door's cracked for several seconds *before* the elevator doors open. We looked back a couple seconds before this and it's the same. Shelia."

The tech took the video back even further.

"Okay, there. See? It opens right there. He then holds that position. As I know you know, those doors are designed to self-close. Meaning that our subject here"—she tapped the male suspect—"was watching and waiting for precisely the right moment to bolt, as if to limit hit time on camera. Dunno about you, Itzhak, but given the total package, I'd have to ask, why's he acting so suspicious? Unless…"

*Valid point.*

But Mizrahi was damned if he was going to concede it to her.

"I get your point, Glass. But you have to admit that the hat prevents us from making a *positive* ID."

With a shrug, she said, "Hey, your call, Itzhak. I'm just trying to be helpful and give you a heads-up. What you want to do with this is totally on you."

She said this in a tone that implied that she was henceforth absolved from any and all subsequent fallout.

He nodded.

"Have any idea what floor he went to?"

"No, but that bank serves floors fifty to seventy-five, so at least that narrows it down for you. Knock yourself out."

He sent her a pitiful headshake.

"That's incredibly helpful, Glass, just incredible. Especially since I wasn't notified until"—he cast an unnecessary glance at his watch—"at least ten minutes *after* the fact. Why the delay? Are you intentionally wanting to piss me off?"

But he knew the answer: the bitch was intent on sabotaging him in the hope of making herself look good. And do it by any passive-aggressive means possible.

She crossed her arms and leveled a retina-coagulating stare at him.

"Don't forget, Itzhak, yesterday you were awarded the dubious distinction of the little boy who cried wolf," she said with an emphatic nod. "*We're* on top of this, Itzhak. How you wish to protect your turf is your business. After all, as you so readily point out *ad nauseum*, your firm's the one being targeted, not ours. Plus, you're always crowing about how Kevlar your security is. Let's see how that pans out."

There's that Queeg reference again. Just like last time, it sapped his resolve to keep from bitch-slapping that silly fucking smirk from her smug pudgy face.

"A piece of advice, Glass. If you're so convinced that that's Gold," he said, with a nod at the screen, "I suggest you bring in as many extra bodies as possible to make sure your ass is adequately covered. Remember, your team's on the line here just as much—if not more—as mine."

She coughed a deep hearty guffaw, wiped a drop of spittle from the corner of her mouth.

"Let's agree to disagree on that last point. Hey, as far as getting in some extra personnel in, I called in the request. Guess what? They assigned me *one* additional body. That's how dire my supervisor sees our situation. What you don't seem to understand is I'm dealing with a huge building full of floor space. I realize it's not quite as vast as your six floors, but hey… Bottom line? You do your job, we'll do ours. We clear?"

He moved a few steps toward the door, preparing to exit her little fiefdom; his not-so-subtle way of letting her know the meeting was henceforth over. Then he paused to say, "You should wake up to the fact that if Gold's crew really *is* in the building and *does* manage to wind up violating our offices, you and your crew will look just as bad as ours."

She laughed again, shaking her head.

"Total moose shit, Itzhak." Then, flashing a sly grin, she added: "Hey, long as we're on the topic, you sure your network's still secure?"

Without batting an eye, he quickly said, "Absolutely."

*Huh? Why would she ask that?*

Eyebrows arched, she nodded thoughtfully.

"Well, in that case, you shouldn't have any problems at all managing the threat."

Itzhak turned and stormed out, feeling the color drain from his face.

*Did that bitch know something he didn't, or was she throwing out zingers just to fuck with him?*

# CHAPTER 38

## Seattle

LOPEZ RADIOED, "FATHER, bad news. They made you in the lobby. That's the latest chatter. They know you're on your way up to floors fifty and above."

*Shit.*

He'd done everything he could think of to reduce the odds of being spotted or identified. Thank God Prisha had found a way to monitor their transmissions.

Arnold began to sort through fallback options. But one overwhelming fact remained: he *was* inside the building now. Hiding. This gave him a definite advantage. Yet he couldn't ignore the stone-cold fact they'd nailed him within, what, a measly two seconds of exposure? Tops. That should tell him something. And it was disheartening.

Mulled it over and decided it was either just a lucky catch by some security guard or *maybe* their CCTV monitoring system had some freaking crazy AI algorithm working on *all* the feeds. Which meant that another attempt on another day would be no different than the shitty situation on this day.

Plus, he wouldn't even consider substituting Lopez, Vihaan, or Prisha for himself. No, not anymore. No, man, this was now his operation. Him against Mizrahi. He was inside now, and it was Game On.

"Want to abort?" Prisha asked over the radio.

"Hold one," he said.

Eyes scrunched tightly shut, thinking hard, he game-played scenarios until finally zeroing in on one. But wanted the group's input before committing to it. Although ideally, they intended to limit radio traffic to essential info, this was an exception.

He radioed: "I still think our plan's solid enough that it's worth sticking to it. After all, I'm inside, right? Anyone have a problem moving ahead?"

No one broke squelch.

"Okay then," Arnold transmitted. "Let's make this work."


Scowling, Mizrahi stormed back to Valchenka's cubicle and halted a mere three feet from him, arms crossed, staring.

The tech casually tipped back in his creaky desk chair, slipped off his headphones, and greeted him with a flagrantly bored expression.

Mizrahi stabbed a finger at him.

"Double-check the network. Make sure it's clean."

Frowning, Valchenka gave two questioning blinks, then said, "I just finished a complete system scan five minutes ago."

Mizrahi recoiled.

"Stop whining. Do it over then. *Now.*"

The Russian glanced from his boss to his headphones, back to Mizrahi.

"Why? Nothing unusual's going on."

*Goddamn insolence.*

Mizrahi wanted to break the geek's keyboard over his disheveled head.

"Not true. There's an invasion in progress. One of the pentesters was just identified sneaking into the building. I know this for a fact because I just saw him on video footage in Glass' office." Pause. "This, of course, means it's very likely they'll try to gain control of our command center, which, as you know,

222

means taking control of our Ethernet network. *Do. You. Understand?"*

These last three words came out e a hair shy of a full shout.

Valchenka responded with a *whatever* look before he nonchalantly rotating back to the three monitors while slipping his headphones back on.

Mizrahi glared at the fool long enough to send a telepathic message of his own before storming back to his office.

Earlier in the day, he'd summoned his only additional guards back to the office to reinforce his present staff. Seemed to be a good call since he was now convinced that at least Gold—and perhaps even more of his team—were now in the building. But he would be damned if he would concede that point to Glass' ugly face. If she didn't give a rat's ass about helping him defend their offices, then he and his team would do so alone. A point he planned to emphasize when writing up his After-Action Report for Collier and the security committee.

The two additional security guards were lolling in two tattered chairs, chatting. They were the team's utility players: available to cover nights, weekends, holidays, or any other odd need that cropped up.

Their chitchat stopped as abruptly as their posture straightened with Mizrahi's entrance.

He quickly briefed them on the rapidly accumulating evidence that the attack was in progress and that recent intel sources strongly indicated that Gold and at least one other of his underlings were now staged in some undefined location within the building, preparing to strike at any time.

He also explained that he believed that Gold was presently holed up in a storeroom or some equally out-of-the way spot until late that night, when most employees would be gone. Only then would they make their final assault. He assigned one guard to assist the tech monitoring the video feeds he'd surreptitiously installed throughout the firm's six floors. The second guard would help him walk random patrols through their offices until morning.

After dismissing them, he leaned back in the chair, closed his eyes, and once again started worrying about what additional security measures he could possibly deploy to keep that squirrelly little dipshit from violating his sovereign territory.

## 3:57 PM

Arnold snapped abruptly from a drifting fantasy to fully alert. He heard the muted slap of footsteps on floor tiles. Leaned forward to peer through the vertical gap between the stall door and its support frame.

A uniformed guard was standing dead center in the white-tiled men's room staring silently at Arnold's black Adidas below the stall door.

*Oh, shit....*

Arnold froze, his heartbeat now a thundering stampede.

A moment later the thick-soled black shoes stepped closer and halted mere inches from the door.

"Everything okay in there?" a gravely male voice asked.

*A smoker, for sure.*

"Excuse me?" Arnold said, glancing around nervously.

Had he been spotted darting in here? Yeah, but that was like over an hour ago, so…

More likely, this was a routine patrol now that they were aware he was in the building and hiding. But, did a review of the videos finger him exiting the elevator? Timeline would be about right…

"I asked, is everything's okay in there?"

*And why exactly does this concern you?*

"Yeah, I'm good. And if you let me finish taking a dump, I'll be even better."

A brief pause, then the shoes turned an about-face to vanish without another word.

Arnold leaned forward to squint through the opening again. Yeah, dude was gone. Gave a massive exhale, wondering now what?

*Well, one thing for damn sure, he'd better get the hell out of here and find another hiding spot, since a ton of time still existed before the party's scheduled kickoff.*

Arnold waited two minutes before flushing the toilet, then washing his hands just in case the dude was out in the hall, ear to door, checking out his suspicions. And if so, what then? Blow past him heading for a stairwell? For sure he couldn't duck into an office.

*Oh man!*

He had no option but to roll the dice and go into the hall for a look. He edged to the door, cracked it, peeked out. At least the narrow swath he could see was guard-free. He took a tentative step into the hall, scanned the rest of area.

*Clear.*

Okay, so maybe the guard was simply on a random routine patrol to ensure that some homeless dude or junkie wasn't camped out in one of the stalls. But on second thought, that didn't make sense...this floor access required a key card.

*Well, true, but said street person could've tailgated a legit employee right out of the elevator...yeah, but given all the layers of lobby security, how likely was that? Not very.*

*What the hell.*

He returned to the men's room, but this time settled into the adjacent stall, just in case the same guard reappeared.

*But dude, your shoes are the same.*

*What excuse you planning to hand him if he pops up again? Irritable bowel syndrome?*

*Good question.*

He'd cross that bridge if and when it arises.

Seated, he checked his watch. Damn, still had waaaay too many hours ahead of him. Not only that, but he'd forgotten to pack his Kindle and the battery on his Surface was almost moribund. Damn. Should've thought to bring a charger. Come to think of it, was there even a 110-volt outlet in here?

With a resigned sigh, he settled in for one goddamn boringly long afternoon.

Just then, he heard the door open.

# CHAPTER 39

## Seattle

WITH EACH PASSING minute, Mizrahi's piss-off factor inched relentlessly closer to unadulterated rage. Should that happen, he risked stumbling into a stupid mistake, and stupid mistakes were unacceptable.

Somehow, he needed to find a way to short-circuit his mounting anger, to vent the tension pressure-cooking his chest. But he could see no release other than to crush that little fucker's throat with his bare hands. Each tick of the second hand increased the unmistakable feeling that Gold was edging closer to his territory. By now, he was dead sure that the little bastard was somewhere nearby hiding in a stairwell, a broom closet, a lavatory.

He felt this as acutely as a full-face whiff of eye-watering ammonia. For him, the unbearably frustrating reality was not having the manpower to post a guard at every access point, and this was forcing him into the risky strategy of concentrating his assets near Gold's anticipated target. Making things worse was the feeling he was overlooking *something*.

*What was it?*

He reran his mental checklist yet again.

Every available team member was on high alert and on

task.

*Check.*

So far, there were no reports of unusual key card activity.
*Check.*

Their Ethernet network remained unbreached.
*Check.*

Or so said the Russian.

Exactly: Or so said the Russian...

This thought began eating away at him like an ear worm.
And with it came concern for the key card reports. Now *that*
was a weakness. For the accuracy and timeliness of those reports
depended completely on Glass' team.

There it was: the weakness he'd known was present but
had been unable to identify. Two vulnerabilities, really: The
Russian and The Cunt.

Did either of those passive-aggressive amateur human
beings have any appreciation for the blowback this would slam
into them should Gold triumphantly strut into Collier's office
with the crown jewels? Did they even comprehend the indignity
of having to apply for unemployment benefits? Or realize that
one egregious blunder could end up haunting his resumé in
perpetuity? Which brought Mizrahi full circle right back to the
key question: had the Russian actually scoured the network for
a breach, or had he done nothing more than a cursory network
look-see from thirty thousand feet?

Mizrahi knew that their network integrity was his greatest
vulnerability. For if Gold *had* breached their firewall...

But there was also the key card issue. Damn. Shaking his
head, he headed back down to Glass' office.

There she sat, kicked back at her desk, the picture of pure
insouciance, sipping from a white paper Starbucks coffee cup.
He struggled to not scream at her.

Instead, he asked calmly as he could muster: "Anyone
reported Gold leaving the building yet?" But he was unable to
mask the edge to his voice.

She carefully set the coffee cup to the right of her keyboard with a bemused smile.

"As I remember it, you were adamant that the suspect wasn't Gold."

*Bitch.*

"No. As usual, you weren't listening carefully. What I *said* was that with the hat masking his face, it is impossible to identify him unequivocally. Those were my *exact* words and I still stand by that. I never said it *couldn't* be Gold."

She tossed him a thoughtful nod.

"Oh." Then, after a beat: "You know, that sounds quite a bit different from what I heard." She feigned a theatrically thoughtful pose. "Perhaps I misinterpreted? Yes?"

"Stop fucking with me, Glass. Whoever he is, he certainly wasn't acting like someone who belongs inside our building, so please, just answer my question. Have you seen that person—whoever the fuck he is—leave?"

She rotated her chair to face him straight-on.

"Itzhak, you can't possibly expect us to track every sketchy person we happen to notice step on an elevator. Since I suspected he *could* be your guy, we duly notified you of our impression, documented the warning in our logs, and in so doing, discharged any and all responsibility to you and your firm. Or do you disagree?"

Her eyebrows arched questioningly.

*Bitch certainly seems to get off on yanking my chain. Don't give her the satisfaction of seeing it get to you.*

"Yes, what you just said is true, but in this particular case, you seemed convinced it was Gold. In addition, we both know he's involved in a pen-test targeting my firm. Therefore, it makes sense for your team to remain on the lookout for him, if for no other reason than as a matter of general building integrity and security. Or do you disagree with me?"

She shook her head dismissively.

"Under normal circumstances this is true, we do operate

like that, but, in this particular case, you made it screaming clear to myself and my witness that you didn't believe it was him, so…"

She shrugged.

Inhaling deeply through flared nostrils, Mizrahi glanced up at the recessed fluorescents, counted down three seconds, then: "For shit's sake, Lorna, I *don't* know that it *wasn't* him, so for the integrity of our building and our law offices please take this threat seriously."

He hated to beg, but he saw no alternative.

After a slow, pensive nod, she said: "I'll take it under advisement."

# CHAPTER 40

## Seattle

ARNOLD ROCKED FORWARD to peer through the gap along the side of the stall door.

*Who just entered? The guard? Crap, too late.*

Whoever it was remained out of his limited field of view, but he heard the steps head toward the urinals. A moment later came a flush, then the splatter of running water, followed by the whine of an air dryer.

With a sigh of relief Arnold settled back onto the commode and tried to relax, but the need for hypervigilance was making that impossible. At least by closing his eyes with his back up against the cool white subway tiles, he could drift into a semi-meditative state for a few seconds. But anything longer than that was flat-out impossible.

In addition to gnawing constant angst over being discovered was a constant gut-churning dyspepsia over Rachael. She couldn't remain as their business manager. It would be...well, awkward. At least for him, it would. Even the optimistic side of him couldn't see any upside to keeping her.

*She had to go.*

But working through the mechanics of how to engineer that was growing uncomfortable. Worse yet, was knowing that dwelling on it in the middle of the creep was, like, totally insane. *Especially* now. Yet for some reason, he couldn't ignore it. Jesus!

*Discuss it with Prisha. Have her do it?*

He ruminated on that a bit.

*Yeah, that's exactly what he should do. After all, she was an associate. And this was supposed to be a partnership, right? And HR was a business issue, right? Most definitely.*

But this decision didn't do squat to alleviate his angst. On and on the rumination churned, the minutes creeping past one by one by one...

## 7:32 PM

Arnold's patience was worn wafer thin. Enough with the waiting. Time to begin the final ascent to the summit. At last.

He felt wonderful to stand and stretch, knowing he could finally leave this freaking stall in this freaking men's room. Time for final preparations.

He inspected the rucksack contents. All items present and accounted for.

*Check.*

Over his shoulder it went.

He verified that the color-coded key cards were in the correct pockets, ready to go.

*Check.*

He assessed his ability to grab the correct card with minimal concentration.

*Check.*

Mentally reviewed the other required items.

*Check.*

"Uncle, sit-rep please," Arnold radioed Vihaan, who monitoring the firm's security video.

"Be advised, two offices in proximity to the target remain occupied. Also, Mizrahi and two other dudes appear to be randomly patrolling all the floors. Your call, boss."

"Roger that. Hold one."

Random foot patrols...an obvious issue that, somehow, he'd mind-farted. Even so, what did he think they would be doing? Especially after being tipped about his presence in the building. Jesus.

On the other hand, they could partially counteract this when Vihaan took down their security video. So far, Mizrahi remained oblivious to two key factors: that they were in the Larkin Standish networks, and he had no idea what the proof of penetration was.

Okay, what to do about the occupied offices? How late were those dudes planning to work? Certainly, not all night, right?

*Well, dunno...lawyers...*

He rocked his neck from side to side, loosening up kinks, the decision making his head feel full of lead. He did a few shoulder stretches, then pulled his right heel up to his butt, counted to thirty, repeated the process with his left heel.

*C'mon dude, stop fiddle-farting around. Shit!*

He radioed.

"We stick with the plan. Our most critical strategy is psych-ops, right? The more they wait, the more bored they'll be. We just need to keep ourselves amped."

*Yeah, easy to say.*

Someone keyed their microphone twice to acknowledge the message.

Although everyone should be on frequency, listening, Arnold radioed Prisha: "Mother, did you copy?"

"Roger. Holding on thirty-three."

The plan called for her to hang out in the women's toilet on the thirty-third floor just as he was doing in the men's room.

"Son?" Arnold asked Lopez, whose task was to keep ears on the firm's radio traffic.

"Nothing's going on, but from what little I've heard, our friend—Lopez was referring to Mizrahi—"sounds beaucoup stressed."

*Nice.*

Smiling, Arnold reluctantly slipped off his rucksack and set it back on the tile floor, bent over, touched the tip of his toes again, held that position for a slow count to thirty. With a resigned sigh, he settled back onto the commode.

# CHAPTER 41

## Seattle—7:53 PM

ARNOLD FINISHED OFF a dark chocolate and almond Kind bar, then washed it down with the last of his bottled water. Checked his watch. Just shy of nine PM. Getting there. Slowly. Painfully slowly.

He opened the stall door and dashed to the sink to partially fill his water bottle and to rinse his fingers, wiping them on his jeans rather than activate the noisy blow-dryer on the off-chance a guard might be nearby on a routine patrol. He wasn't sure how much more of the mind-numbing waiting he could tolerate. Certainly much of the fantasized pen-testing glamor was being sullied by this gig.

Mizrahi barged through Lorna Glass' open office doorway.

"I want your staff to conduct a detailed sweep of the two floors above and below us while we sweep our floors. This is the only way we'll know those assholes aren't an imminent threat."

Glass typically left for home at five PM sharp, but this evening she was hanging around to personally man the fort. A concession she'd agreed to only after finally squeezing a molar-gnashing admission from Mizrahi that she *was* correct that the

235

suspicious figure caught on camera *was* Arnold Gold.

She considered his demand for all of half a second before shaking her head.

"No can do, Itzhak."

Mizrahi reared back.

"Why not?"

She chortled.

"Oh, for Christ sake, man. You know the answer to that, so why bother to even ask? No way am I about to neglect this entire building just because you may have a security test on your hands."

*Oh, it's Miss Hight and Fucking Mighty, now.*

Mizrahi rubbed the stubble on his right cheek, rethinking his approach to securing her help. It would be tough, but if you didn't ask...

"I understand your concern, but I guarantee that we'll all feel more comfortable about this...this situation...if we combine forces for one concerted sweep through those floors." He paused, then added "If we do that and come up clean, well then, I'll feel good enough to stop pestering you."

This last was said with a note of forced levity, a ploy he reserved for special situations like this. Ha-ha-ha.

To his surprise, she nodded.

"Alright, sold. I'll do it. But on *one* condition, and one condition only. I want it unequivocally agreed that once this special sweep wraps up, my crew will resume *routine* duties. This means no more special manpower-consuming sorties. In other words, this will be it for going out of our way to help you do your job. Is this clear enough, Itzhak?" Her eyes drilled him. "I really don't want to have to repeat it an hour from now, or anytime else tonight."

Shocked at the harshness of her reply, Mizrahi found himself facing a knotty dilemma: she just agreed to help him search the area of concern, which was good.

*But should he exercise this one-time option now or hold it in reserve until later?*

Tough question. Just how strong was his conviction that Gold *was* hiding in the building? Strong enough to burn up this one-time offer now? Huh. The more he considered it, the less sure he became. He didn't even know, for example, if Gold had been awarded the contract.

Fact was, he didn't have one concrete confirmatory scrap of evidence to support his assumption. What's more, his only evidence that Gold might be in the building was a gutfeel; a gutfeel based on two seconds of inconclusive CCTV footage. Simply put, he didn't have hard-core objective proof to support his belief. Was he really willing to squander this one opportunity *now?*

Mizrahi's tongue flicked over his lips.

"Perhaps it might be prudent to delay this until we have further evidence of Gold's whereabouts...but I still believe it's very worrisome that no one's seen him exit the building."

"You absolutely sure you want to hold off?" she asked, eying him askance. "You were so gung-ho just a second ago."

*Go ahead, throw her a bone.*

"Considering our limited resources," he said, purposely using the plural possessive, "you may be right to hold off *for a while*, at least. Let's see what shakes out in the next couple hours. Agreed?" Without waiting for an answer, he pointedly pushed up his sleeve to glimpse his watch. "We're heading into the quiet hours now. If Gold's planning to move—which I have no doubt he is—it'll be soon."

"Okay..." Glass said with an unsettling questioning shade, as if possessing proprietary information.

Mizrahi didn't like the sound of that. It made him uneasy.

He stormed from her office.

A half hour later, Mizrahi was back in her doorway, his growing edginess now hovering gravely close to the tipping point.

"I say we sweep those floors *now*," he insisted.

Glass studied his face for a moment, nodded twice, as if resolving a conflict.

"Your call, Itzhak," then was out of her chair, moving around the desk, radio in hand. "I'll accompany my team."

He fell in behind her, suddenly having trouble keeping up, her eagerness layered on her unsettling tone, all of which triggered an abrupt jolt of buyer's remorse.

*Had he jumped the gun on this, his one shot?*

"Father," Lopez radioed, "building security's conducting a sweep of the floors directly above and below the firm, *including* the toilets."

*Here we go. Showtime.*

Arnold radioed.

"Mother, drop down to twenty-nine. I'll head up to fifty-four. Hold there. Copy?"

"Roger that, but don't forget, security is undoubtedly all over any key card activity, especially this time of night, so odds are they'll be looking at *any* usage. What I'm saying: if forced to use a card *other* than our planned attack, just make damn sure it's one from the other firm. Copy?"

"Roger that. Try to stay within your stairwell. Doubt they have the manpower to sweep the floors *and* stairwells."

During the entire operation, their plan called for Prisha to operate within the south stairwell while Arnold worked the north shaft.

"Okay team," Arnold said, "time to rock and roll. Everyone still have solid copy?"

After receiving confirmation from them, he started up the stairs, two at a time, the exertion incredibly invigorating after so many long hours cooped up in a freaking toilet stall.

*Well, there was also the adrenaline surge from knowing they were finally underway, that all their chips were now on the table.*

Hit the fifty-fourth-floor landing, pulled out the first key card, checked that it was the right one. He radioed.

"Mother, all set?"

"Roger that."

"Okay, here I go."

He swiped the key card over the magnetic sensor and watched the red LED wink green. The lock disengaged.

*In for a penny…*

He opened the door an inch, counted off two seconds, shut it, then stood perfectly still on the landing, listening. Stone silence. Then he climbed again, up two more flights to fifty-six, where he repeated the process of opening and closing the fire door with the same key card.

He stood, gripping the purple tubular railing, leaning into the center of the shaft, head cocked slightly, scanning for the slightest noise echoing along the concrete shaft.

He heard nothing but a reverberating dead silence.

# CHAPTER 42

## Seattle

MIZRAHI'S EARBUD CAME alive with Glass' voice.

"Itzhak, the north stairwell door on fifty-four was opened just now."

He was in the firm's thirty-fifth- floor security office, fidgeting, shifting nervously leg to leg, peering over the shoulder of his seated IT technician, intently watching a CCTV monitor as it cycled routinely through two-second segments of pans of the firm's empty halls.

The tech could stop on a particular camera if something caught his attention, but so far nothing had.

*Huh. Did an employee step out onto a landing? This time of night? A smoke break?*

Although the building was supposed to be smoke-free, tamped-out butts commonly littered an occasional landing during routine inspections. A couple of months ago, he'd noticed an empty red Folgers can serving as an ashtray.

*Or was this Gold's opening move?*

Mizrahi never even thought twice about how Gold might get his hands on a key card. For hackers, stealing restricted-area access was *de rigueur.*

"Okay...." His mind was now accelerating through

multiple scenarios, questions ricocheting inside in rapid-fire sequence. None good. "Got an ID on it?" he radioed back, referring to the key card.

Her answer was immediate: "Emerald Town Insurance."

Thought about this.

"Is there such a firm in the building?"

"There is."

*Huh. Still…*

"Have your team investigate it, Lorna."

A noticeable pause, followed by: "No, Itzhak, I suggest *your* team investigate it. At the moment, our hands are busy keeping tabs on this entire building. You, on the other hand, are responsible for only six floors. It's a simple matter of manpower."

He silently mouthed *Fuck you* before calmly speaking.

"I would if I *could,* Lorna, but apparently you forget that our key cards can only access our floors."

*So there!*

Silence.

"*Fine,*" she said grudgingly. "But keep in mind, we're not at your disposal this entire friggin' night. You shot your wad earlier this evening. My advice? Stay on top of things."

"Thank you," he said as calmly as possible through gritted teeth.

*Yeah, it was Gold.*

He started picking in his left nostril with the nail of his little finger, a nervous habit of his since childhood.

# CHAPTER 43

## Seattle

STANDING ON THE stairs up from the fifty-sixth-floor landing, Arnold leaned over the rail to monitor the barely audible footsteps and muffled voices echoing up the concrete shaft from below.

The good news: they weren't growing louder.

He fought an almost overwhelming urge to flee higher but didn't dare move for fear that the slightest noise might alert that person(s) of his presence. His thundering heart was already masking the muffled voice. He began to purposefully inhale slowly to calm himself and to keep from hyperventilating.

He was dying to know what was going on in the south stairwell, but for obvious reasons he didn't dare whisper unless it was a flat-out grab-your-ass-and-bail emergency. He swiped sweat beads from his forehead with the back of his hand, glanced at the glistening moisture, then blotted it on the thighs of his 501s.

Moments later, the voices vanished, leaving him in creepy absolute silence. He blew a soft sigh of relief.

*Was this a trick?*

He stayed motionless, head angled, listening straight down the shaft.

*Nope, nada.*

Five minutes later Lopez's voice popped up in his right ear.

"A sweep of floor fifty-four turned up nothing."

Arnold double-clicked his mic to acknowledge the message, his jaw muscles still taught. At this point they were restricting voice traffic to essential transmissions only, to prevent accidentally doubling on each other. From here on out, the caper hinged on flawless communication.

"Am thrilled to report," Lopez added, "that Ms. Glass isn't particularly enamored with der Fuehrer Mizrahi."

After a muted chuckle, Arnold whispered.

"Good. Stay on plan."

# CHAPTER 44

## Seattle

AFTER SLOWLY CREEPING back down to fifty-four, Arnold paused to listen again. After ten seconds of eerie echoing silence, he carefully removed the same key card as earlier, double-checked that it was the correct one, then swiped it over the reader.

The lock released and he repeated the process.

*Perfect.*

Then he was moving again, streaking two stairs at a time back up to the fifty-sixth landing, where he stopped to listen for a reaction.

"Itzhak, be advised of another entry, north stairwell, floor fifty-four. Same door. Same ID as last time."

Glass' radioed words caught him in the middle of another routine sweep of their offices. He halted abreast of the elevator doors, mulling over this latest news. Although he'd been excluded from subsequent pen-test negotiations, he reasoned that if Gold's team *was* now under contract, the highest-probability confirmation targets would probably be the room containing their network servers (which he knew Gold had seen) or Collier's office.

Of the two, he believed Collier's office was the more likely target, which was why he was focusing his patrols nearby.

"Itzhak, did you copy?"

"Yeah, yeah, I did," he radioed with a dismissive wave before returning to the issue of the door openings.

*Were they for real, or just one of Gold's ploys? Risk deploying an asset to check it out, or hold fast?*

A moment later he radioed.

"Glass, I think it's a fair assumption that those entries are probing activity associated with the pen-test. Agreed?"

After a brief hesitation, "Agreed."

*But she didn't sound like she gave a rat's ass.*

Mizrahi dug his finger into his nose and inhaled deeply.

*Man, could she piss him off!*

"Fine. Look, whatever. The point is, we have every reason to believe we now have pen-testers inside our building, and I don't think there's any controversy about their target. For the record, I'm officially asking your team to help us apprehend them. Do you copy this request?"

"Record? There *is* no fucking record. Get it? Oh, and by the way, we *are* helping you. We *have* been helping you since we reported that first sighting, the one in the lobby. *That* was us helping you. But all you did rant was and rage about it, after which, let me remind you, you finally had to concede that I was right. And now? We give you additional information and what the hell do you want to do about it? Huh? Argue some more. But this is beside the point. The point is, we *are* assisting. We're monitoring CCTV coverage of the building in addition to conducting routine foot patrols. I even added one overtime person tonight. We can only do what we can do. I just can't fathom why you refuse to acknowledge this."

"I understand all that. But if you agree that a security test is underway, why can't you concentrate your assets on floors adjacent to ours? Why spread them out throughout the building?"

"Jesus fucking Christ, Itzhak, listen to me, and listen carefully because I. WILL. NOT. Repeat this again: I simply can't commit resources to assist you just because you may have hackers evaluating your security. Boom! And that, sir, IS FINAL. Your security is your job. I suggest you take care of it and keep me advised."

*Cunt.*

## 9:05 PM

Arnold checked his watch. Again. He'd been sitting on the switchback between fifty-four and fifty-five long enough now. Time to press on.

He whispered, "Status on thirty-five?"

Lopez answered, "Perfect timing, dude. One occupant just turned off his lights and is waiting for the elevator. But the bad news is that I think I see an increase in random security patrols on that floor, but it's only my impression."

Arnold massaged the back of his neck, weighing the pros and cons of continuing now or waiting.

"Only Mizrahi's dudes, right? Or are there others?"

"Just Mizrahi's."

"At the expense of the other floors?"

Lopez hesitated.

"Again, can't say for sure, but that's my impression."

*Hmmm. Had Mizrahi somehow discovered what he and Collier had agreed on for proof of penetration? Or was this just a lucky guess? Was Lopez's impression accurate?*

He thought about that.

*Naw, the lawyer learned from his initial mistake and wouldn't have shared that information with the security committee.*

Arnold believed Collier was dead serious about obtaining an accurate security assessment. So yeah, the more he thought about it, the more he believed that Mizrahi was simply making an insanely lucky guesstimate. *If* in fact, he really was concentrating their patrols on that floor.

Arnold whispered, "Mother, reposition to forty. Continue as planned."

"On my way."

Arnold crept down to forty, putting him and Prisha on the same level but in opposite stairwells. Once in position, he listened hard.

Only dead silence.

He waited sixty seconds more before whispering.

"In position?"

Prisha: "Roger."

Arnold wiped his sweaty palms against his thighs, sucked a long deep breath, hoping to calm his banjo-string nerves. From here on out, success relied on perfectly synchronous timing with a dash of good luck. Each move needed flawless execution if they were to produce the intended effect.

He whispered, "Son, status report?"

"Clear," came the crisp monosyllabic reply.

One word, loaded with anxiety.

"Ready, Mother?"

She broke squelch twice to indicate yes.

Arnold nervously checked the time, but it didn't even register. He realized what he'd just done and shook his head.

*Calm the fuck down, dude.*

He whispered, "On the count of three..." while readying his key card.

"One...two...three!"

He swiped the card across the sensor as Prisha was—hopefully—doing the same, unlocking the north and south stairwell doors on the same floor in synchrony.

The moment the LED flashed green, Arnold was off, climbing two stairs at a pop, all the way to floor forty-one. There, he halted on the landing, with a white-knuckle grip on the railing, as he scanned the heavy dusty silence of the long vertical rectangular shaft.

He realized he was holding his breath, so he inhaled deeply

through his nose.

"Itzhak," Glass radioed, "be advised that *both* north and south stairway doors were opened *simultaneously* on forty with the same—I repeat—*same* key card."

Mizrahi was standing dead center in Collier's office, having just checked his iPhone images from this afternoon, comparing them to the room's present appearance. No, nothing appeared to have been moved or misplaced. Good. Gold hadn't made it here yet. *If, in fact, this is his target.*

He opened his mouth to yell that opening both doors simultaneously was impossible but hit his tongue brakes before he sounded like a fucking idiot. Gold. Had to be. That little shithead. Of course. Steal a card, clone a copy or two. Put two of his people in the stairwells and coordinate by cell phone. No problem. A perfect example of a psych-ops mindfuck.

"*Now* are you convinced Gold's in the building, Glass?" he said, unable to smooth a biting sarcastic edge from his voice.

"For shitsake, Itzhak, point made."

Finally. He'd been correct from the start. She, on the other hand, was just stupid.

Warmed by her concession, smiling broadly: "Do you also agree there is at least two of them?"

"What the fuck's your point, Itzhak?"

"My *point*, Glass. Is that this forces us to be more aggressive now. Which is precisely the point I've been trying to make all night."

"Go ahead, knock yourself out, but we've been down this road too many times already."

*Yeah, right. You two-faced bitch.*

Now what? Sweep both stairwells again?

For what? They would be long gone from that landing by now. Besides, his team didn't have the manpower to play cat-and-mouse with them in addition to guarding the offices. And no way would Glass agree to redeploy her precious manpower from her exalted position of Lorna-the-Protector of the entire fucking building. In fact, she was probably getting off, fantasizing over the stress this was causing him. However, he would be remiss to not check the fortieth-floor landing.

Hold on. On second thought, now that she was a believer, maybe she would help by conducting another sweep. He knew he was pushing his luck with another manpower request, so he decided to use a more conciliatory tone.

Keying his radio.

"Is it possible for someone from your team to check floor forty for me? I'd sincerely appreciate it."

No immediate response.

Finally: "Make you a deal, Itzhak: we'll sweep stairwells thirty up to thirty-four if your team clears your floors *including* the corresponding landings. In addition, I'll reposition my two lobby guards closer to the elevator alcoves. I just requested they work overtime. This is the best I can do for you, man. Copy?"

*Closer to the elevators? For what, to kiss those fuckers goodnight as they were leaving the building?*

He nodded, satisfied that she finally understood the stakes involved and had done something.

"Thank you, Lorna. I mean that."

And he did.

# CHAPTER 45

## Seattle

"GOT SOME BREAKING NEWS," Lopez radioed to the group. He summarized the hot-off-the-press over-the-air negotiations between Glass and Mizrahi.

Arnold asked the group: "What do you think, stay on plan or wait until after the search?"

"Great question," Prisha said, but left it at that.

This would be his call.

Arnold ran through the ramifications. The main objective of their guerilla warfare prod-and-vanish strategy was to fatigue, anger, frustrate, and disorganize coordination between the two security teams to improve the odds of success. Problem was, there was no way to know if their strategy was succeeding. But the tactic still seemed logical enough to not abandon it.

*Just keep the faith, dude. The plan's solid. Well, hell, in for a penny...*

"Stick with the plan. Standby."

"Roger," Prisha responded.

Arnold kept an eye on his watch while mentally visualizing the time it would likely take for Security to patrol the relevant floors, including checking offices, restrooms, etc. Then added three minutes, just for drill.

*Okay, time...*

Then, just to be super cautious, he tacked on an additional three more minutes: watching the red second hand creep at what had to be an accurate yet annoyingly slow speed. His attention bounced from the watch face to the insidious stillness of the concrete shaft; back and forth like a tennis match. As the second hand finally completed the third revolution, he felt a flush of satisfaction for having exercised patience, for having resisted the urge to just push ahead with the plan so they could get on with it. Patience had never been his strong trait.

A quick glance up and down the flights, then a deep breath...okay, time. The plan called for them to creep back down to the thirty-sixth floor now.

He radioed, "Ready?"

"Roger," Prisha answered eagerly.

"Okay, go."

Cautiously he started down, hand sliding over the cool purple railing, ears alert for the slightest sound, his heartbeat galloping again. He reached thirty-six without incident, then waited an additional minute to ensure that Prisha was positioned. And besides, there was no need to push it.

Another glance at his watch, more out of habit than necessity.

He slipped off his rucksack and dropped to his right knee. One by one, he removed the needed items, placing them on the unfinished concrete: a roll of fifty-pound-test fishing leader and his red, five-bladed Swiss Army knife, which he opened to the biggest blade before setting it next to the leader.

He studied the two items for a moment, knowing something was missing.

*What?*

*Ah, yes: Scotch tape.*

He rummaged through the rucksack, found it, set it next to the leader, reran the checklist. Leader, knife, tape. That it?

*Oh, shit, the key card.*

Yikes, how could he forget such a crucial item? This rocked his confidence.

He set out the key card and rubbed his tingling palms together. He squinted at the door, then back to the assembled material.

He reached for the key card when—

*Thump.*

*What?*

Head cocked, he scoured the stillness for the sound.

There! Barely audible. Reverberating up the concrete and steel shaft. If not for such absolute stillness...

He zeroed every available inner-ear cell into the heavy echoing silence, searching for the slightest reverberation...

There! Again.

Scarcely perceptible but distinctly detectible. Enough to register. Enough to catalog? Perhaps.

*What? A footstep?*

Yeah, that's exactly what it was.

Heart jackhammering his sternum now, he realized he was hyperventilating, so closed his mouth and held his breath. Carefully, slowly, he stood, took hold of the handrail, leaned only far enough over to sight straight down the slit left between flights of zig zagging purple railings, down through the bare concrete shaft.

*Holy shit.*

A hand on the railing was sliding slowly, relentlessly upwards, coming toward him. What, three landings down?

Whoa. Then he could make out faint labored breathing and a muffled repetitive clink; perhaps a wedding ring striking the metal rail? He pulled back, exhaled a wide mouth silent breath, inhaled another lungful. He could feel droplets of sweat dappling his forehead. He slipped off his glasses, and his palm wiped his face.

*Calm the fuck down, dude.*

Now what? He chanced another peek over the railing.

There was the hand again, but now only two and a half flights below him, laboriously plodding upward.

*Think.*

Okay, well, the dude was obviously slow and out of shape.

Time advantage, Arnold. But did he still have enough time?

Put his hand over his mouth, whispered, "In position?" hoping the throat mic would transmit his words.

Prisha double-clicked.

"The floor clear?" he asked, figuring Lopez would realize the question was for him.

"Yes, as of thirty seconds ago."

Arnold picked up the key card from the cement and whispered, "On three. One...two...three!"

The lock disengaged with a click loud enough to echo all the way to freaking Tacoma. Arnold pulled the heavy steel door open only far enough to keep it propped with his left foot, then started a mental stopwatch without a clue as to how long it might take for Mizrahi or his proxies to respond.

*Stop! Just stay on the point, dude.*

He started in, working fast as possible, methodical, zoning in intently on each move, figuring it was better to burn some extra seconds than to risk a stupid, time-wasting slip-up. He spooled off an estimated six feet of leader.

*Enough?*

*Well, shit, you'll find out.*

He used the Swiss Army knife to cut the length before pressing the back edge of the blade against his thigh, snapping it shut, then he crammed it in his rear pocket. Done. He tossed the roll of leader back into the rucksack, leaving only the Scotch tape and the rucksack on the concrete.

Forcing himself to work quickly yet precisely despite an increasingly tingling spine and spasming asshole, he looped one end of the translucent leader around the horizontal push bar as close to the lock as possible then secured it tightly in place with a double square knot.

He grabbed the Scotch tape, tore off a good three inches, and taped the knot securely to the bar. He burned an extra second running his thumb and forefinger around the tape to convince himself that it was stuck as tightly as possible to the metal, then he pulled the monofilament straight down until it was taut.

He inspected it to convince himself it was secure.

*Fifty pounds? Yeah, that's the rating.*

He pulled harder, tugging the push bar down until he saw the tang withdraw far enough into the latch to open the door. Perfect. The leader's fifty-pound rating appeared strong enough for what he needed...at least for this preliminary test. However, given the angle required and the edge of the metal door, the question was, would it break when it came to the actual act?

*Yo, dude, keep moving.*

Left hand now holding the door open, Arnold scooted back a few inches to carefully snake the leader under the bottom edge of the door, trying like hell to keep from abrading it against the metal. Jesus, his mental stopwatch was ticking louder and louder with each rapidly evaporating second, pumping more adrenaline into his arteries, pushing his anxiety off the freaking chart. A drop of sweat dripped off his nose.

*Where was the dude on the stairs?*

Forget him. Just focus on getting the job done.

A voice echoed from below, the words indistinguishable. Had to be the out-of-shape guard, probably receiving word that this door was just opened. Which might get him moving faster. If he could. But from the sound of it...

Shaking away the thought, he focused instead on methodically threading the leader along the bottom edge of the door toward the right corner, directly below the hinge. Once there, he pulled the remaining length up the side of the door until it was straight, then glanced at the Scotch tape...

*Aw, fuck.*

There he was, left hand holding the door, right hand

holding the leader, glancing from one hand to the other with no freaking idea how he was going to tape that sucker in place. The footsteps echoed louder and louder along with the ticking of his mental stopwatch.

*Jesus, dude, chance it.*

Still crouching, he shifted position enough to push his right toe against the leader to keep it from coiling back under the edge of the door the moment he let go. Then he carefully let the door reseat in the jamb. Not too bad, only a soft click.

*No turning back now. You're totally committed.*

The footsteps grew louder with each second.

With his left hand holding the leader in place, Arnold blindly reached behind him to where the Scotch tape should be, brushing it with a fingertip, then grabbing the spool. Holding one end of the tape in his teeth, he pulled off about four inches and tore it free.

He stuck the free end to the side of his cheek, allowing the rest to dangle while stretching the leader taught along the side of the door as much as possible. He wanted to smooth out the strand but he was pushing his luck to the absolute limit as it was, so he ended up just slapping the tape over the last couple of inches, securing it an inch or two from the bottom hinge.

He stood, giving it a final glance from a more normal perspective. No question you could see it, but only if you knew exactly what you were looking for. But a passing glance? A person would probably go right past. Especially if said person was looking for an intruder.

Well, hell, no time to try camouflaging the sucker anyway. Even if he had a clue how to do that. Which he didn't.

Still fighting an anus puckering urge to streak up the stairs, he dumped the roll of tape in the rucksack and slung it over his shoulder.

He whispered, "Go!"

Then he was jetting stealthily up toward forty-one, fast as his legs could transport him. No way that huffer struggling up the stairs had a prayer of catching him now, not if his breathing was any indication of his fitness.

Assuming, of course, that one of Mizrahi's crew didn't come through the door on the next landing…

# CHAPTER 46

## Seattle

"MOTHERFUCKER!" MIZRAHI BELLOWED, his open palm slamming the desktop with a deafening *bam*, rippling the oil slick of stale black coffee in the last half-inch of his stained Seahawks mug.

He and two team members were just returning to his office after wrapping up yet another methodical sweep of the thirty-fifth floor, entering each conference room and office and flicking on the recessed ceiling lights, verifying that no one was crouched in shadows. That was when Glass had radioed that, once again, both stairwell doors were opened simultaneously with the same key card.

*Goddamn Gold. Clearly, that little turd was trying to skull-fuck him.*

And successfully, too.

Mizrahi's head felt dangerously close to exploding, his blood pressure flirting the limits of blowing an artery. Exasperated and annoyed, and for lack of any better way to express his frustration, he just simply shook his head. Fuckers.

Both of his security guys stood fidgeting in place, eying him warily, awaiting instructions, everyone now acutely aware that Gold had just given both security services the middle finger salute.

Eying them, Mizrahi barked, "What?" as an unequivocal challenge.

Flashing a wide-eye *I'm innocent* expression, John Nusbaum muttered, "Didn't say a word, Sir."

"Bullshit. You didn't have to." Then, stabbing a finger at him: "You were thinking it. Stay on task, Nusbaum."

Nusbaum shuffled in place, mumbled, "Want me to go down, check it out?"

Mizrahi rolled that around a moment, deciding...

"No. I'll do it. You two move up to the next floor and sweep it but let me know *immediately* if anything, I repeat, anything, looks suspicious. Understood?"

"Loud and clear."

Nusbaum started for the south stairwell, his partner falling in beside him as Mizrahi moved into the hall just outside his office.

*Elevator? Stairs?*

The stairs would be quicker, plus it would eliminate any sound as the elevator arrived.

After pushing into the north stairwell, he quickly descended to thirty-six, stopped on the landing to listen and survey the area. Not a soul in sight. Eerily silent. Was Gold nearby? Waiting, listening, sensing? He didn't pick up the presence of another person, which didn't surprise him. Really hadn't expected to find anyone. Not this long afterwards.

He walked down to thirty-four and unlocked then pulled open the heavy steel fire door to the Larkin Standish reception lobby. Holding it open, he paused to survey the immediate area. No, didn't see anything suspicious, but...he began to experience a vaporous intuition that someone had entered here recently.

He turned and carefully let the fire door seat as quietly as possible on the off chance that Gold, or one of his team was close enough to hear its muted click. Then he stood still, studying the empty hallway, listening intently for unusual sounds. Nothing. He went back up to thirty-six, still convinced this was Gold's target.

The lights in the one office remained on, but the others were now uniformly dark, leaving only hall lights that cast a decidedly ghost-town feel over the deserted corridors and offices. He tilted his head back slightly to sniff the air but registered nothing more than the musky odor of vacuum cleaner dust. Still, couldn't shake the feeling of a pen-tester nearby. On this floor? Out on the stairs? Where?

He glided silently and quickly straight to Webster Collier's office, flicked on the lights to scan the room. Nope. Not here. And there was no real hiding place either except for...he moved to the desk, leaned over to check the footwell. Empty.

*Huh.*

Cocked his head and sniffed again like a preying wolf.

Nothing.

Disappointing. But...he reminded himself, Collier's office was just a guess as to what the target might be.

*Still...*

In the hall again, he rescanned the empty hall in both directions. Nothing other than the one lit office.

*Huh. Could it be?*

He walked to the doorway to look inside.

A junior partner must've caught the motion, for she glanced up from her screen, fingers poised over the keyboard.

"May I help you, Itzhak?"

"How long have you been at your desk?"

"All evening. Why?" she asked, a shrug in her voice.

"Have you seen or heard any activity over the past ten minutes or so?"

Her posture straightened in the ergonomic desk chair, a concerned expression suddenly painting her face. She began studying him with probing eyes.

"No, why?" A questioning tilt of the head. "Is there a

problem?"

He flipped a trivializing wave.

"Not really."

"Not really? Yet, you asked it with concern all over your face, so let me ask again: *Is* there a problem, Itzhak?" as if she knew he'd not been honest.

Mizrahi weighed his answer.

"Not if you haven't heard or seen anyone."

He watched her study him a moment longer before reluctantly returning to her monitor, then immediately back to him.

"Hold on a moment, Itzhak. Let me rephrase this: *should* I be concerned?"

*Tell her? Why not?*

At this point any additional eyes and ears working for him would be an advantage. He hesitated, making it seem as if he was seriously debating what to confess, but in reality, was actually trying to recall her name.

"Officially, I've been instructed to say everything's fine," he said in forced sincerity, then cast a quick glance into the hall behind him as if wary of an eavesdropper. He turned to her again with his best conspiratorial concerned-for-the-firm's-welfare expression, lowered his voice in mock discretion. "Just between you and me, Building Security believes we—meaning our firm—has a vulnerability test underway and are hoping to shut it down before it goes any further."

He even threw in a keep-it-to-yourself wink for a brilliant touch of authenticity.

She nodded with what appeared to be relief, then muttered, "I'll let you know straightaway if I hear or see anything." She returned to her keyboard and monitor.

"Thank you."

Back in the hallway he glanced right, then left, strategizing his next move. Gold could be hunkered down in one nearby, waiting patiently for them to drop their guard. If, in fact,

Collier's office was the target.

Or...Gold and a minion could very well be out there in the stairwells, relying on their bush-league simultaneous-door trick to lull him into lowering his guard. And since Gold's little game required two team members, capturing either one would be enough to shut down the test. And now that he thought about it, what was to say that Gold didn't simply catch an elevator and shoot straight back to the lobby and on out of the building, planning to return and keep repeating this same trick night after night until they could simply walk in to finish the invasion?

*Huh.*

Yeah, for all he knew Gold was no longer even inside the building. But he seriously doubted this. He believed that Gold was being truthful when he let slip his need to return to Honolulu soon, so odds were, this was the pen-test.

Plus, to purposely allow himself to be caught on camera only to leave the building didn't fit with the sophomoric simultaneous-door diversions. No, the only way for tonight's events to make sense was for Gold to still be nearby, perhaps just on the other side of that door, waiting for an opportunity to strike. The longer he considered this twist, the more sense it made. In fact, the little shit could be hiding on one of their floors right now. Leaving him no option but to keep looking until Glass confirmed that Gold had left the building.

Back in the center of the main hall—the most central area on the floor—he radioed his security team instructions to continue their routine floor sweeps while he meticulously searched thirty-six again. He turned a slow three-sixty, critically looking for likely hiding spots.

Besides the various offices, there were also two lavatories and three utility closets, but the closets were inaccessible with his key cards. Had Gold been canny enough to swipe one? He considered this. No, his group wasn't experienced enough to come up with something that wily. He certainly wasn't suspicious enough to call for one of Glass's crew to come open the closets for him. And besides, he had the definite feeling she'd turn him down anyway.

Where to look now? He'd just checked the south stairwell and the one lighted office...why not go ahead and recheck the north stairwell and the two lavatories? Only then would he begin looking in the offices off the two side halls.

Mizrahi pushed open the heavy steel fire door into the north stairwell, crouched to thoroughly inspect the striker plate on the lock to see if, when opening the door, Gold had packed enough material in it to keep the lock from seating when the door shut. Nope, the lock wasn't jimmied or tampered with. Holding the door open with his left hand, he stepped onto the bare concrete landing and looked up and down but couldn't see further than the landing above and the stairs leading down. Certainly, neither Gold nor a team member was out here...

*At least not on this landing....*

Slowly, he studied the stairs. Nothing. Yet, he still sensed an unmistakable vibe. That the little turd *was* nearby. Standing perfectly motionless, still holding open the substantial steel door, he listened for the slightest telltale sound...but could hear only the faint distant hum of the HVAC. The more he absorbed the absolute stillness in the stairwell, the more he felt Gold's presence.

Stepping back into the main hall, he watched the door shut and lock automatically on its own. But just to make sure, he pushed on the door. Nope. Solidly locked. It hadn't been jimmied. For a long moment he stared at the door, convinced there was more to the simultaneous door opening trick than just psych-ops. But for the life of him, couldn't decide what that might be.

Finally, reluctantly, he turned to inspect the offices bordering the halls to this floor.

# CHAPTER 47

## Seattle

AS ARNOLD CREPT stealthily up another flight toward fifty-one, he heard the steel fire door bang against its hinges somewhere below. On second thought, *just* below. He froze in place, every sense hyper-alert.

*Guard or employee?*

Stupid question. This time of night, it had to be a guard. No way to know how many floors down, but as loud as it was, it was close.

*Did they notice the fishing leader tied around the push bar?*

Jesus, if so, the entire caper was probably doing the backstroke straight down the drain.

His heart—which had been using his sternum as a conga drum—was now hammering like a freaking piledriver, the patina of sweat from scurrying up and down stairs morphing into heavy droplets.

Fuuuuuuck!

Eyes scrunched tight, he scoured the mausoleum stillness for telltale sounds or other hints of what was happening on the landing below. But the only perception he could pick up from the silent still void was a vague scent of concrete dust. Still…he swore he could feel body heat radiating up from the flight immediately below, as impossible as that was…

Opened his eyes and glanced down the stairs, the stark LED brilliance reflecting off the walls forcing him to squint. Once adapted, he saw nothing but concrete, stairs, and ugly purple. Yet he swore he could still sense body heat. He imagined a guard on the landing below, motionless, staring upward to where he stood, listening, reacting to exactly the same perverted, imagined sensation.

Seconds passed. Followed by more seconds…

Finally he caught a very faint metallic *click*, then more eerie silence.

Did the guard actually retreat into the hall, or was he still on the landing, lying in wait like a jungle predator laying a trap?

*Chance a peek over the railing at the narrow rectangle between the zig-zagging stairway or continue to creep up?*

Arnold pictured himself cautiously leaning over the railing, only to come face to face with a guard doing exactly the same thing.

*Jesus. Get a freaking grip! Just keep on trucking…*

Slowly, deliberately, he raised his right foot to the next step up, cautiously shifting his weight onto it, then did the same with his left, repeating the process again and again, gradually creeping up the flight while maintaining an intense focus on the stillness, cautioning himself to not drop his guard.

On the landing of fifty-one, he waited, listening.

Concrete silence.

In a barely audible whisper, he said: "Mother, sit-rep?"

"Holding, south stairwell, forty-one," she whispered back.

"Copy."

"Be advised," Lopez reported, "not all is copacetic with the troops."

"How so?" Arnold's interest piqued.

"There's some friction zapping back and forth between security teams."

Although he hadn't planned on this occurring—on account

of it simply didn't dawn on him—if that ended up a byproduct of their psych-ops, well hell, he wasn't going to complain or beat himself up over it.

He whispered, "Totally tubular, dude. Okay, we wait them out now."

Three minutes later, standing with his back to the elevators, having personally inspected every goddamn office on the floor, Mizrahi radioed Glass.

"Hey Lorna, we just cleared all our floors. Again. You have anything?"

No reply. Which pissed him off even more.

Eventually, she radioed, "Glad you checked in, because I was about to let you know I'm ready to shove off and do not— I repeat—*do not* want to be disturbed by you under any circumstance until I'm back at work. Not even if Gold commits seppuku in the middle of Collier's office. Got it? I fully intend to kick back with a frosty twelve-ounce Rainer and ask my wife about her day...and for once, actually listen. I just turned over the reins to D'Angelo, our regular three-to-eleven shift super. You know him, don't you? Well, he's in command as of now." After a beat, she added, "Don't worry, he'll notify me if I need to know about anything, but I'll be accepting calls only from him."

Mizrahi gnashed his molars again. The bitch was shoving her total disregard for his situation right up his nose. She, Brittney Griner, and the whole perverse gaggle of muff divers—

"You're getting royally boned up the tailpipe on this one, Itzhak," she added with a chuckle.

*Fuck you, bitch.*

He took his thumb off the transmit switch and holstered his radio.

*We'll see how you feel about it, next time, bitch, when I sit on intel. We'll see how smug and arrogant you are.*

*Focus.*

*What else can I do now?*

Once again, he considered updating Collier about the attack in progress. But again, he decided that doing so risked too much blowback should he become suspicious about his source of information, especially knowing that it'd been a mistake to include him in the first pen-test discussions. No, it would probably be best to wait and say nothing until the dust settled, when he was assured of tonight's outcome.

What next? Perhaps thirty-five again? The server room?

*Aw, yes, the server room.*

That could just as easily be Gold's target. Good, he once again had direction. A glance at the elevator, then the stairwells.

Having just inspected the north stairwell, why not walk up the south one for the sake of thoroughness?

# CHAPTER 48

## Seattle

ARNOLD'S WATCH SHOWED 1:00 AM straight-up.

*Jesus, it took long enough.*

He whispered, "Mother, what's your take?"

"All quiet on the southern front."

Arnold cast an anxious glance up and down the stairwell; a nervous habit acquired since he'd settled in on this landing. No movement. No sound except an episodic, barely perceptible rumble coming through the concrete, possibly from the elevator shafts. He believed his hearing was increasingly acute in such mortuary stillness. If the rumbles were actually from elevators, they seemed to be growing less frequent. Which was good news, right? Probably.

*What now? Wait? If so, for how long?*

Or proceed?

He radioed: "Son, status report?"

"I'm hearing nothing but routine traffic from building security and nothing between them and Mizrahi. Those dudes have been, like, radio silent."

Arnold massaged his temples, trying to decide: this good or bad?

267

*Had to be good, right?*

Or was Mizrahi trying to lull him into a false sense of security?

"Uncle, status report?"

"That office's still occupied. A cleaning crew's just starting in on thirty-four."

*Well hell, either go for it now or wait until the cleaning crew finishes thirty-five.*

Blew another breath.

*Ah hell, showtime.*

Arnold began creeping back down to the thirty-sixth floor.

# CHAPTER 49

## Seattle

ARNOLD MOVED SWIFTLY and silently onto the bare concrete of the thirty-sixth-floor landing, then stopped, left hand white-knuckling the tubular metal rail, scanning for sound. He caught only the soft regular swoosh of the pulse in his right ear. No smells other than the dry concrete and his own sweat. No change in the harsh LED lighting. Everything exactly as it had been his last time here.

*Too freaking good to be true, right?*

A chill at the base of his tailbone began to scintillate up and down his spine.

Spent another five seconds analyzing the same auditory void, boosting his confidence, convincing himself that no one else was out here on the stairwell.

He dropped into a crouch and inspected the fire door.

*Holy shit!*

The fishing leader appeared untouched, still there, taped to the door, looking exactly as he'd left it. He was in business. His heart was now galloping even faster.

Wait! What if Mizrahi noticed the jerry-rigged door opener and had stationed some three-hundred-and-fifty-pound ex-biker dude on the other side, just waiting for him to open it?

Okay, but what were the odds? Especially considering there'd been no radio traffic from Mizrahi about it? Had to be really damned low, right?

Yeah, probably, but...

He whispered, "Uncle, status report on thirty-six?"

"Crew's just about finished, looks like."

Okay, encouraging. Arnold removed his glasses, massaged the bridge of his nose, glanced at the leader again, thought about it a second time.

"And security?"

"Last seen heading into Mizrahi's office. Otherwise it's, like, radio-silence."

Kneeling, butt on his heels, Arnold leaned forward and carefully peeled back the scotch tape, freeing the leader from the door. He laid the clear filament on the bare concrete landing, left hand at the ready to stop it from curling up under the door the moment he let go. Aww crap: the moment he released it, it did just that. He grabbed it before it could make its way under the edge of the door. Hmm, hadn't counted on having to hold it like this. He thought about it, then shifted positions so that his left foot would pin it to the concrete, then he knelt on his right knee to free both hands.

Arnold slid his backpack off and dropped it beside his left foot. He pulled out a six-inch-long wood dowel into which he'd carved a shallow groove around its middle.

After wrapping two loops of leader around the shallow center groove he'd carved into the dowel, he tied a double square knot to secure it in place, making a weird looking, but functional handle. No longer concerned with the leader coiling under the door, he set the dowel on the concrete.

*Damned sweat!*

On his brow. On his hands. Dripping down his chest. Plus, he was breathing like a freaking sumo wrestler. He wiped both palms on his thighs, sucked in a slow deep calming breath, said a silent prayer that this next tricky part might actually work.

Taking particular care to prevent the edge of the steel door from abrading the leader, he threaded it to a spot he estimated was directly below its attachment to the push bar. Was the filament strong enough?

Kneeling on the concrete, butt on his heels again, he picked up the dowel in his right hand. Palm up, leader snaking between his middle and ring fingers, knuckles barely above the unfinished cement, he slowly began pulling straight back, the filament immediately snapping arrow straight.

Wait. Everything was completely wrong. Without easing up the tension the leader; he stopped pulling to assess his position. Well, to begin with, his knee was absolutely killing him, what with grinding into the cement like this. And this position was certifiably insane: no mechanical advantage at all, especially with his elbow already behind his shoulder, making it impossible to apply more force.

*Stupid, stupid, stupid.*

He backed up, this time with both knees on the hard concrete to distribute his weight so he could pull straight back with his arm instead of his back. Repositioned now, he began slowly increasing tension, the laser-straight fishing line screaming taut.

*Jesus, am I pulling on a concrete cinderblock?*

This triggered another thought: what if Mizrahi had noticed the leader and had removed it from the push bar and tied it to, say, the leg of a chair? Wouldn't that be the ultimate Fuck You! The image was so absurd that he laughed.

*Stop screwing around, dude. Focus.*

Cautiously, he increased the tension, and glimpsed his watch.

*Holy shit, the minutes were evaporating faster than alcohol on hot glass.*

"Yo, father, your man's starting to patrol thirty-six again."

*Fuck!*

Mizrahi was down the hall on the other side of the door.

By now, his knees, right arm and shoulder were a medieval choir of agony: once again. This wasn't working. He glanced at the death grip he had on the dowel, knuckles almost scraping the concrete, the bow-string leader straining. Shit, he was leaning too far forward, the angle awkward as hell, *and* one hundred percent of his weight was grinding his knees into the cement. Everything about his position was totally FUBAR.

There had to be a better way. But what? He didn't want to ease up on the leader again for fear of fatiguing it even further.

What if Mizrahi comes toward the door? Well, his only option would be to put the dowel on the concrete and sneak back up the stairs and pray that 1) he doesn't notice it if he opens the door; or 2) the leader will survive another go at pushing the extremes of its tensile strength. Or maybe he should just go for it now. Sure, hiding on the stairs would be the safer play. But how many times could the leader cycle through this much stress without snapping?

He had no clue. But really didn't want to find out.

"That office still occupied?" he whispered.

"It is…wait-wait, hold one…she's coming out, but with the lights still on…she's heading for…ah, man, just went to the ladies' room."

Arnold imagined hearing the filament screaming for mercy and he laughed a painful cynical snort. Then he thought: fuck it, just go for it. He took a deep breath and pulled harder.

With gritted teeth he pulled, his knees now the overriding voice in the chorus of pains.

Wait. Was that…*yes*, the faintest give.

Or was this just hope duping him?

Another glance at the leader, another prayer, pulling…a…bit harder…wait, definitely a hint of give.

A fractionally harder pull, then, *click*. The door unseated a half inch from the jamb.

Freaking *hallelujah*.

*Whoa, not so fast!*

He now faced a holy-shit dilemma: here he was, both hands clutching the dowel, straining at an ungodly angle to keep the door slightly ajar, his arm and back muscles nudging the point of collapse…so, how the hell could he keep this steel fire door from slamming shut the moment he grabbed for the handle? No clue. But he did know he couldn't hold this bad boy steady with one trembling arm, even for one second.

*Was it possible for one hand to keep it open long enough to grab the handle with the other? Was he fast enough?*

He'd better be, because he sure as hell couldn't maintain this tension for much longer.

His left hand shot out for the handle.

# CHAPTER 50

## Seattle

"D'ANGELO, YA MIGHT wanta come take a look at this," the security tech told D'Angelo Black, the supervisor who'd relieved Lorna Glass.

Black glanced from the scheduling spreadsheet on the glowing monitor to the tech in the doorway of the cramped office.

"Why, what you got?"

The tech wore a puzzled expression.

"There's some super-hinky shit going on in the north stairwell of thirty-six. Thought you might oughta take a look-see…you know, given the pen-test warning and all…"

Black's first impulse was to blow it off but didn't want to give the impression of neglecting his supervisory duties, so he nodded, stood, scooted around the corner of the desk, and began trailing the tech to the room where the CCTV footage—both live and recorded—was viewed on multiple high-def monitors.

On the night shift, their primary focus was the lobby, its exits, and the garage. Less so the stairwells and elevator alcoves. Especially the garage, where they occasionally had to evict a homeless squatter while trying also to keep a lid on vehicle break-ins—window smash-and-grabs—since the street entrances were never closed.

"There," the tech said, pointing to his workstation monitor.

D'Angelo bent over for a closer look at the screen, where a young male with a backpack was kneeling in front of the fire door, bent into what looked like a painfully awkward position. His first thought was that he was watching a homeless guy jerk off, then he realized that the guy was pulling something else. Wasn't having much luck with it, either.

"Ah, so..." the tech said, scratching the crown of his head, "whatcha want me to do about it? I mean, radio Itzhak? After all, that's his floor..."

D'Angelo checked his watch, anxious to return to the office and waste no more time on this.

"Very true, it is his floor."

The tech shuffled, looking down, checking out his own sneaks.

"Uh...that mean you *don't* want me to let Itzhak know?"

D'Angelo sighed, crossed his arms, peered over the tops of his glasses at him.

"Yo Stu, couple things. Mizrahi knows all about the pen-test in progress. He's been aware of it all day. Made a big stink about it to Ms. Glass. That's how come *we* know about it. According to her, he demanded she pull all our manpower to sweep several floors for him. Why she accommodated that prick's a total mystery, but you know how he gets. Me? Shit, I would've told that asshole to take a flying leap." He grinned. "Guess that's why she's boss and not me."

He was turning to walk back to the office when Stu asked, "So you're sayin' what, do nothin'?"

His tone smacked of amazement.

"Yeah, Stu, that's exactly what I'm telling you. Mizrahi's aware he's got a test underway. He's also the big kahuna in charge of their security." He pointed an index finger toward the ceiling. "A point he never ceases to emphasize. We assisted him once already tonight, which—in my opinion—was one more than he deserved. When Ms. Glass turned things over to me, she made it very clear that for the rest of the night he's on his own. After all, this is supposed to test *his* security, not ours."

# CHAPTER 51

## Seattle

ARNOLD'S FINGERS WRAPPED around the metal door handle a microsecond after his ears registered the solid steel click of the lock seating securely, but the significance didn't really sink in until the door refused to budge. Solidly locked. He tugged again as if willpower could overcome reality. Nope.

*Goddamnit.*

He was tugging on a firmly locked steel door.

Defeated, he dropped onto his butt to stare at his situation. Now what?

*Well, for one thing, dude, get up. Don't get caught sitting here on your ass.*

Lopez's voice materialized in his ear.

"Mizrahi's coming straight toward you, man. Get outta there. *Now.*"

*Shit.*

A frantic glance at the dowel; the clear fishing leader knotted securely around the center groove.

"*Arnold*, you copy? Dude's almost at the door now, man…"

Arnold surveyed his workspace. Other than the dowel and leader, the area was clean; all the evidence secured in his rucksack.

"*Dude*, you copy me, or *what?*" Lopez asked with growing urgency.

"Copy," Arnold whispered while scooting up the stairs two at a time, streaking toward the thirty-seventh-floor landing.

He was in mid-stride when he heard the all-too-familiar metallic snap of a latch. He froze, one foot on the next stair, the other on the step below. He slowly withdrew his hand from the railing in case Mizrahi glanced up. He covered his mouth and nose with his palm to muffle his labored breathing, and slowly leaned to the left to wedge his shoulder against the wall, moving as far from the tubular railing as possible, every ounce of concentration now on his ears.

Silence.

Slowly now, taking extreme care to make no sound, Arnold turned far enough to sight down this half of the zig-zag flight: nothing but railing, stairs, and concrete. And deathly silence. Good thing he'd made it around the switchback...

Click.

*Whoa. For real?*

Slowly, Arnold pivoted around to face down the stairs and listened but heard nothing but stone-cold silence.

He whispered, "Lopez, sit-rep?"

"He's back in the hall and doesn't look happy."

A surge of confidence flooded his body, and he took a slow tentative step down. Stopped. Listened again. More silence. Two more steps. Process repeated. Still nothing.

Arnold rounded the one-hundred-and-eighty-degree switchback, then trotted the zag portion of the flight to the empty landing. Amazingly, the door had simply pushed the dowel to the side as it swung open.

He stood, hands on hips, trying to decide how he would get the freaking door open., knowing that the longer he stood here dawdling, the higher the odds of Mizrahi discovering him. Especially with the freaking overhead bubble cam recording him. Speaking of which…WTF? He glanced up. Yep, there it was, right above him. Jesus. His stomach backflipped. He glanced back at the dowel, still trying to decide the optimal way to open that sucker.

Crouch, don't kneel. Those freaking knees simply couldn't tolerate that again. And move further back to gain some real leverage. The problem was deciding what angle would give him the best chance of catching the heavy door before it could shut. Although crouching wouldn't be as stable as kneeling, the higher angle would allow his hands to be closer to the handle.

Close enough to grab it in time?

This time he squatted and held the dowel with both hands. He took a moment to make sure his position felt stable, then started to pull slowly straight back, knuckles skimming concrete. The line went taut immediately. He continued slowly applying deliberate incrementing force, fearing that a sudden jerk would snap the filament. The new position was certainly proving to be more awkward balance-wise but it would definitely be a superior angle for The Move.

Then he heard the latch click. Ah, first problem solved.

Slowly, deliberately, he pulled the door a half inch from the jamb.

*Good enough? Hmmm…*

Wouldn't hurt to give himself a tad more space. He increased the tension, moving the door edge a half-inch more. Then, struggling to keep the door away from the jamb, he slowly raised both hands until the leader angled up almost forty-five degrees, which had the disadvantage of making it more difficult to keep the door from closing but shortening the space between his hands and the handle, this new position now forehead-thumping obvious.

*Ready?*

Go for it.

# CHAPTER 52

## Seattle

ARNOLD'S LEFT HAND shot out, catching the edge of the cold steel door a fractional second before it mated into the jamb. He tugged it open far enough to drop the dowel and grab the handle with his other hand, and to keep from scissoring his fingertips against the jamb.

He paused for a deep breath, then repositioned his hands to relieve the strain on his shoulder girdle. He shuffled his feet into a position that allowed him to wedge his left shoe between the door and jamb, now freeing his hands.

"Got it," he whispered, while glancing up at the black glass CCTV bubble and mugging a defiant grin, his mind flashing on the opening credits of *The Wire*, the one in which the kid shatters the surveillance camera lens with a dead-on rock throw.

Hhe heard a double-click response, probably Prisha.

"Mizrahi just left the office and is heading toward the south stairwell," Lopez radioed.

Arnold blew a sigh of relief. Maybe Mizrahi was heading up to one of the other floors.

Left foot still propping open the door, Arnold gritted his teeth and pushed up onto his sore right knee, put his ear to the opening and listened for telltale sounds. He heard only silence, confirming Vihaan's report of an empty hall.

He fished the Swiss Army knife from his back pocket, opened the blade, and cut the leader from the push bar. Wadding it into a ball, he crammed it and the dowel into his left rear pocket, then slipped the knife back into his right. He scoped out the narrow swath of hallway visible to him.

*Damnit.*

The lights were still on in that one office.

He whispered, "Has that office worker returned yet?"

"Nope," Lopez answered. "She's still in there."

Then, Arnold was up, opening the fire door just far enough to squeeze into the hall, turned and closed it as soundlessly as possible. He was now officially inside the hallowed halls of Larkin Standish.

There was no turning back.

# CHAPTER 53

## Seattle

D'ANGELO CONTINUED SWIVELLING back and forth in his desk chair, massaging his chin, taking unabashed perverse pleasure in watching the CCTV feed of the thirty-fifth-floor north stairwell, where that white boy was finally able to finagle the fire door open and wedge the tip of his kick into the crack far enough to check out the action in the hall.

*Where was Mizrahi? The exalted one? The Savior of Security?*

Now, in the moment of Larkin Standish's greatest need.

The night-shift supervisor smiled in satisfaction as the intruder slipped into the thirty-fifth floor of the law office and closed the door behind him. The intriguing question now was, would Mizrahi ever admit to Lorna Glass that he'd been had? He decided that that item would be impossible to hide, for ultimately a report would have to be filed. Once that happened, regardless of whether Mizrahi caught him before he escaped, his security had been breached. He wished he could be there to see how that played out.

Still smiling, he switched to the monitor with the spreadsheet for next month's schedule.

Arnold dashed to the lighted office, stopped just to the left of the doorway, and peeked in. He saw an unmanned desk, two guest chairs, and a small couch and a large window framing myriad city lights. No closet. Plain, functional, utilitarian.

"She's out of the can now," Lopez warned.

Arnold glanced over his shoulder at the hall. Not in sight. Yet.

But would be any second. The other end of the hall dead ended. Trapped.

*Fuuuck.*

He darted into the office, wedged himself into the narrow triangular space between the couch and wall one second before he heard the clickety-clack of her high heels heading toward him, then, a moment later, the squeak of a chair spring.

Slowly, noiselessly, Arnold scrunched into a fetal position on his left side. He was squeezed into an extremely tight space, just feet from the desk if viewed from the doorway. Worse, the dust down here was tickling the back of his nose, getting dangerously close to triggering a cough or sneeze. Arnold covered his mouth and nose with both hands, fighting the urge to purge the dust.

*Jesus, how long was he going to be stuck here?*

Anyone's guess. He resigned himself to one long drawn-out wait.

Ten plus minutes later, Lopez was in his ear with: "Mizrahi's back on your floor, heading straight toward you."

*Shit. Had a camera caught him running into the office?*

A moment later he heard a knock, followed by a somewhat gruff male voice say, "Seen or heard anything unusual?"

A female voice answered with a hint of annoyance, "Unusual? Like what?"

"Someone other than the cleaning service."

A two-second pause, then: "Why? Is something going on? Something I should know about? *Should* I be concerned?"

Her voice rose in volume with each syllable.

"No, ma'am, no need for concern, but Security told me

that the unauthorized individual seen entering the building earlier today has not yet been seen leaving. This, by the way, is the reason I'm staying on duty...to make certain our offices are adequately protected." A brief pause. "But you didn't answer my question. Have you seen anyone?"

Several seconds of silence ensued, followed by: "Do they *suspect,* or do they *know* this suspicious person remains inside the building?" she asked with lawyerly precision.

Mizrahi hesitated a beat.

"As I just said, they observed a suspicious-looking person enter the building earlier but have not seen him exit. I'm just being overly cautious. Please don't read anything more into it because there's no need for concern. In fact, I'll keep a particular eye on this floor and your office."

"I really don't like the sound of this. I think I'll pack up and finish from home. May I call you once I'm ready to go?"

"Certainly. If you would like, I'll stand right here and walk you to the elevator."

Arnold heard what sounded like a desk drawer sliding open.

"The elevator? No, Itzhak, I want you to escort me *to* the parking garage *and then* to my car and then make sure I'm safely locked inside before you leave me. This time of night, it shouldn't take you but a minute or two."

Emphatic. Unequivocal. Direct.

"No problem. I'm more than happy to walk you out."

He heard the drawer slide shut followed by the squeak of the chair spring.

Totally tubular. Being able to work while Mizrahi was escorting Ms. Bigwig to the garage removed a gonzo weight from his shoulders in addition to being an incredible stroke of good luck.

Heard movement, then moments later the recessed overheads went dark.

Silence.

Arnold peeked around the edge of the couch; saw hall light angling in. That, in addition to reflected ambient city light from the windows, was enough to see around the office. From his limited vantage, it appeared like the woman was indeed gone.

He whispered, "See them?"

"Yep. At the elevators. I'll let you know when they're off the floor."

"Roger that."

Arnold heard the distant ding of an elevator chime.

"They're on the elevator now and the door closed. Where are you?"

"Hold on."

He slowly wiggled from his hidey-hole, stood to scan the office more comprehensively.

"I'm in the office the lawyer just left. Still clear?"

"Far as I can see."

Yeah, well Lopez couldn't see all the hall, so...Arnold approached the door using a peripheral route to limit being seen by anyone out there. This angle offered a view of the hall to the south, which was clear. He darted to the opposite side of the doorway and scanned the hallway to the north. Also clear. He mentally rehearsed his next steps since they would be the kill shot.

"Uncle, copy?"

"Roger," Vihaan answered.

"Cut their video feed and let me know the instant it's off."

"Roger. Hold one...here goes...okay, they're blind."

Arnold streaked straight for Collier's office via a route furthest from the CCTV bubble, reached the doorway and ducked into his darkened office, phone in hand, already opened to the camera app, ready to go.

*Did they see him?*

For sure he'd momentarily passed through the absolute periphery of the camera's view.

*Then again, did it really matter?*

The moment Mizrahi's security cams went down, they'd know damn well they were in the process of getting royally boned. Meaning; he'd better get this part wrapped up and boogie on out, pronto. Where was Mizrahi now? At the lawyer's car? On his way back? Speaking of which, what about his other two Larkin Standish techs?

*Forget about that crap. Get on with it.*

He snapped a picture of his watch with Collier's office in the background to document the time and location. Made sure the image was exactly what he needed. It was.

He was about to snap a selfie with the picture of Collier's wife held next to his face when Lopez said, "*Security!*"

Arnold glanced at the door to the hall. Empty.

"Where?"

"Heading straight for you."

*Shit!*

He glanced around frantically. No place to hide.

He glanced at the desk.

No not that old cliché.

But...with no other option, he dropped to his hands and protesting knees and started crawling for.

Lopez said, "Looks like maybe just another routine sweep, but he'll be on top of you in, like, three seconds."

Arnold keyed his transmitter, pushed the desk chair away from the footwell, then backed in until his butt was up against the kick panel.

"Good luck, dude."

*Jesus.*

Not enough room to fit all the way in, leaving his head and shoulders protruding toward the floor-to-ceiling windows, desk chair out at a weird angle but with no place to move it...and he was now hearing footsteps growing louder. If the dude noticed the chair....

He went still just as a high-intensity light swept across the room, followed by: "Unit Two...yeah, nothing...roger that...on my way."

Arnold couldn't believe it: lucked out again?

*Too freaking good to be true.*

Arnold waited five full minutes—timed to the second on his watch—before he considered so much as a muscle twitch. Then, before risking a peek around the edge of the desk, he emailed the two critical photos to Prisha and Lopez just in case he got nailed on the way out. The main goal of the caper could now officially be scratched from the to-do list. The only problem now was to figure out how to boogie out the door without anyone knowing diddly squat. If he could pull that little white bunny out of his hat, it would be the ultimate one-finger salute to Herr Commandant Mizrahi.

"How we doing in the hall?" he asked.

"At the moment, clear."

"The video feed back up?"

"Not yet. Why?"

"Go ahead, put it back up. That might distract them for a moment while I try to sneak out."

After scrambling back onto his feet, he spent a moment to tenderly massage his bruised knees, then crept to the door, poked his head just far enough out to check the hall. Clear.

"We're good," he whispered. "Which way out?"

Prisha radioed: "I caught an elevator. No problem."

*Seriously?*

Hey, why not? But he saw no upside to brashly standing in full view of the CCTV for however long it took for an elevator to arrive. Best to sneak out a stairwell, maybe get as far down as thirty-three before riding the rest of the way. With key card in hand, he was about to streak for the north stairwell when an elevator dinged.

*Mizrahi? Back already?*

*Well duh! Dude's had more than enough time to escort her to the garage and get back up here.*

*Screw it. Go.*

287

The south stairwell was the closest. He headed there, knowing that one of Mizrahi's techs could undoubtedly see him on CCTV now, but so freaking what? At this point it was a foot race. He reached the door, fobbed himself into the stairwell and started flying down, taking stairs as quickly as possible without stumbling.

He was just hitting the thirtieth-floor landing when Lopez's voice popped up in his earbud.

"Bogies on both stairwells."

"What level?" he asked, still moving, not skipping a beat, flying step to step, as fast as possible.

"Just entered off thirty-five."

Okay, good, he had a massive head start.

"Anyone lower?" he asked.

"Yeah, your friend."

Fucking Mizrahi. Arnold stopped to listen for footsteps coming toward him, but the stairwell was disconcertingly quiet. *Hmmm....*

He started down again, but now at a normal pace, because at this point, why rush? And besides, he could catch his breath while keeping an ear out for footsteps echoing along the concrete tube.

*After all, what could Mizrahi to do now?*

Especially with him way out of his jurisdiction. If there were such a thing. And building security? What were they going to do? What law was he breaking?

Good question. Had no idea. Still, he was grateful to be carrying his personalized SOW.

He whispered, "Still heading down the stairwell. Keep me informed." Then he thought of something: "Their eyes and ears back up now like I asked, right?"

"Oh, shit, I got distracted," Vihaan said. "Okay, there, it's up."

Arnold passed floor twenty, continuing his descent at the same rate, but pausing every now and then to listen more closely.

Lopez radioed.

"Bad news. Your friend's in the lobby over by the door to the garage stairs waiting for you and isn't, like, in a particularly excellent mood over this."

"So what? What's he going to do? Arrest me? Fuck it if the dude can't take a joke."

He radioed his number-two.

"Prisha," he said, no longer seeing a need to disguise identities. "Say they catch me now...what can they do other than escort me out of the building?"

"Not a damn thing that I know of. They certainly haven't caught you in the act of committing a crime. Uh, why? You expect that'll happen?"

"You out of the building?"

He swore that by now she probably was but didn't want to make a wrong assumption.

"I am. Almost back to the car."

"Good. I'm going to Facetime you. Standby one."

He stopped long enough to connect with her on Facetime.

"Start recording this, okay?"

"Roger that. You're being recorded."

Staring directly into his camera, Arnold stated his name, date, location, time, and the purpose of the recording, then continued recording himself walking down the stairs.

He tried two key cards, but neither unlocked the door to the present floor, so he continued down two more flight before radioing.

"Vihaan, do me a favor, will you? Call Mr. Davidson and have him stand by, just in case, okay?"

"Roger that."

Arnold was stepping onto the eighth-floor landing when an idea hit: this battle of wits with Mizrahi had become way too personal, morphing into a gonzo point of pride. He would be damned if he would let that asshole nail him. He sorted through his cloned key cards until he found Collier's, swiped it across the card reader and saw the LED flash green. He opened and closed the door, repeating this process for the two levels immediately below before picking up his pace again.

"Yo, dude, security just radioed Mizrahi to ask if Collier was in the building. That you?"

"Yep. He answer them?"

"Hold one."

Arnold was moving past floor five now.

"He said no, that's one of your diversions. He asked security to check it out while he covers the lobby elevators."

"Copy."

Arnold kept going, but more deliberately now, making sure to move as quietly as possible since the stairwells exited on either side of this elevator core. When he reached the lobby level, he stopped to listen, but heard only the familiar dense silence of the concrete. Unlike the other floors, this one didn't require a fob for exiting in case of an emergency.

He took hold of the door handle, straightened his posture, threw open the door and strode straight for the front doors, throwing a slack-jawed security guard a jaunty salute with one hand while recording everything with the other hand.

He waved at Mizrahi over by the door to the garage stairwell, and yelled, "Nice to see you again, Itzhak. Was it as good for you as it was for me?"

Then he pushed through the door into the early morning chill.

# CHAPTER 54

## Seattle

SOON AS HE cleared the front doors and was on the sidewalk, Arnold stopped Facetime and radioed Prisha.

"I'm out. Where're you?"

"At the car. Why?"

"Just checking. Be there soon as I can get up that stinking hill."

Arnold turned for a final close-up of the familiar massive structure, only this time processing it through the tinted lens of intimacy. During the past week, he'd studied every facet of the building the team could dredge up, yet so many details remained obscure and mysterious, never to be known by him, leaving in him an inexplicable urge to know more.

He knew, though, the next big job Gold and Associates landed would be equally as distracting, be it a pen-test or not. For the moment, though, he felt sad about walking away from such an emotionally impactful experience, but was hit by an effervescent rush of exuberance, along with tear-evoking joy, of knowing they had just completed their first official pen-test.

Successfully, too.

He stifled the urge to whoop and jump and fist-pump air. For numerous reasons, but primarily because if Mizrahi were watching from the lobby, he didn't want to rub it in any more than he had. And he actually felt a pang of regret for his snide parting shot in the lobby. Totally uncalled for. Anyone involved in the creep knew exactly what went down. That's all that really mattered.

But still…it felt mind-blowingly awesome.

He glanced up Madison Street, just as the traffic light turned green, not that there was much traffic this time of early morning.

*Jesus, what a slog.*

Rounding the corner, he saw the car with Prisha, Lopez, and Vihaan on the parking strip, Prisha with her butt up against the front fender, chit-chatting, goofing off, coming down off the high of successfully completing their inaugural creep. Grinning, he approached the group, hand raised to high-five each one like a TD celebration.

Once finished stinging each other's palms, he announced: "Man, am I, like, stupor-inducing ravenous."

"Me too," Prisha echoed. "I'd kill for a big fat greasy cheeseburger about now."

"With bacon," Lopez added with a laugh. "Plenty of bacon."

"Sounds about right," Arnold said, stomach now growling in anticipation. Problem was… "Anybody know a place open this time of night?" This particular aspect of late-night Seattle life had atrophied significantly since his relocation to Honolulu. Not that he'd been one to be out partying at this hour anyway.

Lopez threw out; "There's always that dump over off Denny…The 5 Point?"

He spoke almost apologetically, as if to say, *Well, you asked.*

Arnold began filing through his memory bank, the name ringing a faint bell of familiarity…then, suddenly dredged it up.

"That scuzzy joint off Cedar? The one with a Chief Seattle bronze, like, right outside the front door?"

"Yeah, that's the place. Hold on, lemme check, see if

they're still open. Used to be twenty-four seven before Covid…"

Lopez said, initiating a two-thumb iPhone search.

The four filed through the doorway into a harsh discordant mix of hard rock, clattering dishes, and alcohol-heated conversations. They stopped to survey the packed early morning diners for an open table. Arnold saw four partiers pushing out of a booth in a far corner and began snaking between chairs and bodies. He scrambled for the booth before anyone else could snatch it, his team members dancing the sideways two-step in pursuit. They settled on seats still warm, the breathed in overheated, humid air carrying tinges of salty fry grease, strong coffee, Lysol, and perspiration. Pretty much exactly what he'd envisioned.

It was one of those offbeat joints that he'd subliminally written off as not his thing, but now, sitting inside, he spent a moment deciding if his imagined image aligned with reality. Not really. Best described as definitely different. Eclectic. With, he suspected, a resolute, highly segmented clientele. A spot that people might describe as having *character*. (Whatever *that* meant.)

This booth, for example: the wall next to him layered with years of political handbills, posters, advertisements, and off-beat bumper stickers, pasted one atop another at haphazard angles. A glowing, white neon sign: PLEASE DON'T DO COKE IN THE BATHROOM—cast a red reflection against the wall on which it hung.

Menus were dealt, followed by moments of decisions, after which an attentive waiter strained to clarify their shouted orders over the background din.

Food and beer were ordered, then served.

Then Arnold announced to the group: "Time to get serious, guys. We need to make a couple major decisions."

They all leaned forward, elbows on the tacky tabletop,

closing up ranks to hear over the ebb and flow of the sometimes explosive background din.

Arnold raised his voice.

"Okay, here's the question: when do we break the news to Collier? I mean, it's Thursday morning now, right?"

He paused to sip his IPA.

Prisha sent him a puzzled look.

"Like, why wait? Why not lay it on him first thing this morning?"

Arnold nodded at her suggestion, swiped a blob of foam off his lip.

"That's one option," he said in a tone that implied that it wasn't his first choice.

Lopez shrugged.

"I don't get it? What's the issue?"

Vihaan simply crossed his arms and frowned.

Arnold said, "Don't you guys want to see how this thing plays out over the next, say, twelve hours, or so?"

Laughing, Prisha slapped the table.

"Yeah, totally, dude!"

Arnold: "I mean what's the downside in waiting to see what happens when Collier hits his office? After all, he's one *very* precise dude."

Lopez looked puzzled.

"So he comes in, sees a couple items misplaced. So what? What's to say the cleaning crew didn't move them? I mean, what am I missing here?"

Arnold: "Yeah, right. Under *normal* conditions. Which these ain't. For starters, he signed the contract and knows we're under a time limit. Just makes sense to keep an eye out for things. But I'm more curious to see out how Mizrahi plays this with his ass now officially in a wringer. He knows he's been got, right? Which means he knows Collier's going to find out, like, soon, like maybe even a few hours from now, especially with building security in on it. There's no way he can sweep this shit under the rug." Arnold poked a finger at Lopez: "Aren't you just a teensy-weensy bit curious to see how it plays?"

Lopez nodded and turned to Vihaan, who looked at Prisha, who looked at Arnold.

"Okay, so how long do we give him before we break the news?"

Arnold hiked his shoulders.

"No set time...this afternoon sometime between, say, noon and four PM?"

"Naw, I say fuck that," Lopez said slicing his palm through the air. "I say lay it out there first thing this morning. Or, better yet, call him now. I mean, like, slam, bam, we did it."

They all laughed, not because what he said was funny, but as a way to unwind tightly coiled nerves. But the laughter quickly trailed off and they began exchanging glances again, as if each was waiting for someone else to render a decision.

Arnold stalled by sipping his beer again, everyone seeming to want to wait for someone else to step up.

When no one did, Arnold said, "How about this: we give him till noon tomorrow and if we don't hear a word, I'll text him the pictures. How's that for a plan?"

Prisha snickered.

"Yeah, I like that. Like it a lot, matter of fact."

# CHAPTER 55

## Seattle

ARNOLD WAS DEEP into stage four sleep when James Brown jarred him awake. He rolled over, squinted at his bedside Alexa: 8:07. Pulled the phone from its charge cord, inspected the screen: Webster Collier.

He smiled. The only reason for a call at this time of morning was that Collier knew.

*The only question was, how? Deduction or from Mizrahi?*

Arnold's money was on deduction. His smile was a full-on grin before he had his legs over the side of the bed, sitting upright with the phone.

"Good morning, Mr. Collier."

A brief hesitation, then: "You didn't, perhaps, pay a visit to my office last night, did you?"

A sparkler of giddy pride ignited in the depths of his chest.

"Yes sir, we did," purposely emphasizing the plural, as in a team effort.

He could hear Collier breathing hard, either deeply annoyed or out of breath from climbing stairs. His money would be on the former.

"We need to discuss this ASAP. In person. Unfortunately my schedule is chockablock until five thirty. Can you meet me in my office then and I'll make sure I'm available come hell or high water."

"Absolutely, sir. Oh, and my Seattle associate, Prisha Patel, will be with me."

"Fine. See you then."

Clearly, the man wasn't pleased.

Arnold and Prisha were perched on uncomfortably hard club chairs as Collier strode commandingly into the reception lobby from the familiar hallway.

They rose in concert, Arnold taking a step forward to intercept the managing partner with, "Allow me to introduce my Seattle associate, Prisha Patel. Prisha, Mr. Collier."

After shaking hands, Collier leaned back, giving Arnold a head-to-toe, then appeared on the cusp of saying something, then nodded, an asymmetric smile flirting across his lips.

"The weight and knee brace...all part of a disguise?"

Arnold nodded confirmation.

"Yes."

Collier shook his head and turned, extending an arm toward the hallway.

"We're in the conference room down the hall, first door on your right. The door's open."

The same small room as his first official visit. As he turned to enter, he saw Mizrahi and the other two committee members at the table, white Starbucks cups in front of each one, Mizrahi's eyes molten lava.

As they slid into two empty chairs, a silence as heavy as sodden wool cloaked the air. Arnold busied himself with inspecting his manicure, then cast a quick sideways glance at Prisha, who was checking stock prices on her phone. Arnold began to suck a space between two upper incisors, waiting for Collier to break the awkward vibe pinballing between the attendees.

After leisurely closing the door, Collier took the sole

remaining chair, flattened his palms on the table and pressed his lips wafer thin. He remained frozen like this for a long moment before clearing his throat, and without preamble, turned to Arnold.

"Please tell us how you were able to access my office last night."

Arnold stole a quick glance at Mizrahi, who was glaring at the yellow legal pad in front of him, back military-straight, hands on thighs, a dyspeptic expression painting his face.

"First, let me say that breaking into your networks, was difficult. Right from the start it was clear that everyone in this office is exceptionally well trained in spotting and resisting social engineering scams. So it took multiple attempts to finally worm our way into…" He caught himself from slipping into tech-speak that no one but Mizrahi would comprehend. "your network. But once in"—he tossed in a shrug of nonchalance—"mapping it was no problem." Which was probably already more than Collier really wanted to know.

"But I want to specifically know is how you physically entered my office," Collier said with more than a touch of annoyance.

Arnold raised a placating palm.

"Sorry sir, but please bear with me, I'm getting there. Having access to your security network was crucial for breaking into your office because we had to be able to shut down your video surveillance."

His peripheral vision caught Mizrahi cringe.

*Uh-oh.*

"Video surveillance?" Collier asked with a puzzled expression. "Are you referring to the CCTV camera above the elevators?"

*You have got to be kidding me, right?*

And there it was. The perfect torpedo. Arnold stared directly at Mizrahi, eyebrows arched questioningly but didn't say a word, the room silent enough to hear a termite fart.

"What video surveillance?" Collier asked, leaning forward now, staring intently at his head of security.

Arnold quickly added, "Before you two gentlemen get entangled in that subject, please let me give you this."

He pulled a manila envelope from his backpack and slid it across the table to Collier.

Without a word, Collier calmly opened it to examine the eight-by-ten blowups of the shots taken inside his office: the proof of penetration they'd agreed upon. Studying the photos, his expression grew darker and grimmer until, without a word, he passed them to Gloria Kim.

To Arnold: "At any time did you open a file or drawer or inspect any paperwork on anyone's desk?"

"No sir, I didn't."

Collier was studying Arnold's eyes intently, as if searching for a flicker of deception.

"How can we be assured you haven't done anything to compromise this firm?"

The obvious question shocked him. He began absent-mindedly finger-combing his hair, scrambling for a compelling answer. Everyone in the room undoubtedly presumed—correctly—that every member of his team was a hacker. White hats now, but hackers, nonetheless.

That made them guilty of snooping regardless of how loudly they might protest. He understood this. Still, being guilty by association pissed him off. Especially since there was no way to prove they hadn't snooped. Proving a negative is often exceedingly challenging. Worse yet, he was totally unprepared for the question.

Sensing Arnold's emotional conundrum, Prisha jumped in.

"Guess you simply have to rely on our word and reputation. But since I'm the only other member of the team to set foot in the building last night, I can assure you we were in and out of there as fast as possible."

She spread her hands, and that was that.

Allen Wyler

"In the meantime," Arnold said, "we should have our comprehensive report submitted to you within a week. It'll lay out everything in sufficient detail for you to have a much better feel for the timeline. By comparing the report with your own internal security footage, you should have more confidence that what we just said is the truth. I was in your office only long enough to take those pictures and hide from whoever checked your office. Once you've had time to read and digest the report, please feel free to institute a corrective action plan and move forward accordingly. We will, of course, be available to assist you in any way possible." Then, after a breath, added: "We have one more thing to add, and it's important."

He removed a small digital Sony recorder from his backpack, held it up like a magician before performing a trick, then said to Collier, "Either your committee has a leak, or your office is bugged. Or both. I say this because Mr. Mizrahi knew exactly when we were hired for the break-in."

He thumbed Play on the recorder. Mizrahi's distinct accent could be heard radioing Lorna Glass and her crew a heads-up that a pen-test was about to occur.

"The bottom line is," Arnold said, thumbing off the recorder, "that the test was done under seriously flawed circumstances. On the other hand, that's irrelevant now that the test is over. I'm just suggesting that you keep this in mind when assimilating the report. In other words, we were able to break in spite of this."

He casually dropped the recorder into his backpack.

Collier turned to Mizrahi: "Can you explain this, Itzhak?"

Mizrahi glanced away.

"Sir, this is neither the time nor the place for this discussion."

Time to exit stage left. Arnold grabbed his rucksack and pushed up from the conference table, Prisha following suit.

"If you or your committee have any further questions, you know how to contact me," Arnold said, motioning for them to

300

stay put. "No need to get up. We know our way out. I believe that at the moment the group has more pressing matters to discuss."

Collier was up out of his chair, motioning the other to remain seated.

"I'll just see our guests out and will be right back to finish this conversation."

# CHAPTER 56

## Seattle

PRISHA SHUTTLED ARNOLD back to his place, making good time heading northbound along Aurora Avenue in amazingly light traffic.

Since leaving the law offices, an unsettling emptiness began to haunt him: the realization of what life would be like without Rachael. He desperately wished he could remain cocooned in the contented cloud of the gig's total immersion. But he knew that their fundamental incompatibilities left no other option than to just deal with the ensuing void; that he wouldn't miss Rachael *per se* as much as the simple joy of having someone to share life with.

No doubt the gig was a distraction from the starkness of living alone. Again. Yes, he could do it. He had done it. And besides, he had no other choice but to do it. After all, he'd done it in the years following his parents' murder. That didn't mean he was looking forward to it, especially now, as he recalled the stark hollow emptiness of the life he'd had when lying low in Honolulu, in that blur of days before Mr. Davidson tracked him down and blew his cover. The days before Gold and Associates became a concept. The loneliness would be worse now simply because satisfaction and contentment are always relative to past experience, right?

"Whatdaya think about offering Ito the position?" Prisha asked.

A subconscious alarm beeped, jolting him back from ruminations. He suddenly became aware of the bridge they were crossing, the gunmetal gray water of the ship canal one hundred and sixty-seven feet straight down, the blur of railings. He replayed her question, scrambling back into his Gold and Associates mindset...slipped off his glasses and squinted, massaging the bridge of his nose.

*Jesus...*

She kept her eyes on the road ahead, allowing him time to answer, the two of them having quickly slipped into that well-worn-pajama rhythm of people who've collaborated closely over years instead of only a few months.

"To tell the truth, that subject hasn't really been a high priority for me these past few days." He thought about these last words, and quickly amended them with: "Guess it's as good a time as any to discuss it. Why, what're your thoughts?"

*When in doubt, punt.*

Lips pursed, eyes on the road, she seemed to gather her thoughts.

"Ya gotta admit, he does excellent work. He's responsive, dependable, and fills a definite niche." Paused a beat, shrugged, added; "Don't really see any reason *not* to bring him on. After all, he can be our boots on the ground over there when you're over here."

"Seeing no reason to *not* bring him on board isn't an enthusiastic endorsement. Or am I missing something?"

A quick meeting of their eyes before her focus returned to the road.

"Just wonder how much thought you've put into it...you've seemed so distracted when we haven't been focused on the creep. Wondered if that's what's been consuming you."

When he didn't answer, she added, "Hey dude, I ain't

stupid. Something other than our creep's been eating at you, so I'm simply flat-out asking, you cold on him now, or what?"

"Naw." He scooted back to the normal position, began staring out the side window again, blankly watching the blur of buildings. "Just personal shit's all."

"Rachael again?"

*Again?*

Was that a hint of disgust in her voice?

"Uh, strike that last remark," she said. "That was uncalled for."

But telling.

"What I'm asking is, do you want to bring him on as our Honolulu associate? After all, thought that was the whole point of recruiting him."

"It was. Still is. But to be blunt, you cool with bringing him aboard as an *associate?*"

She shot him another glance, then back to the road. An associate—as opposed to employee—would draw an equal share of the profits. Made an enormous difference.

"Isn't that what this discussion's all about?"

"Yeah, it is," Arnold agreed.

The problem was that his emotional conflict cut deeper than simple regrets over Rachael. It went like this: Gold and Associates was *his* baby. Each new associate relinquished a fraction of the company from him. Something he was finding extraordinarily difficult to do.

*For sure, dude. But that's how companies grow. And you want this company to be really good, right?*

Although his rational self realized that delegating responsibility was essential to growing a healthy, viable legacy, an amorphous protective segment of his psyche still grappled with the idea of diluting the *Gold* by increasing the *Associates*. Perhaps this was something he could discuss with Mr. Cain. He must've experienced similar qualms when first taking on partners in his law firm.

After several seconds of silence: "There an issue, dude?"

Arnold shook his head.

"Naw, not really."

"Okay, but that sounds less than definitive and certainly not enthusiastic. What? You want to punt? Is that what you're saying?"

Shaking his head again, he sighed.

"Naw, you're right. He's perfect for that slot. I'll offer him the job soon as I'm home."

"You sure you're down with it, dude? I mean..." she asked, eyebrows raised with skepticism.

"Yeah, seriously, I am."

# HONOLULU

# CHAPTER 57

## Two Weeks Later

STRETCHED OUT ON back his back deck chaise, laptop on thighs, eyes shut, drifting lightly in that delicious no-man's-land somewhere south of wakefulness but still north of sleep, cotton candy breezes ruffling his hair…

"Three Hearts in a Tangle" broke the bliss.

Arnold fumbled the phone from his cargo shorts, grappled it into proper orientation and blinked at caller ID. It was unidentified. He almost didn't answer it, assuming it might be a spam call, but then decided what the hall, he could always block the number if it were. Chance looked up at him, having had a nice snooze interrupted, ready to stand if Arnold did.

"Hello?" he answered lamely, scrambling for mental traction, setting the laptop on the table before he sat up.

Then: "Mr. Gold?"

He recognized Mr. Collier's tenor immediately.

"Mr. Collier?"

"Yes."

"Yes, sir, what can I do for you?"

"Is this a good time to discuss an urgent business matter? If not, I'd like to schedule this at your earliest convenience? Things are moving very quickly, so I'm anxious to talk. It's extremely important."

Arnold glanced out over the ravine defining the rear property line, across to the exposed lava formation on the other side, to gently swaying palms and dusty scrub, and zeroed in on the almost level spot where a certified asshole had taken a shot at him a couple years ago. So many changes in life since then...

*Was Rachael all settled into her old bedroom in the family house? He missed her. Terribly. But...*

"Not a problem Mr. Collier, I can talk now."

"Excellent." Pause. "We just finished a rather lengthy partnership meeting."

Arnold detected a rhythm emerging. There was also an unfamiliar edge to the managing partner's voice, a herky-jerky awkwardness instead of his typically smooth lawyerly flow.

"The entire meeting focused on one issue, which is what I wish to discuss now." Another pause. "The partners—in a rare show of unanimity—were *extremely*, and rightfully, I might add, disturbed and upset over the findings in your report. Not only the findings *per se*, but the speed with which you gained control of our most sensitive and confidential files." Pause. "In addition, we were gobsmacked to discover that our offices *had been* under unauthorized video surveillance for some time now."

Arnold heard Collier inhale audibly and realized the cause for his atypical tone and rhythm: the man was seething mad, like, hyper-gonzo pissed.

"Needless to say, we're all *extremely* upset."

*No shit.*

"Would Gold and Associates be interested in exploring the possibility of assuming management of our IT infrastructure?"

*Wow.*

Arnold began to palm-wipe his face and in the process knocked off his glasses but caught them before they could bounce off his leg onto the wood deck.

"Wow. That's amazing, Mr. Collier..."

"Is that a yes? Because if so, I want to move this discussion to the next level ASAP. Frankly, your report has affected us profoundly and we're all extremely uncomfortable with our present situation, especially now being aware of the extensive surveillance system throughout our offices."

Arnold was up now, pacing, phone to ear, finger combing his curly black hair, mind going at Mach III rabid bat speed but knew he needed way more information before going too crazy.

"I guarantee we're interested in discussing this further, but what exactly do you mean by assume management of your I-T?"

"Exactly that. A management role. We are considering letting Mizrahi go if we can secure a suitable replacement to assume his responsibilities. In essence, we're offering Gold and Associates the right of first refusal."

*Double Wow.*

"I'm flattered to be asked, Mr. Collier, but before I can possibly agree to further discussions, I need to have my partners brought up to speed and Ms. Patel involved. I'm sure you understand."

"I *do* understand, and I don't mean to pressure you, but when might I expect an answer?"

"I'll be back to you within the next twenty-four hours. Is this acceptable?"

"It is. Arnold...oh, may I call you Arnold?

"Certainly."

"Please know that we're all extremely anxious to negotiate a mutually beneficial agreement."

"Yes, sir. I'll be back in touch as soon as I have word. And as I said, I truly appreciate the offer."

After ringing off, Arnold stared blankly across the ravine at the sniper spot again while weighing the offer. In reality, almost any good pen-test can expose at least one or two vulnerabilities no matter how tight the security.

Any network of computers and devices—such as printers, modems and routers—create opportunities for intrusion in disconcerting numbers.

*And besides, what's to say his team would do any better than Mizrahi?*

What would happen in, say, six months when Larkin Standish clandestinely employed another pen-test team to evaluate Gold and Associates? No, as attractive as this offer might be, it was not without serious pitfalls. Then again...

Jesus, management. Decisions. Worry. Why had he ever in his wildest dreams wanted to run his own company?

He punched the speed dial on his iPhone, listened to it ring.

Prisha answered. "Yo, dude, s'up?"

"We need to talk."

Allen Wyler

# Acknowledgements

I am extremely grateful to the following resources:

Jonathon Tomek, CEO and Co-Founder of MadX, https://www.madx.co/

Ryan Jones, Co-Founder and CTO of Digital Silence www.digitalsilence.com

Printed in the USA
CPSIA information can be obtained
at www.ICGtesting.com
LVHW090404301123
765058LV00012B/668